PRAISE FOR
MIMI LEE READS BETWEEN THE LINES

"I haven't loved a cat in a book this much since I read the first *The Cat Who Could Read Backwards* by Lilian Jackson Braun a hundred years ago.... Mimi is a delight and I can't wait to hang out with her again."

—Poisoned Pen

"This is catnip for fans of talking cat cozies." —*Publishers Weekly*

"[*Mimi Lee Reads Between the Lines*] will appeal to readers who enjoy Vivien Chien's Noodle Shop mysteries, with their Chinese American heroines, as well as similar family dynamics and portrayals of savvy businesswomen." —*Booklist*

"If you love an intriguing mystery with an appealing protagonist, a wisecracking cat, and lively family dynamics, you must read the Sassy Cat mysteries by Jennifer Chow. I'm so glad I found this fresh new voice in the cozy mystery world."

—Sherry Harris, Agatha-nominated author of
the Sarah Winston Garage Sale mysteries

"I love Marshmallow! He is once again my favorite character in this series . . . he really saves the day in this book. Overall, *Mimi Lee Reads Between the Lines* is another great entry in this cozy cat mystery series. Four stars!"

—Diane Reviews Books

"Add in the talking cat as well as a new fur baby—this book was a fun read that cozy fans are sure to enjoy." —Books a Plenty

"A cracking, fun, and lighthearted cozy mystery."

—Brianne's Book Reviews

"A lighthearted cozy mystery with a cute kitten, a matchmaking mama, fun foreign fare, parent problems, a set-up sister, one panicky principal, and a cheeky cat."
                                                    —The Avid Reader

"I enjoyed this lighthearted cozy mystery, second in the Sassy Cat Mystery series. The fascinating mystery had me stymied, the characters are well defined, and I appreciated how close-knit Mimi and her family are. . . . I highly recommend this cozy mystery!"

—Open Book Society

PRAISE FOR *MIMI LEE GETS A CLUE*

"Mix an intrepid dog groomer with a sarcastic cat, add a generous dose of Southern California, sprinkle with murder, and you get a cozy mystery that's bound to please."

—Laurie Cass, author of the Bookmobile Cat Mysteries

"A fun, charming, and totally unique mystery featuring lots of adorable pets (and one particularly snarky cat). Mimi Lee is a winning heroine with a hilarious family, especially her meddling, marriage-obsessed mother."
                        —Kerry Winfrey, author of *Waiting for Tom Hanks*

"I laughed out loud more than once reading *Mimi Lee Gets a Clue*, the first book in the new Sassy Cat mystery series. Mimi Lee is feisty, determined, and lots of fun—and I love Ma, her matchmaking mother. The story features an intriguing mystery, and Marshmallow, a talking cat that only Mimi, as his owner, can hear.... Sharp writing, a main character I'd happily be friends with, and a talking cat. What more could a reader want?"

—Sofie Kelly, *New York Times* bestselling author of
the Magical Cats Mysteries

"Chow's charming debut is an adorable mystery perfect for pet lovers. Mimi's authentic family grounds the story amidst the glitzy and glamorous backdrop of L.A. I devoured it in one sitting."

—Roselle Lim, author of *Natalie Tan's Book of Luck & Fortune*

"Chow smoothly mixes intrigue, romance, and humor. Cozy fans will have fun." —*Publishers Weekly*

"A frothy, fun series debut." —*Kirkus Reviews*

"Pet lovers will be delighted by this fun and yet suspenseful mystery.... The balance between suspense and humor is perfect and makes this read a page-turner." —Book Review Crew

Mimi Lee

CRACKS
THE CODE

Jennifer J. Chow

BERKLEY PRIME CRIME
NEW YORK

BERKLEY PRIME CRIME
Published by Berkley
An imprint of Penguin Random House LLC
penguinrandomhouse.com

Library of Congress Cataloging-in-Publication Data

Names: Chow, Jennifer J., author.
Title: Mimi Lee cracks the code / Jennifer J. Chow.
Description: First edition. | New York: Berkley Prime Crime, 2021. |
Series: A sassy cat mystery
Identifiers: LCCN 2021006726 (print) | LCCN 2021006727 (ebook) |
ISBN 9781984805034 (trade paperback) | ISBN 9781984805041 (ebook)
Subjects: GSAFD: Mystery fiction.
Classification: LCC PS3603.H696 M54 2021 (print) |
LCC PS3603.H696 (ebook) | DDC 813/.6—dc23
LC record available at https://lccn.loc.gov/2021006726
LC ebook record available at https://lccn.loc.gov/2021006727

First Edition: November 2021

Printed in the United States of America
1st Printing

Book design by Alison Cnockaert

For Ellie, because you asked so nicely.

CHAPTER

one

AH . . . THE TRADEMARKS of a Los Angeles summer day, an intoxicating combo of scented tropical sunscreen and giddy laughter, came through the open door. I spied pedestrians strolling across the palm tree–lined plaza through the plate-glass window of my pet grooming salon, Hollywoof. They must have been heading to the nearby beach, because they wore variations of swim attire, from the tiniest scraps of bikinis to thick blanket cover-ups with wide straw hats perched on top of their heads.

A loud bark refocused my attention on my canine collie customer. The Lassie look-alike rested a few feet away from her celebrity twin's golden star embedded in the floor—my shop had its own Bark of Fame walkway. The collie also stood a careful distance away from my dozing Persian cat, Marshmallow, who liked to nap and protect his coveted sunny spot.

This would be a short appointment, since the dog's owner had requested a quick styling session. The woman sat on a cream pleather bench in the waiting area, uninterested in the doggie film showing on the large-screen TV across the way. She flicked through a glossy magazine in a lazy manner. When she crossed her legs, the multiple sterling silver anklets she wore chimed gently with the movement.

I nodded to my colleague, Nicola, who sat near the cash register, to let her know I'd be going to the back room with the dog. However, in the throes of TGIF laziness, she seemed enamored with her phone and kept scrolling on it, not bothering to glance up. She might have been hard at work looking for the latest casting call. The searchlight that aimed down on the reception area highlighted her classic beauty, as if she were on stage. Her gazelle-like stature and beautiful symmetrical face really should have been a shoo-in for callbacks, although she said her bulbous nose gave her "bad luck" and ruined her chances of being a movie star. I thought that if she could deliver her lines with more emotion, she could've gotten cast.

I walked the collie down the hallway past the side room with its holding space of crates, ready for extra animals to wait in during our busiest of days. We entered the back area where I kept my professional grooming equipment. I passed by the stainless steel sink because the dog didn't need a wash, but I hooked her leash on to one of the grooming tables. Using a pin brush, I fluffed up her luxurious fur. Before too long, I'd managed to create a hairstyle that would've rivaled the best blowout.

When I returned to the front room, the dog's owner snapped shut her magazine and blew a kiss at the dog with her red lacquered lips. From her purse, she pulled out a spray bottle labeled "Purified rose water." She spritzed her collie and rubbed her hand against the dog's fur. "There, much better. Looks less puffy like that and more beach-tousled."

Marshmallow woke at the woman's commenting. He yawned and examined my handiwork. "Wow, Mimi. You really nailed the bedhead look."

I choked back a laugh. I'd gotten used to Marshmallow's sassy personality over time. And his telepathic ability. When he'd first been given to me by my younger sister, Alice, I figured I'd been overly stressed by opening Hollywoof and had imagined his voice in my head. Turns out he actually had a knack for "speaking human." Though I'd never quite mastered cat language, which meant I still had to address him out loud. Not that I'd let anyone see me talking to a cat. I'd never even told my family or boyfriend about Marshmallow's special talent.

The collie's owner went over to the cash register. She had to tap her long fingernails against the glass jar of homemade dog biscuits to get Nicola's attention. Nicola immediately dropped her phone and served the customer.

The lady and her dog passed by me as they headed toward the exit. "Thanks for the furstyle," she said.

When she exited, the bell above my store's door rang out with a loud jangle.

"She didn't leave a tip," Nicola said and frowned. "Figures. Reminds me of my old job." She used to be an assistant to a famous producer's wife, Lauren Dalton, and she'd hated being treated like a doormat.

"Well, it's a new day," I said. "A beautiful one at that. Look at the amazing sunshine streaming through the window." It did look a little like molten gold from this angle.

Nicola rolled her neck, making the stretching appear like an elegant dance, complete with fluttering swan arms. "I'm incorporating more dancing into everyday motions. I think it'll help with me getting cast."

I had my doubts about that, and I also saw Marshmallow twitching his whiskers in amusement.

"Mimi, I'm going outside to practice some more moves in the plaza," Nicola said. "Besides, we're almost closed for lunch anyway."

I enforced a mandatory break hour starting at noon. The perks of being the boss of my own business. Although I wouldn't have started my shop without a healthy infusion of cash from Hollywoof's benefactor, Pixie St. James. "Dance away," I said to Nicola.

She nodded and skipped out the door while waving jazz hands.

Marshmallow puffed out his white fur. "So, what are we having for lunch, Mimi?"

I shrugged at him. "*I'm* eating a mini chicken pot pie. You had a large breakfast, so I think you'll be fine. Plus, Dr. Exi talked about your weight on our last visit."

"What does that man know?"

"He *is* a vet."

Before we could argue any more, the bell above the door jingled. Oops, I'd forgotten to lock up. I'd have to tell this customer about our schedule. Some newcomers didn't realize we took a lunch break. However, when I checked on the visitor, it was someone I recognized and had been thinking about only moments earlier.

"Pixie," I said and greeted her with a hug. She smelled of her usual signature pumpkin spice fragrance.

After the embrace, though, I held her at arm's length. "You look refreshed." Her brown hair appeared professionally styled, but she wasn't wearing her typical pantsuit. Instead, she'd opted for a flowing white summer dress, which made her tanned skin all the more prominent in contrast.

"I've been to the island," she said.

"Which one? Catalina?" Less than an hour away by ferry, it was a haven for Angelenos. In fact, I'd met Pixie there last summer when I'd saved her shih tzu from the choppy waves. She, in gratitude, had given me the capital to start up this business.

"Of course. And I brought you a little something from my travels. Actually, it's for Marshmallow." She winked at him.

"Finally, some acknowledgment," he said, as he crept up close to her.

Pixie bent down and gave him a love pat on the head. Then she pulled a fish-shaped toy out of her purse and dropped it on the ground before him. It must've triggered something since the toy started quivering.

"Is it going to move? Will he need to chase it?" I asked.

My cat stuck his nose in the air. "An exercise toy. How could you have read me so wrong, Pixie?"

"Great," I said to Pixie with a straight face. "He needs to work some layers off."

Pixie's lips formed a surprised circle. "Oh no, Mimi, this device is for you to operate. It's a fish-shaped cat massager so you can pamper him. I remember how much he loved that massage mat at my place."

Marshmallow yowled with mirth. "Now that's the ticket, sister."

I picked up the trembling fish with its massaging bumps, and turned it off. "I'll save this for some other time," I said, going behind the counter and dropping it into my purse.

Marshmallow growled. "You're on lunch break right now. Plenty of time to give me a good massage."

I ignored him. "Have a seat," I said to Pixie, gesturing to the pleather benches.

She smoothed out her dress and sat down on one bench, and I

leaned back on the other. Marshmallow decided to jump up next to me and curl up there, ready to listen in on our conversation.

"Was your trip for business or pleasure?" I asked. As CEO of her own tech company, Pixie worked hard, and she'd been known to schmooze with her clients at different locations. I'd run into her at a country club once and wouldn't be surprised if some important client had asked her to meet in Catalina for a round of golf.

"Both," she said, giving me a wide smile. "A few months ago, I closed escrow on a house in Catalina. I've been renting it out as a vacation home and was just meeting up with my property manager."

"A place in Catalina." I whistled. "That's a nice investment."

Her brown eyes glowed with enthusiasm. "Yes, and I can have a second home to visit anytime I want. Or to lend to friends."

"That's super generous of you."

"In fact"—she leaned forward and clasped my hands—"I had a sudden cancellation in the middle of next week. You know, it's really hard to get a spot around July Fourth. Why don't you stay there for a few days, all expenses paid by me? Consider it as an early anniversary celebration of Hollywoof's opening."

"Wow." My words left me. I'd love to have a vacation, and Catalina was such a serene place. I could probably close shop for a short period, or maybe Nicola could run it while I was gone.

"So, what do you say?" Pixie asked.

"I'd love to," I said, dreaming about a romantic getaway with Josh. "Could I maybe take a guest?"

"I thought you'd never ask," Marshmallow said. He nudged my side and trained his charming baby blue eyes on me.

I stroked him. Well, I could humor my cat for the time being. "Maybe two guests . . ."

Pixie tapped her chin with her forefinger. "Bringing your cat along is an excellent idea. As Marshmallow explores the old house, you can jot down detailed notes. I'll make sure everything is cat-safe and then I can advertise the place as pet-friendly."

Before we could figure out any more details, Pixie's phone rang. She frowned at the caller ID. "Odd. I don't recognize the number."

I watched as she excused herself and stood closer to the front door. "Yes, this is Pixie St. James."

She mumbled, "Sorry, the name doesn't ring a bell."

Pacing back and forth, she said, "I'm afraid I can't be of help."

She hung up the phone and turned to me with a slight frown. "I don't know why some woman would be contacting me about a stranger I've never even heard of."

From beside me, Marshmallow gave a soft hiss of sympathetic outrage.

"Anyway"—she pasted a bright smile on her face—"can you check with Josh on his availability? Once you two agree, I'll arrange all the details."

* * *

Focused on telling Josh the exciting news after work, I spent the afternoon in a whirlwind of doggie sudsy baths, blueberry facials, and stylish headbands. Before I knew it, the clock had struck six, and I strapped Marshmallow into his carrier to make our way home. The 405 freeway yielded no major traffic hiccups (a welcome change of pace), and I made it home by seven.

Since Josh and I were neighbors, I figured I could easily find him in our shared complex, Seaview Apartments. However, I didn't see Josh's vehicle in the communal carport parking area. Not that it should surprise me. He usually worked long nights at the law office to get in all those billable hours.

After getting some fast Chinese food delivery from Wok On, I ate my dinner perched on my IKEA couch. Thank goodness the fabric was washable because sweet-and-sour sauce wouldn't complement the lime green color.

I kept glancing out the window at the courtyard, an open area with a few potted ferns, waiting for Josh to appear. Finally, I saw him cross the space to head toward his apartment, unit number one. I grabbed a few wrapped fortune cookies to go and ran out the door—but not before Marshmallow slipped through the closing crack. "Someone's gotta chaperone you kids," he said.

"Jealous much?" I asked as I smoothed down my wrinkled T-shirt with the image of a dabbing dog.

I called out Josh's name before he could enter his apartment. Not that I minded the back view of him.

When he turned around at the sound of my voice, my heart skipped a beat. Ever since the day we'd met in the laundry room of our complex, I still grew excited each time I saw him.

"Mimi," he said, his voice brightening with pleasure. He paused. "And my man, Marshmallow."

My cat curved his tail into a question mark. "I'll try to take that as a compliment."

"Come on in," Josh said, unlocking his door and opening it wide.

Marshmallow and I entered Josh's tidy apartment. I didn't know how he could live so neatly. I'd never seen any dirty laundry in sight, and sparkling clean plates always sat lined up in a bamboo dish rack. His living space also gave off a whiff of his signature scent, a heady dose of pine.

"Make yourself at home," Josh said, waving his hand around.

"Don't mind if I do," Marshmallow said, making his way over to the dining table featuring an outline of the humuhumunukunukuapua`a fish. He curled up on one of the chairs there.

I took a seat beside my cat and traced one of the scales on the table. The detailed wooden furniture replica was a loving gift from Josh's parents to remind him of his home state of Hawaii, where the two of them still resided. "We won't stay long, Josh," I said. "I just wanted to give you a special invite in person."

"To what?" He stood near me, and I raised my head to take in his curious gaze.

"Pixie bought a house on Catalina Island, a vacation home. She invited us to stay there for a few days and check out the island."

"A vacation together?" His voice dipped low and intimate.

Marshmallow growled.

I gave Josh a sheepish grin. "Kind of. But I told Pixie I'd take Marshmallow, too. She wanted to make sure the house is pet-friendly enough and market it as such. She's already renting it out to people, but there was a last-minute cancellation for next week."

Josh draped his arm around me. "Sounds wonderful."

I bit the inside of my cheek. "The only thing is the open dates land at the beginning of the week."

"Well, then I'll have to work doubly hard and shift my schedule around." Josh removed his arm from my shoulder to pull out his phone and examine his calendar app.

We locked down the dates for next week and agreed to clear our schedules. "I'm sure Hollywoof will manage fine without me," I said and paused to give him a probing look. "Are you sure you'll be okay at work? Your law firm isn't known for its lazy work ethic."

He tapped a few notes on his phone. "I'll let my bosses know. They should be fine with it. And, besides, I have a paralegal now."

"Really? That's news to me," I said.

He shrugged. "She got hired this week and is already a very efficient worker."

"Oh, okay. What's her name?"

"Gertrude," he said.

Marshmallow slunk onto my lap and purred up at me. "All the Gertrudes I've seen on TV are grannies."

Now I was thinking about a little old lady shuffling paperwork at Josh's law firm, and I stifled a laugh. I felt grateful that Josh and I could spend a little R&R together, with an emphasis on the resting part. After all, it was hard to imagine anything terrible happening in such an idyllic place.

CHAPTER

two

I LOUNGED IN BED on the weekend. *This is how it'll feel on the island,* I thought, except with the sea breeze tousling my hair. I sat up in my bed and blinked at the strong sunlight streaming in through the window. On Catalina Island, there would also be the added enchantment of knowing that I had no other duties whatsoever.

Marshmallow crept through my open bedroom door and launched himself on my bed. "About time you got up," he said. "I'm starving."

I bustled around in my robe, getting breakfast—er, brunch—ready for the both of us. Meanwhile, I called up Nicola to tell her about my impromptu vacation this coming week. She seemed less than enthused about managing the store on her own but still agreed when I dangled overtime pay as an incentive for her.

Then I texted Pixie, telling her that Josh and I would be free to take her up on her generous offer.

Excellent, she replied. Come by to get the keys.

Marshmallow finished devouring his kibble and jumped onto the kitchen counter, where I'd been eating a bowl of cornflakes, to literally put his nose in things. He scanned the text message from Pixie—that's what I get for having a cat who's able to talk and read.

"I'm coming with you to see her mansion," he said.

"Yes, I know how you love visiting Pixie," I said, and my cat calling it a mansion wasn't that much of an exaggeration.

Marshmallow stretched out across the counter. "Not my fault you 'forgot' to massage my back the other day, even with the new gift. I'll have to make do with Pixie's high-tech mat."

Thankfully, my cat didn't continue griping as we drove up the Hollywood Hills. Maybe the fact that he didn't get carsick, even on the winding roads, helped improve his mood.

The expensive houses barnacled to the side of the hilltop looked dazzling in the golden sunshine. Pixie's house, though, still stood apart from the rest with its unique oval design.

After we parked and Pixie had greeted us, Marshmallow didn't stop to goggle at the columned hallways or pause on the travertine floor but made a beeline to the massage mat near the kitchen. He closed his eyes in bliss as it turned on. Even after Gelato, Pixie's cute shih tzu, scampered across the floor to reach my cat and started yipping for his attention, Marshmallow kept his eyes shut. He gave a contented purr in Gelato's direction to quiet down the pup.

Pixie and I remained near our pets in the kitchen area. I sat down before her gorgeous mother-of-pearl inlaid breakfast bar on one of her fancy bar stools with ergonomic cushioning.

"Homemade iced tea for you, Mimi?" Pixie asked while peering into her massive fridge.

"Yes, please." I loved her beverage concoctions. She often added a twist to her drinks, like fresh herbs from her garden or hexagonal ice cubes. This time around, she layered hand-whipped milky foam on top of my iced tea.

She herself sipped seltzer water infused with pineapple-ginger syrup as we talked. "Hope you enjoy your stay in Catalina," she said. "The vacation house is a lovely three-bedroom done up in the Art Deco style with a great view of Avalon Bay."

I clinked my glass against hers. "It's been forever since I've had a proper vacation, Pixie. Thank you."

"Don't mention it." She reached over to a side table, grabbed a sealed envelope, and slid it over to me. "I've placed the key inside, along with directions to the place."

Glancing at Marshmallow relaxing in the corner, I suddenly realized how I could stop him from putting a potential damper on a romantic trip with Josh. "It's too bad we have to take the *ferry* to Catalina," I said. "The bumpy ride will take about sixty minutes."

Marshmallow turned his head my way and hissed. "You mean we're going to be surrounded by water on all sides for a whole hour?"

"I hope we don't get seasick," I added.

Pixie sucked in her breath. "Why, Mimi, you can't possibly be thinking about taking a *boat* to the island."

"How else would I get there?" I started licking the foam off my iced tea. It tasted like victory and nutmeg.

"With the company jet, of course." She smiled at Marshmallow. "And that way, you won't have to leave your poor kitty behind."

Marshmallow let out a contented sigh and stretched his whole body across the mat.

Wait—what? I shook my head at Pixie. "Really, I don't want to inconvenience you."

Marshmallow gave a soft growl. "Come on, Mimi. You promised."

"It's no bother," Pixie said. "In fact, I insis—" Her phone rang.

Checking the caller display, she said, "I think the area code is from Catalina Island, but it's not my manager. Could it be spam?"

From his corner, Marshmallow licked his lips. I, too, started thinking about Josh's homemade Spam musubi.

Pixie let the call go to voice mail and then clicked on the message. We could all hear the replay:

"Miss St. James? This is Lavinia, head of the cleaning crew for your rental property. I didn't have time to come into the home until today, but something strange is going on. The last tenant left some of his stuff—and there's this weird blue stain on the carpet." Her voice grew flustered. "I can't reach Lloyd. Could you try and contact him? Thanks."

Pixie bit her lip after the message ended. "Lloyd Webster's my property manager." She tried his number right away. No answer.

"Bad reception maybe," I said.

She rang him again. No luck. Pixie drained her glass of seltzer water.

I tried to allay her fears. "There's probably a reasonable explanation. Maybe he's taking a coffee break. Try one more time."

She redialed and hit the jackpot.

And even though I didn't have my cat's sharp hearing, the man's voice was so loud I could eavesdrop on the whole conversation without straining.

Pixie's usually smooth voice grew brisk. "I've tried calling you several times already."

"Sorry," he said. "My ringer volume was on low."

"Is everything okay?" Pixie asked.

The man belted out, his voice even louder, "Why wouldn't it be?"

14

She explained the message from the cleaning lady and what the woman had found in the vacation home.

The voice on the other end grumbled. "I'm not surprised."

"Really?" Pixie raised her eyebrows.

"That renter wanted to stay longer at the last minute, and I put my foot down—hard. But the guy probably didn't listen and made some mischief at the house."

Pixie looked skeptical, but she said, "You'll take care of this, right, Lloyd?"

"Don't you worry. I'll talk to the cleaning crew and make sure to track down this Dav"—he stumbled over the word—"Dwayne and make him pay."

She hung up and stood staring into space for a moment.

"What's odd is the last renter was supposed to have already left yesterday morning," Pixie said. "Lloyd never told me the man had wanted to stay longer. And with the sudden cancelation from the next set of renters, he could've extended his time without any hassle. Although then I wouldn't have been able to offer you a vacation."

I shrugged. "I wouldn't have even thought about going to Catalina if you hadn't brought it up."

She frowned. "This is not the first miscommunication I've had with this manager."

"Who ran the rental house before?" I asked.

"I did, but it took too much time. In fact, all the contracts and marketing materials still have my contact info on them. Lloyd offered to give me a free trial run of his skills for one month, and I agreed. He has such an impressive résumé."

No wonder there'd been communication issues. My dad always said there was no such thing as a free lunch. (He worked in finance before retiring, so he had the proper expertise.) He told me that money always came from somewhere—and it looked like it'd leaked right through Pixie's fingers through the incompetence of her new hire.

The idea of free lunches made me hungry, and my stomach started growling.

Pixie gave me an apologetic look. "Unfortunately, all I have in the fridge are power shakes."

"That's okay. Marshmallow and I should get going anyway." I peeked at my cat, who'd gone comatose on the mat.

Pixie laughed. "Leave him with me while you get some food. And take your time, Mimi. I don't have any plans to go out today. Not with this Catalina house issue."

"That would actually be really great—thanks, Pixie." I wouldn't mind getting some lunch without needing to worry about where to keep Marshmallow while I ate. A craving for piping hot roti suddenly hit me.

Like Ma, though, I didn't like eating alone, and one more person meant I could order extra food sans guilt. I texted my sister to see if she'd meet up with me.

Roti Palace?

She messaged back. You know I'm in.

•   •   •

When I reached the stylized restaurant mimicking an open air food court, I spied my sister already seated at a fluorescent yellow plastic table with matching chairs. I bet the Roti Palace owners had wanted to emulate a bustling hawker atmosphere through their brightly colored dining furniture.

Alice stood up as I approached and hugged me. At the same five-foot stature, I didn't need to reach up for her embrace. Strangers always wondered if we were twins, given our similar petite frames and oval faces with elfin ears. Only our hair set us apart—Alice kept hers in an efficient bob with bangs while I often tried to tame my own unruly shoulder-length black hair into a flattering style.

My sister smiled at me as we both sat down. "I can never get enough of the food here," she said. "It's always super *shiok*."

Sometimes Ma's words from Manglish, a combination of English and various languages found in Malaysia, where she grew up, crept into our vocabulary.

"I agree. Everything is delicious at this place." Roti Palace served delicious roti flatbread, kind of like a multi-layered crepe. I liked to dip mine in curry sauce.

After we ordered, I decided to get an update on my sister's summer life. "Are you enjoying your break off from school and wrangling five-year-olds?"

She gushed with pride. "Oh, but the kids in my kindergarten class this past year were so amazing."

"You say that *every* year."

"And it's true each time." Her light brown eyes didn't hold even a glimmer of sarcasm.

I shrugged. Managing a classroom of kids felt like it'd be an anger management exercise for me. I much preferred a roomful of dogs—or cats.

"Looking forward to anything these next couple of months?" I asked.

She pulled a few napkins from the dispenser on the table and arranged them into a neat stack. "The usual summer schedule. Catching up on my to-be-read book pile and binge-watching Korean dramas."

I tugged at my earlobe, hating to impose on her despite her easygoing plans. "In that case, would you mind checking on the shop next week? Nicola will be there, but I'd feel better having someone check in on her in case she needs help."

"Oh." Her eyes widened. "Is everything okay at Hollywoof?"

"Everything's fine," I quickly assured her. "It's just that I'm going on a trip with Josh to Catalina Island for a few days."

She clasped her hands in delight. "Sounds lovely, Mimi, and oh-so-romantic."

My cheeks grew hot, and I dropped my gaze to the table.

"Who's going to take care of Marshmallow?" Alice asked. "Do you want to me to keep him company?"

My mouth quirked. "No need. He's invited along. Pixie has a new house in Catalina that she's allowing us to stay in. Marshmallow's presence will help her qualify the place as pet-friendly."

"Okay, so I can help check on Hollywoof for you . . . but I have a favor to ask in return." She took one of the napkins from her stack.

Huh. My sister never asked for assistance. Sometimes I wondered if it was an inherited family trait. "What do you need, Alice?"

"A wingman, er, woman." She folded the napkin into an origami heart.

"Interesting." I leaned forward. "For what?"

"Ma's entered me in a speed dating event."

My mouth dropped open.

Alice continued, "Say you'll come." She whipped out her phone, tapped away, and pivoted the screen for me to see.

I re-read Ma's text. She did have some strange matchmaking

schemes, like the time she tried to set me up with that Chinese food delivery guy, but "Superpowered Speed Dating"?

"Who even knows what that is?" Her wide eyes pleaded with me.

I held my hands up in surrender. "Fine. It's a deal." Whatever Ma had been plotting, I'd make sure to be there to help my little sis out.

CHAPTER

three

MARSHMALLOW EXUDED A good mood the next morning. It seemed like the extra massage and pampering had relaxed him enough to lower his usual grumpiness level. I'd enjoyed my own lunch outing yesterday with Alice and hummed as I set out his morning dish.

The "Chapel of Love" ringtone broke into my peaceful mood. I'd reserved this precise song for matrimony-minded Ma. I decided to put her on speaker because she typically talked in a loud voice, and I didn't need to lose my hearing anytime soon.

"Mimi," she said, her voice booming even more than usual. "I speak to *mei mei* yesterday night. Alice tell me you go to Cat-alina."

In the background, Marshmallow purred his approval. "That's how the name *should* be pronounced."

"I can't believe she told you already." What had Alice been thinking?

"She say she so busy, must watch pet shop this week. Cannot audition for date show—aiyoh!"

I rubbed my ear. "Are you referring to, like, a TV dating show?"

"Yes. It call *Old Maids*."

No wonder my sister had begged off. She'd probably used taking care of my shop as a prime reason to get out of another of Ma's match-making schemes. "They're airing a show with a title like that on a major network?"

"What 'major network' ah?"

I watched Marshmallow finish his last bite of kibble and retrieved his bowl. "You know, it's the big TV stations like ABC, NBC, etc."

She made a sound like she was sucking on a pickled plum. "*Old Maids* on YouTube."

Okay, that explained the egregious name.

I heard the reproach dripping from her next words. "Cat-alina not safe, Mimi."

Plopping the empty dish into the sink, I said, "It's a resort island, Ma. Seems pretty safe to me."

"I see on news, major network that man go missing. Havoc!"

Was there a way I could reassure Ma somehow? I pulled out my ace card. "Well, I'm not going alone. Josh will be coming."

"Oh? Josh and you two *pakat* and put heads together for this?" Her voice trilled at the pair of us scheming to plan a private trip. She even repeated my words about Josh coming along in an excited manner.

My dad's voice bellowed across the line. "What?!" Then his voice got muffled. Ma must've pulled the phone away because now all I heard was whisper-arguing in the background.

Dad had always been overprotective of us girls. He'd been golfing a lot since retiring, but he'd bought those clubs when we were pre-teens— in anticipation of warding off possible suitors. Turned out that he needn't have worried, at least given the lack of boys knocking down the door to see me during my adolescent years. Alice, on the other hand, had had secret admirers and love notes, but she'd never chosen to rebel against the no-dating-until-college rule.

Ma finally came back on the phone. "Sorry lah. Need talk to your dad more."

We hung up, and I turned around to find my cat staring up at me. "It'll be an exciting time at the next Family Game Night, huh?" Marshmallow said.

I cocked my head at him. "The one set for July Fourth?"

He gestured at my phone with his paw. "Yeah, bound to be fireworks."

Like a bad omen, Marshmallow's words sparked a sudden literal call for help. Pixie texted, Can you come over? Police are on their way.

What had happened? Once I'd gotten Marshmallow into the car and strapped him in the carrier, we hurtled down the streets. A dozen different scenarios flooded my brain, each situation worse than the last. Did she get robbed? Was Gelato hurt? Could this be a life-and-death matter?

When I arrived at Pixie's house, I knocked on the door. "It's Mimi."

Pixie opened it, and while she didn't seem to be in any immediate danger, her face appeared paler than usual. She seemed unharmed, though. Gelato sat near her feet and yipped a warm welcome to Marshmallow.

I enveloped Pixie in a huge hug that my dad would've been proud of. Maybe his bear hugging talent had passed down a generation. "What's going on, Pixie?"

"I received a call from a Detective Brown. He wanted to chat, and I automatically said yes. But I know you've had some scuffles with him before..."

"It was smart of you to text me." I felt my jaw tighten. The last time I'd been privy to one of the detective's "friendly chats," he'd been pegging my sister for murder.

Pixie invited me over to her immaculate kitchen. She pulled out a few glasses from a cabinet, but left them sitting empty on the breakfast bar counter as she stared distractedly toward the foyer.

A few tense moments passed with her clutching onto the glassware before the doorbell rang. She hurried to let in the detective, Gelato nipping at her heels like a fierce little guard dog.

I heard Detective Brown's voice thunder in the air. "May we both come in?"

Had he brought along a partner? That was new.

A yip from Gelato and a responding sweet purr answered my question.

Marshmallow and I glanced at each other.

"Nimbus," I said as my cat nodded.

"Hope you don't mind," the detective said to Pixie. "I just came from the vet's."

"Not a problem," she said.

Detective Brown had brought over the stray kitten I'd found hanging around Roosevelt Elementary, the school where my sister worked. I'd named the kitty myself after I'd washed off the dirt and discovered a soft gray ball of fluff underneath. Even a hardened cop like Detective Brown couldn't resist her cuteness, and he'd soon adopted Nimbus.

Pixie and the detective walked into the room with measured steps. Nimbus scampered into view and said hello to Marshmallow, greeting him with a nose rub.

When Detective Brown spotted my presence at the breakfast bar, he stopped in his tracks and stared at me. A muscle in his neck twitched. "Miss Lee. What are you doing here?"

"I'm a friend of Pixie's," I said. "After all, she gave me the capital to open up Hollywoof. And friends always have each other's backs."

I didn't know if he'd heard my aggressive verbal promise of support for Pixie, but he straightened the lapel of his gray suit jacket. It looked free of fur, so he'd either excessively lint-rolled the thing, or the kitty fur happened to match the fabric.

I pulled out a stool for Pixie to sit on. She settled in the ergonomic seating and cradled the shih tzu on her lap. Kudos to the excitable pup because he managed to stay still and provided her with much-needed emotional comfort.

Detective Brown remained standing, a power move if ever I saw one. I excused myself to rummage in the kitchen for beverages. Maybe Pixie would feel calmer with a drink in her hand. However, I didn't know how to make any of her fancy concoctions and had to settle for a large bottle of purified volcanic water. I poured some into the three glasses on the counter.

The detective ignored my attempt at hospitality. He leaned against the countertop and narrowed his gaze at my friend. "Pixie St. James," he said, "have you ever been in contact with someone named Davis D. Argo?"

She gave a no-nonsense stare back at the detective. "No. Never."

Marshmallow and Nimbus showed up for the questioning party, and the gray kitty rubbed herself against Pixie's ankles. Pixie, in turn, reached down and stroked the kitty's head.

Detective Brown leaned closer to Pixie and towered over her. "You might know the man better as 'Dwayne A.'"

Pixie's eyes widened.

"I take it you recognize that name?" Detective Brown said as Nimbus continued to endear herself to Pixie's legs.

Marshmallow twitched his whiskers. "I know what you're trying to do, Detective Brown. Good cat, bad cop. But it won't work on Pixie because she's innocent."

I piped up. "Stop badgering the witness, Detective." Sometimes Josh's legalese slipped out of my mouth by accident.

Pixie sipped her volcanic water and composed herself. She straightened her back and said, "I've got nothing to hide. I do know the last person you mentioned. This Dwayne fellow rented my house on Catalina Island."

The detective rubbed at his stubble. "Did you have any problems with this individual, Miss St. James?"

She focused her gaze on the clear contents of her glass as though searching for an answer there. After a short pause, she said, "He was supposed to have vacated the premises a couple of days ago. When the cleaning crew went to clean the house for my next guests"—she avoided eye contact with me, maybe not wanting to involve me in this—"they mentioned he'd left some of his belongings and had deliberately ruined the carpet with a blue stain."

Detective Brown gave a low whistle. "So the man didn't want to agreeably leave your rental property?"

In a calm voice, Pixie said, "I'm taking care of the situation."

"I know," Detective Brown said. "I've recovered a threatening letter that you wrote to Davis."

Pixie opened her mouth, but no sound came out.

Marshmallow hissed.

"What letter?" I asked.

"I have in evidence a note telling Davis to get off Miss St. James's property 'on pain of death.'"

"What? Who speaks like that?" I said. It sounded like a line from an old movie.

"Apparently," Detective Brown said, "Miss St. James does."

I glared at the cop. "Where's your proof?"

He reached into his pocket, took his phone out, and showed me the image of a document. I scanned it, focusing on a name in cursive at the bottom of the letter. He then presented the picture to Pixie. "Is this your signature, Miss St. James?"

She jutted her chin at him. "It looks like it—but I didn't write that note."

I moved toward the detective, craning my neck, and peered again at the image on the phone. "The rest of the document is typewritten," I said. "It's not even in Pixie's handwriting. Doesn't that seem suspicious to you?"

"I call this letter a solid lead," Detective Brown said.

"To what?"

"Davis Argo recently disappeared after making a trip to the island."

My hand flew to my mouth. Ma had been talking to me about someone going missing on Catalina Island—and it'd been Pixie's renter.

Detective Brown's face shuttered. "Yes, it's already been broadcast on the news." He turned to Pixie. "I believe that Davis's sister even phoned you to ask about him."

Pixie gave a slow nod, and I remembered the call she'd received the other day from an unknown number.

I blurted, "Maybe the guy drowned in the ocean. Disappeared when his Jet Skiing went south." A tragic accident was sad, but at least it would get the detective off my friend's case.

Detective Brown's face grew grim. "The man's not missing anymore."

Pixie wrinkled her nose. "If he's been found, then why are you here questioning me?"

Detective Brown gave a short cough. "Yes, we did discover him—dead."

CHAPTER

four

"DEAD?" PIXIE ECHOED the detective's words. "What do you mean?"

"He was murdered," Detective Brown said. The sudden ice in his tone made me shiver. Even Nimbus meowed out in alarm.

I drew in a breath. "When? And how?"

"The details of his death remain under wraps," the detective said. "And, Mimi, for your own good, don't try to investigate."

Did I have to remind him that I'd practically handed him the culprits on a silver platter for two of his cases?

He pulled his attention away from me and moved on to needling Pixie. "Perhaps you remember more about your dispute with Davis Argo now that the truth is out."

I wondered if Detective Brown was referring to the murder and making an insinuation against my friend. Taking his glass, I moved it away from his reach. No need to quench his thirst for anything, whether gossip or water.

Pixie looked the detective in the eye and said, "I didn't have any major issues with Dwayne—uh, Davis—but my property manager did."

Detective Brown furrowed his brow. "What manager?"

She ran her hand over her cropped brunette hair. "The one I hired on a trial basis this past week."

"How conveniently timed," he said.

She ignored the detective's comment and whipped out her cell phone. "You can ask him for further details. I'll send you his vCard."

Detective Brown blinked at her. I bet he didn't have any idea that a vCard meant an electronic business card. And that he didn't know how to use Bluetooth to receive the data.

I cleared my throat. "Pixie will need your contact info to send it over by text or email."

"Right." He fished in his jacket pocket and plopped his own real-life business card on her breakfast bar.

Seeing the rectangular cardstock lying there, I wondered how the detective even had jurisdiction for Catalina. Was he collaborating with their police department? How could I tease out the answer? "Detective Brown," I said in an innocent manner, "is Catalina Island supervised by Los Angeles County for police enforcement?"

Marshmallow whacked his paw against my ankle. "Real subtle there, Nancy Drew."

The detective stared at me with his ice blue eyes. "I repeat, no digging, Miss Lee."

I gulped.

Marshmallow gave a soft meow. "Told you so, Miss Obvious-Lee. I should be the one taking charge around here."

Hmm. Not a bad idea. I motioned toward Nimbus, and Marshmallow caught the hint.

"I'm on it," he said. "That little kitty might spill something."

Thank goodness Marshmallow could speak to other animals. On his list of communication hits so far were cats, dogs, and birds.

Marshmallow managed to entice Nimbus to follow him to the massage mat area. Maybe the pampering would make the questioning more productive.

I tuned back in to the human conversation to find Detective Brown tying things up. He stopped leaning over Pixie and said, "I'll be sure to look into this matter some more."

Pixie plucked the detective's card with her fingers. "Please do. You won't find any evidence of my involvement in your case."

"Be aware, Miss St. James, that it was your house the victim rented and your correspondence he received last, as far as we are aware." Detective Brown brushed his hands off as though finished with a solid verdict.

My eyes narrowed as he said goodbye in a stilted manner and removed Nimbus away from Marshmallow's company.

The detective marched his way back to the entrance. Pixie and I followed right behind him. I was ready to literally shove him out the door if needed.

After he left, we stayed in the foyer, staring at the closed door. Pixie's shoulders hunched. "He doesn't believe me," she said.

"Because of an obviously faked letter." I stopped myself short of rolling my eyes.

"Where did he even get that from?"

A worry line creased Pixie's forehead. "Honestly, I have no idea. How would someone have gotten my signature in the first place? And why would they forge a letter with my name on it?"

"I still can't believe he suspects you," I said. "Anyone who's met you knows you wouldn't hurt a soul."

Pixie's eyes got a faraway look. "The timing's tricky, though, because I *was* just on the island."

"That was a coincidence." I put my hands on my hips. "We'll have to change the detective's mind, but it's not the first time I've had to deal with him."

I corralled her back to the cozier kitchen space. Pixie sat on a stool at the breakfast bar and massaged her temples. "This vacation rental is starting to look like nothing but trouble."

I clicked my tongue in sympathy. "Well, I'll be going to the island soon, and I'm sure I can get some answers for you." I brushed away the quick image of a disappointed Josh, who was looking forward to quality time with me, but I hoped he'd understand.

Pixie stopped massaging her forehead to peer at me. Her eyes misted up. "You're an amazing friend, Mimi."

My Catalina vacation probably wouldn't be restful. After all, I only had a few days to gather the evidence needed to prove Pixie's innocence.

• • •

Back home, as I prepared to pack for my trip to Catalina, I touched base with Marshmallow to hear about what he'd discovered from Nimbus.

"Not much," Marshmallow said as he curled up on my bed next to my closed suitcase.

"But she's a detective's cat. Nimbus didn't know anything?" I zipped open the suitcase.

Marshmallow placed a paw over his eyes, as if in disbelief. "She said she wasn't paying much attention to his work. But she did fill me in on her latest escapade with a ball of yarn and her favorite brand of cat treats."

Shaking my head, I marched over to my closet and started rummaging through possible clothing choices. Tees and shorts would be the best bet for the forecasted warm temperatures, but would I also need a fancy outfit in case of a candlelight dinner?

Marshmallow shifted on the bed, and I sighed. Probably not, especially with a third fur wheel around.

Misinterpreting my irritation, Marshmallow said, "Don't worry. I gave Nimbus some pointers. Told her to eavesdrop on his conversations, sniff him for clues, that sort of thing."

I shook off my previous frustration. "I admit, that's good advice."

Marshmallow purred.

I placed my clothes into the suitcase and wondered if I should pack a swimsuit. Not like there'd be much time for snorkeling if I devoted my trip to snooping instead. I turned to my cat, remembering something he'd mentioned about Nimbus. "You said she wasn't paying much attention, but did she provide you with any tidbit of info?"

Marshmallow nodded. "She said her owner left her alone until midnight one day."

"Could he have been traveling to Catalina? Using the ferry can be a whole day affair."

"Also, Detective Brown took a long shower afterward. It's a shame humans don't have an easier bathing option—they'd be less stinky company that way." Marshmallow started grooming himself while I double-checked to make sure I'd tucked deodorant into my toiletry bag.

Had the cop taken a long shower to wash away the filth of a crime scene? Or perhaps he'd gotten seasick on the ferry ride.

Thank goodness Pixie had taken care of my travel arrangements. It'd be a treat to fly to the island on her private jet instead of resorting to a bumpy ferry ride. I reexamined my packing and closed the suitcase. "Ready to get your sleuthing on, Marshmallow?"

"As ever, my dear Watson."

CHAPTER

five

JOSH, MARSHMALLOW, AND I experienced a smooth flight. My cat, uncharacteristically, stayed quiet during the short plane ride. I darted glances at him in his airplane carrier as I told Josh about the situation Pixie had found herself in.

From above, Catalina Island appeared like a mountainous hulk in the middle of crystalline blue waters. Squinting, I could spy the curve of the horseshoe-shaped Avalon Bay. Although Catalina also offered more rugged terrain, most people associated the island name with the bustling city of Avalon.

We drew closer to the land, passing over the beautiful residences and the iconic Catalina Casino building, which housed an elegant ballroom that used to offer first-run feature films. However, our plane could only land at Airport in the Sky, which sat atop a plateau. Its long runway was surrounded by numerous mountains, and we had to take a shuttle to reach the residential area of Avalon.

Finding ourselves without a car, we decided to rent one of the ubiquitous golf carts to travel around the island. It was either that or take a taxi. The golf carts appeared everywhere, standing in orderly lines, like vehicle soldiers, ready to battle the roads for us.

We made our way over to Pixie's rental home, our little golf cart chugging up a steep hill to do so. The GPS led us to a tasteful house painted in delicate dove gray. We parked and approached the entryway, where a cheerful welcome mat with hibiscus flowers printed on it greeted us on the doorstep.

Unlocking the house and stepping inside, we found ourselves surrounded by a vibrant interior. Josh offered to put away our luggage while I continued to goggle at my surroundings.

In the living room, I found overstuffed furniture bursting in sunshine yellow. They seemed even brighter positioned on the pure white fluffy carpet. I bet the entire place would be no less of a bold architectural statement.

Marshmallow, freed from his carrier, swished his tail and said, "I call dibs on this spot." He padded his way past a tall glass case filled with trinkets over to a location near the expansive window, where rays of happy sunshine floated in. He curled up on a zebra-patterned area rug while I wandered over to look through the sparkling clean glass of a huge window. I soaked in the view, an amazing panorama of glistening water speckled with boats.

I felt Josh come behind me and place his hands on my shoulders. I'd probably be able to pick out his touch blindfolded. There was a certain way he curled his fingers around my shoulders that made me feel cherished, like he was holding on to something valuable.

The view looked twice as grand when we marveled at it together. I loved the majestic curve of the bay and how the boats cheerfully gathered in the shimmering water.

Josh eased his hands off me. I felt a wave of dismay as he broke the physical connection. He pointed outside.

"Look at that refreshing water," he said. "I bet it'd be magnificent to go snorkeling. Maybe catch a glimpse of the state fish."

"The humuhumunukunukuapua`a?"

"No." He laughed. "*Your* state fish."

I drew a blank. I'd lived all my life in California but couldn't for the life of me recall ever learning that factoid. My memory instead surfaced with an image of the grizzly bear.

"It's the garibaldi," Josh said. "A bright orange fish."

"I was just about to say that."

"Sure you were," he said in a teasing tone. "You want to take a look around the rest of the house? You know, venture beyond the living room? Everything's done in the Gatsby style."

"Right," I said. "Since you're so knowledgeable about the Great American Novel." He often told me how he had daydreamed through his high school English classes.

A snarl interrupted us before we even started to move. Marshmallow glared at the zebra rug before him. "The best spot in the house is ruined by a rank smell."

"What is it?" I crept closer to my cat.

Marshmallow vacated his spot. "I hope that it's not actually skunk fur disguised as zebra."

I flipped the edge of the rug up. A faint whiff of smoke released in the air, but more disturbing was the bright blue stain on the otherwise snow-white carpet.

I remembered what the cleaning lady had mentioned to Pixie. Perhaps she hadn't been able to scrub out the vibrant color. "What would leave such a mark?" I said.

Now beside me, Josh wrinkled his nose. "Paint ball?"

But it didn't look like paint—it was less liquid in texture and more powdery.

From the corner of my eye, I noticed Marshmallow peering wide-eyed into the glass case nearby. "There's something else," he said.

I moved to join him and stared at the display shelves. The collection seemed to be an array of belongings from famous people who'd lived on the island.

Relics, all labeled, included Bob Hope's cuff links and Clark Gable's cigarette case. I noticed an empty space on the middle shelf. A nearby slip of paper read, "Marilyn Monroe's headscarf." But no fabric lay in that bare spot.

I blinked at the missing item a few times before I decided to take charge of the matter. Pacing around the house, I dialed Pixie's number.

She picked up on the first ring, sounding a bit breathless. "Is everything okay? Did you get there safely?"

"Yes, we're all settled. And it's a really nice house, but . . ."

"You hate the décor," she said.

"No, it's not that," I said, admiring a fan-shaped golden mirror on the wall.

"The decorator made sure to try and keep the originals as much as possible. She said the Art Deco style would be a draw for vacationers."

"The house has great personality." I wandered over to a bathroom, which had an actual claw-foot tub and checkerboard flooring. "But I'm actually calling about your glass cabinet."

Her tone brightened. "My curio case. I wanted a mini museum-quality display in the home."

"Excellent picks, too." I paused. "Did you happen to take one of the items out when you last visited the island?"

"Of course not. They're a collection and supposed to stay together. Why?"

I gulped and headed to the kitchen to get some water for my suddenly dry throat. "The headscarf worn by Marilyn Monroe . . . it's gone."

She drew in her breath as I crossed under a looming chandelier, a veritable sunburst of crystals. I began searching in the kitchen cabinets for a water glass.

Using a hushed voice, Pixie said, "I won that in an auction."

"Is it worth a lot?" I asked, extracting a glass and filling it with tap water.

"Four figures."

The water flooded the glass before I remembered to turn off the faucet. I managed to steady my voice. "For a flimsy piece of fabric?"

"Imagine holding fame in your hands," she said.

"I don't see signs of it anywhere in the living room area," I said. "Someone really must have been a Marilyn Monroe fan."

"A shame," she said. "Can you go report it to Lloyd, my manager? He works at the Catalina Chalets office. I always met with him at the rental home, but the business shouldn't be too hard to find in such a small town."

"I'll go ahead and follow up with him."

Pixie thanked me, then added, "Don't get too caught up in figuring this scarf thing out. Make sure you spend time enjoying your break on the island."

I made a noncommittal murmur as we ended our conversation. Then I searched online for the Catalina Chalets office.

CHAPTER

Six

JOSH INSISTED ON coming along with me to pay a visit to Lloyd. "The guy sounds shady," he said as he maneuvered the golf cart across the bumpy ground. We parked in the downtown area, where I couldn't help but be charmed by its small village feel. I knew the shops had been constructed to appeal to tourists, with their picturesque windows and candy-colored signs, but I still delighted in strolling down the cobblestone paths.

Catalina Chalets, though, wasn't located on any such cheerful main street. Instead, it lay hidden down a side alley. The storefront corresponding to the address also didn't match the business name. Instead, the sign read, "The Job Joint."

Josh and I looked at each other, perplexed.

I shrugged. "Might as well go in."

He nodded. "Even if it's the wrong place, someone should be able to point us in the right direction."

The Job Joint seemed to be a career center of some sort. A fair amount of desks appeared in orderly lines. Beleaguered individuals sat in chairs across from placement specialists, who flipped through ancient Rolodexes or tapped away on computer keyboards, depending on their ages. In the rear left-hand corner, I also noticed a space called "Dress to Impress." It was sectioned off by a full-length curtain like a dressing room. I figured it must be some sort of work clothes closet.

Josh and I remained standing near the entrance of the business, taking in our surroundings. He swiveled his head back and forth, maybe trying to find a clue as to where the actual Catalina Chalets office was located. Meanwhile, I half raised my hand, like a timid schoolgirl, and tried to attract the attention of one of the busy employees around us.

Finally, a career specialist finished with his client and got up to greet us. He had dark, inky hair and horn-rimmed glasses, and his lean frame reminded me of a long-distance cyclist.

"I'm the owner of The Job Joint. Are you two lost?" the man asked. "We don't usually get couples coming in here looking for work."

I could picture a thought bubble floating above his head that read, "Pesky tourists."

Josh spoke up. "We're looking for a business called Catalina Chalets. The address we mapped out brought us to this location."

The man adjusted his eyeglasses and said, "My brother Lloyd runs that fledgling company out of the back room. I'll show you."

No wonder Lloyd had had such an impressive résumé to give to Pixie. I bet his brother had provided big-time help in crafting it.

We passed by the desks of every staff member in the room before reaching the back of the building, where we stopped before a nondescript wooden door.

I raised my eyebrows. "How does anyone ever find this company?"

The man chuckled. "Lloyd has a handful of clients, and he always goes to *them*." He rapped once on the closed door and then left us standing there on the threshold.

The door opened with a squeak. Although the man before us had the same inky hair as his brother, the physical similarity ended there. Lloyd had the broad body of someone who'd played football in his youth (and maybe still did in his spare time). He wore a seersucker suit that might have been fashionable back in the 1950s. Still, it fit him well, and he kinda pulled off the retro vibe.

The man stared at the pair of us with wide eyes. "Who are you?"

I extended my hand to him. "I'm Mimi Lee, and this is Josh Akana. We're friends of Pixie St. James, and she's letting us stay at her place for a few days."

He gave a curt nod. "She did mention that."

"Um." My eyes darted around the small office with its light beige walls, cobwebbed in the highest corners. A wide particleboard desk and a swivel chair took up most of the space. Loose papers, a clunky desktop, and an ancient inkjet printer sat on the table's surface. In the dusty corner of the room stood a copy machine. The only warmth in the tight space was a dejected-looking wilting plant on the messy tabletop. Of course, there weren't any guest chairs to sit in.

"We need to report a missing item from the rental house," I said.

"What?" His coal eyes locked onto me. "How can that be?"

It almost sounded like he blamed me for losing (or taking) something of value.

Josh stepped up to him and said, "We just discovered it when we checked in and called Pixie right away. She recommended coming over here."

"Hmm." Lloyd sat in his computer chair and hunched over his desk.

He picked up a pencil and a random piece of paper. "What exactly is gone?"

"A headscarf worn by Marilyn Monroe. It was supposed to be in the display case."

He ground his teeth together. "That could be worth a pretty penny."

I suppressed my groan. Yeah, didn't I know it.

Lloyd scribbled a note on the paper before him.

I peeked over his shoulder. "'NJD's headscarf'?" I read.

"Norma Jeane was Marilyn's name when she lived here on the island."

Josh cleared his throat. "Do you think this should be a matter for the police?"

"Eh," Lloyd said. "They're probably too busy with that missing man case."

Dead man, I corrected him in my head. If only he knew how serious the matter really was. Instead, my manners won over, and I wished him a good day as we left.

My mind remained on the valuable Marilyn Monroe memento. It still bothered me that it'd been snatched out of the display case. Someone would've needed access to Pixie's vacation home to have done so. Who would have been there most recently? The cleaning crew came to mind.

• • •

I got the head of the cleaning crew's phone number from Pixie, and we managed to squeeze in time to see Lavinia between scheduled cleanings. However, we had to meet her at the current place she was tidying up while she packed away her supplies.

We only caught a glimpse of Lavinia when we arrived at the house, a picturesque cottage. She reminded me of an army sergeant, with her commanding voice and her heavy footsteps. She flicked her hand in the direction of the porch when she noticed us. We dutifully moved over there to wait until she was available to talk.

While we sat down on the cute porch swing close to a flower garden occupied by fairy statues, Lavinia and her team bustled by us, wielding feather dusters, mops, and rubber gloves. The crew tossed everything inside a van labeled, "Clean as a Whistle: in business since 1991."

Then Lavinia turned her attention to us. She marched over to our swing and stood there like a human concrete pillar, as she towered over us. I couldn't help but fixate on her squat legs and hefty forearms. "So, you two are staying at one of the other Catalina Chalets?"

Josh gave a confused smile. "'Other' Catalina Chalets?"

"Yeah." She jerked her thumb at the cottage. "The others like this one, owned by richies from the mainland? I have to clean all four of them on the island. Along with half of the other rentals on Catalina."

"We're staying at the home owned by Pixie St. James," I said. "The Art Deco–style chalet."

Although Lavinia may have exaggerated the number of homes she cleaned, she probably did tidy more than a few of the vacation rentals here. If she'd stolen from any of the owners, I figured she wouldn't have been able to keep her business running for so long. I could pick her brain about the current theft.

"Did you happen to notice anything odd in the living room when you last cleaned Pixie's home?" I asked.

She crossed her substantial arms over her chest and grunted. "Let me tell you. The mess that last tenant left . . ."

Guess she didn't see anything out of the ordinary with the display case. Maybe talking more about the living space would jog her memory. "We did see the blue stain on the carpet," I said.

She harrumphed. "I don't know what he was doing, but the color soaked in deep into the fibers."

Josh used his smooth lawyerly tone. "I'm sure you did the best that you could, Lavinia."

"Of course. We're not called 'Clean as a Whistle' for nothing."

"We noticed that you placed a zebra rug over the stained area," I said.

Her nostrils flared. "The blue color looks horrendous. I couldn't stand seeing it any longer, so I moved the rug over a few feet. Plus, the scorch mark was a huge eyesore."

Josh and I looked at each other with our eyebrows raised.

"Wait, did it catch on fire?" I asked Lavinia.

"Already doused by the time I came," she said.

Josh shook his head. "Still . . ."

Lavinia made a kicking motion with her foot. "Glad to be rid of that last renter. Leaving his stuff behind like castoffs for us to throw out."

I tugged at my ear. "What's that?"

"His pile of junk lingering in the house," she said.

In his excitement, Josh rocked the porch swing, making me wobble. "Where exactly did he leave his stuff?" he asked.

"By the grill. I didn't haul it out to the bins because it's not trash day yet. Besides, maybe he'll call up Lloyd, wanting to get it back, and then I'll be in trouble."

I almost bolted up to search the property right away, but Josh placed his hand on my shoulder to keep me still.

Lavinia squinted at us. "At least you two lovebirds seem like you won't leave a mess. Too busy being holed up in your bedroom." She chortled.

Josh snatched his arm away from me, and I felt myself turning red as the driver in the cleaning van leaned on the horn.

"I must've lost track of time," Lavinia said. "It's off to the next job."

Josh and I stood to leave as well, but I felt unsteady as I got to my feet. More from an emotional rollercoaster than the sudden rocking motion of the porch swing. Lavinia's teasing comment had left me unsettled.

Lavinia had called us "lovebirds." But Josh and I had agreed not to take big steps in our relationship, so we hadn't even said the L-word to each other yet. "I really like you" was the closest I'd ever let loose, and ditto for him. After Lavinia's comment, Josh had pulled his hand away from me pretty quickly. Were we really going at a leisurely pace or headed for a relationship slowdown?

CHAPTER

seven

THANK GOODNESS LAVINIA had thrown us a bone by divulging information about the junk Davis had left. At least I'd have a distraction at the rental home.

When we returned, the patio was dappled with the late afternoon sunshine. The grill hood shone like it'd been polished to perfection. In this gentle setting, it felt like the trash bag couldn't contain anything too sinister . . . could it?

Josh and I both stood about four feet away from the black garbage bag. I wished I had X-ray vision and could see inside without actually touching it.

"I'll let you have the first peek," I said, urging him toward the bag.

He gulped. "Ladies first?"

We stood there frozen before Marshmallow barged in.

"What's with the wax museum stillness?" he said. "It's like someone died around here."

I squealed and jumped in the air. "What if . . . it's the missing man? Or parts of him in the bag?"

Josh furrowed his brow. "What exactly did Detective Brown tell you again?"

I grumbled. "Not much."

Marshmallow sighed. "You two scaredy rats. I'll check out the sitch." He padded over to the bag and sniffed at it. "Can't smell anything rotting, must not be something organic."

Nudging the bag with his head, he continued, "Feels hard, kind of like pieces of equipment."

"What could it be?" I edged closer to the bag while Josh put his arm up to barricade me.

"We don't know what's inside, Mimi," he said. "Could be dangerous."

I nodded at Marshmallow. "He doesn't seem scared. And don't animals have a sixth sense?"

Marshmallow purred. "Or at least a lot more sense than humans."

Inching forward, I fumbled with the knot on top of the bag with shaking fingers. Josh joined my side, and his presence helped steady my nerves enough to untie the bag. I pulled it open wide but squeezed my eyes shut to prolong the reveal.

In that short time gap, I heard Josh shifting beside me. "What are those?" he asked.

Opening my eyes, I tried to take inventory, but the contents looked murky inside the bag. Flipping the bag on the side, I managed to dump the top item out on the deck.

A canister almost rolled away from me, but I stopped it with my foot. "What is that?"

Josh sucked on his teeth. "A smoke grenade."

"Yikes." I stepped back.

"Don't worry, Mimi. It's not a weapon. They're used for, like, weddings. You know, to make plumes of colorful smoke."

Marshmallow hissed. "A smoke grenade could have caused the blue stain on the carpet."

"Oh, this smoke grenade might explain the scorch mark," I said.

Josh motioned to the bag. "May I?"

I heaved it over to him. "There's definitely more stuff inside."

Josh used the light from his phone to illuminate the contents and studied them all. "Looks like there's a cache of sparklers and fireworks in here."

"That makes a lot of sense. It is pretty close to July Fourth." I frowned. "Guess this wasn't such an important find."

"Except that fireworks are illegal on Catalina Island," he said.

Josh's brown eyes glittered. I wondered if we were thinking the same thing. If Davis had deliberately smuggled fireworks into Catalina, what kind of crowd did he hang out with? The dangerous type, who played with fire—and perhaps, lives?

"We should tell the police," I said.

"I'm on it." Josh used his cell phone and put the call on speakerphone, no doubt so we could both hear.

When someone from the department answered, Josh and I both tried explaining at the same time. We stumbled over each other's words. Finally, the disinterested voice on the line said, "It's too late in the day for someone to follow up on your report, but I'll be sure to take down your contact information. An officer will be by sometime tomorrow."

After providing the address and giving our thanks, Josh hung up. Meanwhile, Marshmallow had scurried back inside the house. I could see him through the patio doors circling the kitchen with a plaintive cry. "Must. Eat. Now," he said.

"Er"—I pointed at Marshmallow—"looks like he's hungry. I think we might need to do a quick grocery run."

As we headed inside, Josh said, "You'd better drive then, speedster."

"Very funny," I said as he handed me the keys.

"It's called a speed limit, not a speed suggestion," he teased.

I peeked at him, but Josh had already pasted an angelic smile on his face. In my peripheral view, I saw Marshmallow rolling on the kitchen floor in silent laughter.

• • •

Josh and I went to the grocery store, where they'd definitely hiked up the prices for the island-bound residents (or at least us tourists). We ended up with a bag of kibble and a few deli sandwiches for dinner.

When we got home, Marshmallow was dramatically sprawled across the kitchen floor in mock agony. "What took you so long?" he said.

"You're welcome," I said, filling up his bowl. Then I pointed to his stomach. "I think your reserves would have kept you from starving."

Marshmallow turned his back on me and focused on his food.

Soon, Josh tapped me on the shoulder, and I noticed he'd placed our sandwiches onto porcelain plates for a much homier feel. He cocked his head at Marshmallow. "Do you always make fun of your cat like that? It's a good thing he doesn't understand you."

I shook my head and said, "I don't think his self-esteem will suffer any."

Marshmallow meowed. "It's not really arrogance if it's true."

Josh and I ate our sandwiches (turkey for him and chicken salad for me) perched on the bright yellow sofa. As we munched, I flipped over the zebra rug with my foot. At the edge of the blue stain, I saw the telltale scorch mark.

Why had Davis been using a smoke grenade indoors when it was clearly a fire hazard? Then again, maybe he hadn't wanted neighbors to nose into his business. Absorbed by my conjectures, I'd finished my entire sandwich while staring at the scorched spot.

When I looked up, I realized that Josh had barely eaten his sandwich. It lay beside him, ignored, while he focused on his phone. His eyebrows were drawn together in concentration as he texted away.

"Um, what are you doing?" I asked.

"Work," he said, as though that explained everything.

"We're eating dinner together right now."

"Are we?" He didn't even look up to speak. "You seemed lost in thought a little while ago."

I bit back a retort since I *had* been thinking about Davis earlier. "Fine," I said, trying to keep my tone light. "What do you want to do tonight?" Maybe we'd snuggle on the couch and watch a show.

Josh mumbled something and proceeded to scarf down his food. Yes, he couldn't wait to spend time together.

"I was thinking about some TV, maybe a movie," I said, edging toward the living room.

"Go ahead." Josh waved me off—and proceeded to make a phone call. "I just have to—oh good," he said to the person who answered, "you're still in the office."

Did he really just . . . dismiss me? I understood work was important, but was he going to ignore me the whole night? Before I could dig any deeper into his intentions, my own phone rang.

My dad's name flashed on the caller ID. I headed to the bedroom for privacy to chat with him.

Dad practically shouted at me when I answered. "Mimi," he said. "Hope I'm interrupting something."

"Excuse me?"

50

He caught himself. "I said, 'I hope I'm *not* interrupting something.'" Only a bunch of nothing.

I spotted my suitcase through the open door of a room and sat on the queen-size poster bed inside. There were about half a dozen pillows on the mattress, so I pushed them around to make space and positioned a tufted ivory one behind my back.

Dad took a deep breath. "To begin with, let me tell you about my day." He proceeded to share about every single thing that had happened to him, from his morning cup of coffee (black with two packets of sugar) to his scorecard on the green (slightly above par) to a reminder about the upcoming Family Game Night (on the Fourth of July).

Then he moved on to asking me about our trip. He peppered me with questions about the flight, the décor of the rental house, and even the weather.

I didn't know how long we'd been talking, but at the end of his questioning, my wrist started hurting. "Dad, I should probably get going."

"Oh wait," he said. "Ma might want to chat with you, too."

I heard her angry whispering down the line. She must have been very frustrated because she clipped her words out in polite formal English: "I do not want to talk to her, Greg. Josh and Mimi require their couple time."

I felt a sudden phantom ringing in my ears, and I didn't think it was caused by holding the phone too long next to my head.

Dad cleared his throat. "Don't forget, you're my little Princess One." (My sister, Alice, was Princess Two.)

"Little" Princess now, huh? Still, I smiled at his term of endearment. "Don't worry, Daddy," I said.

He murmured a good night and hung up the phone. When I checked the time, I realized that I'd been on the phone awhile.

I returned to the living room to see Josh furiously texting on his phone. He mumbled something about a missed filing, and his eyes didn't even flicker my way.

Marshmallow sat on a couch arm and gave an exaggerated yawn. "His legal droning is starting to put me to sleep."

I debated on pulling Josh away but couldn't fault him for a good work ethic. I really hoped we could spend time together tonight, though. "I'll be in the bedroom," I said. "Get me when you're done."

He stopped texting, glanced at me, and kneaded his forehead. "Just trying to put out a work fire. It'll take maybe fifteen more minutes?"

An hour of web surfing later, and I lay alone on top of the lacy comforter in the bedroom staring at the ceiling. To be fair, I'd varied my pose by checking out the faded wallpaper stamped with leaf prints and hung with various framed sepia photos.

Us time wouldn't be happening, I thought as I brushed my teeth and climbed back into bed with my favorite pj's.

A shadow peeked over the edge of the bedroom door, and hope bubbled up inside me. But a soft meow revealed it to be Marshmallow lurking at the threshold.

My shoulders slumped. "He's still working, right?" I said.

Marshmallow's blue eyes glittered. "More room for me then." His tail swished as he crossed the room and jumped onto the bed.

I closed my eyes, attempting to block out the world and the sting of unmet expectations. Marshmallow stretched himself across my chest. I could hear the soothing rumble of his purring.

The vibration started making me drowsy. Besides the purring, I heard this reassurance from him as I fell asleep: "Sleep tight, pussycat."

CHAPTER

eight

WOKE UP WITH the taste of fur in my mouth. Blech.

Blinking, I spied Marshmallow nestled on top of the pillow next to my head. He emitted little contented purrs and definitely looked sweeter (and more innocent) when asleep.

I assessed my hair in the mirror in the checkered bathroom. Somehow it was bedhead times one hundred. Not even bothering to tame the strands, I threw it up into a ponytail.

Passing by the other bedrooms, I looked for signs of Josh. Nope. Eventually, I found him collapsed on the living room sofa. The length of his body extended over the cushions, and one arm dangled off the couch, almost trailing along the carpeted floor. I noticed his cell phone lying on the zebra rug, an island of technology adrift in the black and white stripes.

I yawned and moseyed over to the coffee maker. It was one of those high-tech pod devices that my dad had never sprung for because of the initial investment cost. I busied myself figuring out the modes and buttons. Thinking of Josh, I searched first for a coffee pod. Rich medium roast, it read. The last one in the box.

Ma had drilled this Confucius saying into my head at an early age: "A heart set on love will do no wrong." A cup of fresh-brewed coffee could be my way to connect with Josh. Then again, why did I always have to initiate?

Since he hadn't gone out of his way to do me any favors, I decided to swap out the coffee for orange pekoe breakfast tea—for me to relish. Why should I reward him when he hadn't spared any time for me last night?

I'd just poured myself a steaming mug of the tea when a heavy pounding sounded at the door. Josh stirred at the noise. His eyelids fluttered, but he fell back asleep.

I peeked through the kitchen window and swallowed. A uniformed police officer stood outside. I hustled over to the door and flung it open.

The policewoman had her fist raised again in mid-knock. Her intense eyes raked over me, and I felt self-conscious in my rumpled pajamas and ponytailed hair.

"Mimi Lee?" she said. "I'm Officer Perkins."

"Cup of tea?" I said, offering my freshly brewed tea to improve her impression of me.

She jutted her chin out. "I only drink coffee. Black."

The same color as her raven hair and onyx eyes, startling against her alabaster skin.

She glanced over my shoulder, her gaze sweeping the room like a searchlight. The barest flicker of a raised eyebrow. Maybe because she'd spied Josh splayed like a starfish over the couch. "Where exactly are the flammable materials you reported?"

Jerking my head to the side, I said, "On the deck."

I slipped out the front door and showed her the way. No fence restricted the access from the road to the side of the house and over to the barbecue area. Maybe the neighbors on this island were all extra friendly here and shared cookouts.

When I pointed to the large black garbage bag, Officer Perkins swooped in. She studied the contents and said, "I'm glad we finally located these."

What an interesting choice of words. "Were you expecting to find something like this?" I asked.

She grabbed the bag of confiscated fireworks with one hand. "Yes, after the complaint that was lodged the other day."

"Complaint?" I sipped my tea and let the caffeine work to clear out the spiderwebs in my brain so I could absorb her words better.

"I wasn't on duty at the time, but somebody at this residence lodged a complaint against some pranksters. Four rowdy guys who'd lobbed a smoke grenade through the window."

I almost spit my tea out at her. Who were these new people who'd been on the scene?

Officer Perkins motioned for me to follow as she carried the bag over to her police vehicle. She stuffed it in the trunk and continued speaking. "We couldn't track down the perpetrators or the fireworks before today. Didn't think they'd stash their stuff here."

I shook my head. "That poor tenant before us. Something else happened while he was here, too. Let me show you."

She glanced at her watch, and her mouth grimaced.

"It'll only take a moment of your time," I said. "And I'll even throw in a free mug of strong coffee."

She relaxed her lips. "Deal."

We walked into the house. From the now empty living room, I saw a groggy Josh with his head stuck in the kitchen pantry trying to find a quick breakfast. At the coffee machine sat a mug waiting to be filled with rich roast coffee.

The machine gurgled away and soon deposited its caffeinated goodness into a spring green mug. What perfect timing. Tiptoeing over, I placed my own empty mug down and stole the coffee.

A few moments later, I presented it with a flourish to the cop. Officer Perkins glanced between Josh and me for a second before shrugging and then accepting the mug.

While I led the cop over to the glass display case, I heard Josh let out a startled exclamation. Guess he'd discovered that his coffee had disappeared. He pivoted, spotted me with a cop, and stole over to the edge of the living room to watch.

I paid him no attention and pointed out the spot where Marilyn Monroe's headscarf had been.

"Odd," she said. "Why take just the headscarf and nothing else?"

"Yeah." I gestured to some of the expensive-looking accessories around the home, like the sunburst mirror. "Wouldn't it be easier to steal some other item? To do a quick grab-and-go?"

"Unless they didn't want the theft noticed." She took a glug of her coffee. "Maybe so they could resell it without anyone knowing it was a stolen item."

They'd definitely be able to get a good price for it. Something about the cop's observation didn't sit quite right with me, though. Wouldn't someone be bound to notice a disappearance in a glass case with labeled entries?

Officer Perkins drained her coffee while I was deep in thought, and she returned the empty mug to me. "Thanks again for locating the missing fireworks. I'll let you go tend to your scowling friend now." She exited the house with quick steps.

I turned around, almost expecting to see a scowling Marshmallow, but of course, it was Josh. He stared at me, caffeine-deprived and irritated. I'd never seen Josh sans coffee. Guess my cat hadn't cornered the market on early morning grumpiness.

"You gave my cup of coffee away," he said. "And it was the very last pod." He raked his hands through his mussed hair.

"Had to do what I needed to." I tried to soften the blow, not needing two grumpy males around the place. "You know how I don't like getting on the wrong side of the law. Coffee helped to butter her up, so to speak."

He jabbed his finger at the empty mug on the kitchen counter. "I see you had time to enjoy your caffeinated beverage of choice."

Josh knew I only drank tea, and I could have told him the cop would only accept coffee to gain more sympathy points, but I didn't.

Instead, in a sweet voice, I said, "Wake up on the wrong side of bed?" Then I slapped my forehead in mock surprise. "Oh, that's right. You ended up sleeping on the couch all night long."

"Tons of work," he said in a scratchy voice. He rolled his neck.

"I didn't realize that this was a work-cation."

"Well, you didn't tell me this would be a *sleuth*-cation."

I stared at him for a beat before stomping over to the kitchen and placing the empty coffee mug in the sink. "I'm trying to help out a good friend."

He followed me with a sigh. "Mimi . . . I just don't operate very well without coffee."

That wasn't quite an apology. I soaped and rinsed out the two used mugs.

He continued, "Let's go take a walk. We can get some breakfast—there isn't much here."

My stomach rumbled in agreement while my mind tried to think of ways to prolong his coffee deprivation. In the end, though, my hunger won out. Besides, a short stroll would help me get away from this rental home, filled with its lingering secrets and fresh conflict.

CHAPTER
nine

STEPS AWAY FROM the rental house we found an eatery called
Don't Egg Me On. Looked as good a place as any, and it was open.
The other restaurants seemed closed for the time being—maybe it was
too early for the owners to start working. Didn't blame them. I liked
making my own hours at Hollywoof and working from ten to six fit my
own non-morning-person personality.

The restaurant was crammed full of customers, and I heard the
sizzle of food frying when we walked in. A harried-looking waitress
asked if we had any luggage, her gaze flickering to a pile of backpacks
and suitcases overflowing a nook near the door. When we said no, she
appeared relieved.

And as we were only a party of two, she let out a huge sigh of relief.
"Finally. A couple. Easy to squeeze in."

We followed her as she wove between crowded tables and parked us in the rear, in a spot so close to the kitchen I wondered if it was legal. I raised an eyebrow at Josh, but he had already busied himself with settling into his chair.

Our waitress (her name tag read "Kendra") tried to offer a perky smile to match her cheerful 1950s dress. Except the peach outfit was already splattered with large oil splotches, and Kendra herself didn't seem so full of sunshine, but more like a brewing storm.

She slapped down a few sticky menus in front of us. "Bon appétit."

"Coffee first," Josh said, rubbing at his forehead.

I didn't even need to glance at the menu. "French toast," I said, pointing at a neighboring table's delectable dish. "With lots of fresh strawberries on top."

Josh kept a grip on his own sticky menu. He liked browsing through all the options before he decided. Was it the cautious lawyer in him?

Kendra gave up on taking both of our orders at the same time. She left us alone to get the coffee and put in my request. In the sudden silence, Josh didn't glance up even once as he read the menu from cover to cover. Then he remained staring at the fine print.

I waited out his long pondering process but finally asked, "So, what did you decide on?"

He startled. "Have you been thinking about things, too? Maybe we should"—Kendra arrived and shoved a coffee mug with steam piping out of it in front of him.

She pulled out a pen and order pad.

Josh stalled. "Do you have a specialty?"

"You're new here, right?" Kendra tapped her pen against the pad. "Haven't seen you around before, and I'm good with faces."

Josh nodded. "We only just got here."

"Well, see how crowded it is?" Kendra made a motion with her pen

to encompass the full dining room. "People come from all over the island to eat here because everything tastes good."

Josh mumbled a chastised thanks and ordered the eggs Benedict.

She turned to leave, but I put a hand up to stop her.

"Wait a minute," I said. She'd noticed that we were new in town,
and Kendra seemed like the observant type. "Do you know anything
about the police being called in because of something that happened on
this street? Heard the complaint was about a smoke grenade . . ."

She stood closer to the table. "Well, I know some guys looking like
trouble walked in here the other day."

I bit the inside of my cheek. "What made them seem sketchy?"

She jerked her thumb toward the front of the restaurant. "Didn't
want to leave their duffle bag with the others. And when they left, the
contents inside clinked against each other."

Not clothes then. Perhaps the same stashed fireworks we'd found?
"Did you happen to notice anything else about them?"

Her eyes looked up at the ceiling as she tried to recall.

"How many of them were there?" I asked, hoping to prompt her
memory.

"That's easy," she said as her eyes brightened. "Four. They even wore
these jackets with 'Fantastic Four' emblazoned on the back. Misspelled
F-a-n-t-a-s-t-i-c-k."

Four. The same number the policewoman had mentioned. It couldn't
be a mere coincidence. I thanked Kendra and leaned back in my chair,
satisfied.

I didn't even mind that I'd be soon eating in awkward silence with
Josh since I would be mulling over the Fantastick Four info. They were
at least a possible new lead in Pixie's case.

When our food came, Josh also seemed caught up in his own

thoughts. He kept mumbling legalese to himself and glancing at his watch.

We ate a quick breakfast, each of us concerned with our individual troubles. Eventually, Josh pushed away his empty plate and focused on me. "Mimi," he said, "I know you've been reflecting on our situation . . . what do you think about ending this trip early and leaving now instead of waiting until the evening like we'd originally planned?"

Excuse me? I stared at the crumbs on my plate.

"There's sort of a work emergency that I need to go back for," he said.

I screwed up the courage to look into his puppy-dog eyes. His pleading made me wonder: Was he really asking to quit our trip early because of work? Or because this vacation hadn't somehow met his expectations?

Either way, I didn't want to spend extra time with someone who didn't want to be here together a moment more. I squared my shoulders. Not trusting my voice, I nodded at him. Then I texted Pixie and arranged for an early departure.

• • •

During the quick flight, Josh and I studiously ignored each other. I listened to an audiobook while he seemed to be drafting something on an actual yellow legal pad. From his carrier, Marshmallow kept an eye on the two of us, but he soon grew bored and decided that napping took precedence over cat-peroning.

We landed in Los Angeles and made our way back to Seaview Apartments. There, Josh stood before my door, bouncing on his feet as if on an awkward (and maybe disappointing?) first date. I wasn't sure if he'd go in for a kiss or shake hands like we'd just finished a business transaction. He opted for leaning forward and giving me a peck on the forehead.

In response, I gave him a half hug and then ushered Marshmallow inside my apartment. I shut the door behind me and slid down its frame. Then I sat there, brooding. It felt good having my back leaning against solid wood for support. "Did you see that?" I asked Marshmallow.

"Huh?" He licked his paw.

"Josh, when we said goodbye. He kissed me—on the forehead. Like some sick child."

Marshmallow blinked at me with his ocean-colored eyes. "Well, no surprise there, sweetheart."

"What do you mean?"

"You two have been about as ready to explode as those fireworks *I* discovered back at the house." He paused. "Ever since last night."

I opened my mouth to argue with him, but my cat was right. Josh and I were on edge.

Marshmallow waved his paw at my still open mouth. "Just talk to the guy. Isn't that what those mouths of yours are for?"

I felt my cheeks flame up. "I wouldn't even know where to start."

"Sheesh." Marshmallow flicked his tail. "If you think two people speaking to each other is hard, try cat-to-human communication."

I nodded and pulled myself off the floor. As I analyzed the trip, I realized that Josh and I had never experienced any sort of impasse before. Maybe because we both avoided tackling issues with those close to us. Ma had once told me the secret to my parents' long marriage was to not argue, and I never remembered them ever yelling at each other in front of us kids.

Josh and I seemed to be that most nonconfrontational of couples: an avoider-avoider relationship. At least with an avoider-arguer mix, the more aggressive person would be able to bring any problems up. And a dual aggressive couple could yell at each other all day long, but at least they'd never hide their hurts. We avoiders, though, would suffer in denial and ignorance, waiting forever for things to blow over.

Even now I really didn't want to set off any "fireworks" in our relationship, as Marshmallow had called it.

"I know what I'll do," I said, putting away my weekender bag.

"Talk to the boy?" Marshmallow said.

"Investigate that fireworks lead," I said in a chipper tone. "It'll be a good distraction."

Marshmallow covered his face with his paws, but I ignored him. Instead, I started googling for more clues.

My cat relented and said, "Fine. As long as you're not a sourpuss around me . . ."

"Marshmallow, I think you're mixing up *our* two personalities," I said, before clicking on links and trying to find mentions of "Fantastick Four."

Hours later, and I hadn't unearthed any leads. Instead, I'd gotten flooded with hits about comic books and a team known as the Fantastic Four. They all dressed in fitted blue shirts with the number "4" written on them (well, except for the giant rocklike man). When I later crawled into bed and closed my eyes, their superheroic images stayed with me.

CHAPTER

ten

HADN'T EXPECTED TO return until the early evening, so I'd already taken the entire day off from Hollywoof. But I couldn't sit in the apartment a moment longer, with Marshmallow giving me constant pitying looks. I jetted out of there, telling my cat I needed to check on the business.

The store bell jingled as I entered, and I smiled at my sister behind the counter.

"Welcome to Hollywoof," she chirped out before she registered my face. Then her eyes widened. She rushed over to embrace me. "You're back!"

My sister's gesture of affection, combined with the white noise of the high-velocity dryer from the grooming area, made my tension drain away. I'd come to the right place to feel soothed.

Alice placed her hands on my shoulders and took a step back to study me. "Wait a minute. Weren't you supposed to get back tonight right before my event?"

I nodded but before I could say another word, a customer barged into the shop. Her mousy brown hair lay disheveled around her face, and her glasses were askew. "You have to help me," she said, pointing to the corgi she had on a leash.

"Is this for a regular shampoo?" Alice said and gave me a pointed look. "Special grooming services are not available today."

I pretended not to notice my sister's nonverbal communication.

The woman adjusted the glasses on her face. "But this is an emergency. I need to make sure Georgie here is all set for my Fourth of July bash."

"It's July third," my sister said. "Wouldn't you want to wait to spruce up Georgie tomorrow for an Independence Day event?"

The woman clipped out her next words. "Oh no. He's a pet performer, and dress rehearsal happens tonight. It's imperative that he gets fitted right away."

Nicola must have finished grooming just then because she reappeared in the front room, struggling with a bulldog in her arms. Her sleeves were soaked, and suds flecked her face.

The corgi owner took a step back. "You do have other trained staff around, right?"

"This one really put up a fight," Nicola mumbled. "Now where did the owner go?"

I straightened to my full height and looked the customer in the eye. "Actually, Hollywoof is *my* grooming salon," I said. "Tell me exactly what you need done for the dress rehearsal."

The woman pulled out a stars-and-stripes costume and a powdered wig from her large canvas tote. "He needs to be ready for his role ASAP, but I can't seem to make the hair stay on top of his sweet head."

She dumped everything into my hands and waited for my verdict.

I studied the wig. "Is this made for pets?"

She made a moue of distaste. "This wig isn't a mere Halloween prop. It's special, made from non-allergenic materials and hand-sewn by a local artisan. Unfortunately, it's sized for human heads, and I can't seem to get it to stay on Georgie. Don't you have some sort of doggie fashion tape?"

I ran through the grooming inventory in my head. We didn't have anything even close to that, but I might be able to jury-rig something out of my existing accessories. "I'll try to help you."

"Thank the heavens." She handed me the corgi's leash and sat down in the waiting area, where she proceeded to pull out a colorful playbill and study it. I noticed Nicola edge closer to her as I walked Georgie to the back room.

Oh, how I missed the grooming world. The scent of apple shampoo still floated in the air, and I breathed the fruity scent in.

I hooked the dog's leash to one of the grooming tables, while depositing the costume and the wig on a nearby counter. No need for him to chew on his outfit and destroy it by accident as I improvised a solution.

Rummaging through my style accessories, I found an old birthday hat with a thick elastic band. Well, sacrifices must be made. I cut the strap off and stapled it onto the powdered wig, making sure that only the smooth parts of the staples would touch the dog's head.

Now, how would I manage to convince the corgi to keep his wig on? If I'd brought Marshmallow with me to the store, it would've been a cinch to have him explain to the dog what was needed through his animal speaking talent. With only my wits to rely on for an adequate answer, I turned to dog training methods.

Positive reinforcement. If I could somehow reward Georgie for wearing the wig, it would reinforce his behavior. Thank you, B. F. Skinner. I just needed to time it correctly.

Popping my head out of the room and into the corridor, I asked Nicola if she was free. Yes, she was sans bulldog now and able to help me. I asked her to bring along the jar of doggie biscuits from next to the cash register.

When she bustled into the room, I explained my plan. Nicola made sure to wash her hands and be ready with a dog biscuit when I needed one.

"Okay, Georgie," I said to the dog, "here goes nothing."

I gently maneuvered his body to fit in the patriotic outfit. Then I placed the wig on his head, tucking his ears underneath the hairpiece and securing it with the chin strap.

"Good boy," I said while Nicola fed him a biscuit.

He gobbled it up. I sure hoped he'd continue to behave well for his food rewards at the dress rehearsal and for the actual performance.

Nicola stroked his back. "You totally look the part, Georgie . . . Washington."

I snorted at the name.

"It's true. That's his role," she said. "I read the playbill. Even though it's a private production, at least fifty people are attending the play. I asked the dog's owner if I could get involved. Be the narrator or do a voiceover or something. I can channel corgi."

"Wow. That's definitely a unique talent," I said, even though I wasn't sure how in demand doggie accents typically were in the industry.

She gave me a low curtsey for my compliment.

As we tidied up, I said, "Hey, guess what I saw in Catalina?"

"Do you mean *who*? Stars love to visit the island."

"Kind of. I saw famous stars' mementoes. Pixie has this glass display case filled with celebrity possessions. You would've loved checking it out."

"Gee, must have cost a fortune for Pixie to collect."

"Yeah." We ambled down the corridor with the presidential pooch in tow to return to the front room. I slowed my steps as I said, "One item went missing, though. Marilyn Monroe—I mean, Norma Jeane's head-scarf disappeared."

"Dougherty," Nicola added. "Norma Jeane Dougherty. That was the name of her first husband when he was stationed on the island." I didn't understand how Nicola kept all those trivia facts floating around in her head.

When we brought Georgie "Washington" to his pooch mom, she stood up and circled him to inspect his outfit at various angles.

"Yes, this will do," she said.

Nicola lifted up the jar of dog biscuits and I pointed at them, saying, "You might want to consider buying a few of those as incentive. Worked like a charm."

The owner said, "I'll take the whole jar's worth. I could use the extra for the doggie cast party afterward."

While I suppressed a smile, Nicola nodded her head in agreement. "Actors should be rewarded well."

My sister tallied the corgi owner's bill at the register. The now much calmer woman paid and took her huge batch of doggie biscuits.

As the owner walked toward the door, Nicola called out, "Go break a . . . paw!"

Both Alice and I swiveled to Nicola, aghast, but the doggie owner seemed unruffled and waved goodbye to us.

"She knew what I meant," Nicola mumbled. I shrugged while Alice nodded.

Then my sister turned to me. "Sorry, I didn't mean to make you work on your day off, Mimi."

"Not a problem," I said. "Hollywoof is my calming place."

Alice scrunched her nose, and I could almost see the thought forming in her head: *What happened that Mimi had to come here to relax?*

I sighed. "Tell you about it when we carpool to your speed dating thing." As a responsible big sis, of course I hadn't forgotten about her forced participation in Ma's latest matchmaking ploy. In fact, maybe I, too, needed an extra boost in the love department right about now.

• • •

Once we entered the building where the Superpowered Speed Dating would happen, I realized that it looked nothing short of a business office. I hadn't paid attention to the signage outside when I'd driven up in the dark, but it could very well be the organizer's actual workplace.

I spied cubicles lined up at the edges of the large room. The open space in the middle held a long rectangular white table, and folding chairs were spaced evenly down its length.

People were definitely dressed up for the event—in Comic-Con-worthy outfits. Now I understood what the "superpowered" part of the speed dating had referred to. Superheroes—and maybe a few villains—milled around the office floor.

A woman in a red spandex Mrs. Incredible suit used a small metal bar to hit a musical triangle. *Ding.*

From beside me, I noticed Alice smile. Maybe the instrument reminded her of music time with her kindergarteners and had put her at ease.

Mrs. Incredible's voice rang out with crisp authority. "Females whose first name begins with 'A' through 'D' will start. I've calculated the attendee numbers, so five couples at a time. Women will sit on the left side of the table"—she pointed with the metal bar—"with the men sitting across from them. We'll do multiple rounds to make sure everyone gets a turn and go through the entire alphabet."

She continued, "You get one minute to chat and jot notes down on your scorecard. Then I'll chime the triangle. Ladies, stay seated, while the gentlemen move down the line."

The "A to D" participants all took a seat. I hovered over Alice's shoulder at the far end of the table.

Her first candidate was the Man of Steel himself. Okay, so *this* Superman only had muscles drawn onto a shirt and had a receding hairline, but that wasn't too bad.

Alice and he said hello to each other in halting tones, and seemed at a standstill for further conversation.

He glanced at me. "Are you her bodyguard or something?"

"I'm here to keep the conversation flowing. So, what's your favorite superpower?"

"That's easy," the man replied with confidence. "X-ray vision."

Oh, that could go to so many troublesome places, but I gave him a pass . . . for now.

He moved in toward my sister, and I could smell his onion breath even from where I stood. "What about you, missy?" he asked.

Who used that word in the twenty-first century?

Alice, to her credit, answered back in a kind voice. "Teaching is my superpower."

Superman leaned back then and even scooted his chair a few inches away. "That's it?" he said. "You could've picked a number of actually cool powers."

I tapped my sister's shoulder twice, a preset code for "no" between us to eliminate the incompatible prospects from the list.

The chime couldn't come fast enough. When the sweet tone rang out, though, I heard the musical note from somewhere uncomfortably close by.

I turned my head to find Mrs. Incredible standing next to me and frowning.

"All participants must be seated," she said. "No tag teaming."

"But I—"

"You're wasting everyone's time." She pointed to an empty chair that she must have just pulled over. "Sit down there."

She was definitely a teacher—or maybe a corporate manager. Used to being in charge, anyhow.

I did as she asked, but of course, I threw off the numbers. At least I could sit here and watch, take a breather.

Mrs. Incredible tutted. "This won't do," she said. She brought out another chair and sat across from me. "I'll be your partner."

The second round started in earnest.

"Um." I fidgeted with my hands in my lap, not sure what to say. And wanting to flee from the room.

"It's easy, pumpkin," Mrs. Incredible said in an encouraging voice. "Think of it like a job interview. Is the person across from you the right candidate for the position you're offering? Let me show you." She took a deep breath and then launched into a series of rapid-fire questions:

"Favorite superhero?" Did Super Grover count?

"Morning bird or night owl?" Hoot, hoot.

"Dream job." Pet grooming, of course.

"Any siblings?" Alice.

Which reminded me. I was here for my sister and I didn't really need to be in the hot seat myself. Once I finished the next interviews, I'd find an excuse to sneak away from the table.

The next three candidates moved along semi-smoothly. There was the space guy, who didn't seem too impressed with my answer about which *Star Trek* episode I liked. "What's the difference between *Star Wars* and *Star Trek*?" I'd asked. Then came an alien with a huge head, a jaw full of teeth, and a long tongue. I stopped answering his questions when he said his chosen character bit people's heads off. Spider-Man stepped up after, but I couldn't understand a word he said through his webbed mask.

Finally, the last guy was dressed as some sort of rock-man, who looked familiar.

I tilted my head up at his bouldered body with a questioning glance.

"The Thing," he said. "From *Fantastic Four*."

I snapped my fingers. "Right."

He appeared to get tongue-tied after that, but I had a question ready for him.

"Have you ever heard of a group called the Fantastic Four, but with an extra 'k' in the word 'Fantastic'?" I asked.

He nodded eagerly. "I know everything remotely related to F-squared stuff. Read about that group you mentioned on a Reddit thread."

Wow. He really must be a Fantastic Four groupie.

He continued, "I can text you the link if you want."

"Could you email it to me instead?" I didn't want him to have my cell number, so I jotted down an email address on a random scrap of paper I found in my purse.

He read it and frowned at the weird jumble of numbers and letters. "Is this a junk account?"

"Okay, you got me," I said. "Sorry, but I'm not really into the costumed superhero thing. But I'm sure a lot of the other women here are. Good luck."

"Thanks," he said, grabbing the piece of paper and grinning at me.

I admired the massive amount of makeup he'd used to create his craggy face before Mrs. Incredible sounded the triangle. All chatter stopped at once.

"A quick break before the next round," she said.

I caught my sister's eye and mouthed, "Time to go?"

She gave me a subtle nod. In the blur of other people's moving bodies, ready to stretch or head to the restrooms, we snuck toward the exit. And we weren't the only ones to do so. I spied Hawkeye, Captain Marvel, and the Joker also escaping the event.

As Alice and I slipped out the door, I heard Mrs. Incredible's voice from behind me mumbling, "Well, I never."

I quizzed Alice about her experience while we carpooled back to Hollywoof. She kept shaking her head and sighing. "None of them were my type." She'd probably experienced the same lack of stellar candidates as me.

After we'd parked near the store, Alice gave me a lopsided grin. "At least I learned to fend off bad prospects by mentioning that I had kids—thirty of them."

Her kindergarteners. Ha. Guess she hadn't needed her big sis to step in. "Sorry I got pulled away from my wingwoman duties," I said.

"No worries." She slid out of the passenger seat. "Too bad you wasted all your time tonight."

But I hadn't. While watching Alice walk over to her car and buckle in, I mulled over the new lead I'd gotten. Maybe I'd be able to track down that gang of four who'd shown up at Catalina with their illegal fireworks.

CHAPTER

eleven

THE THING WAS true to his word because the next morning I found a link emailed to my junk account. Clicking on the hyperlink took me to a discussion of the Fantastick Four on Reddit.

Scrolling through the comments, I found an entry about trademark infringement. A contributor had captured the F4 wannabes wearing matching jackets inscribed with "Fantastick Four" on their backs. It was a grainy photo, but the poster had mentioned capturing the gang at Alondra Park.

I knew exactly where that was located. In fact, I'd strolled around the lake there a few times, watching the ducks (or geese, depending on the season) paddle around the water. I'd found it a serene place despite the exuberant yelling from the kiddies swimming in the nearby lap pool or running wild around the Splash Pad play area in the summertime.

Located in Lawndale, the park wasn't too far from my parents' house, so it made for an excellent pit stop before this evening's scheduled Family Game Night. And as I didn't have anything else planned for the day, I had plenty of time to wait for the gang of four to show up. I sure hoped Alondra Park was a regular haunt of theirs.

I parked my Prius in the wide-open asphalt lot. Marshmallow groused about how I was leaving him behind to investigate solo, but I blew him a kiss. "Come on. Cats aren't allowed in the park. Besides, you'll have a great view from the hood of the car."

He did love napping in that spot after the engine had created a toasty spot for him to rest.

"Plus," I said, "I don't want you endangering any squirrel lives."

As I walked toward the large manmade lake, I spotted a line of palm trees standing regally and waving their fronds at me. I saluted them before continuing to trudge along the perimeter. It was a long walk around the edge of the water, and the lake seemed more opaque than I remembered it. Perhaps it was murkier from the many birds that commandeered the area. I tried to sidestep all the bird droppings that decorated the walkway.

As I made my way around the walking loop, I didn't see a group of four mischievous souls. Instead, I spied moms holding back their rambunctious kids from jumping into the water. A few elderly folks power walked past me, and squirrels with bushy tails scampered around the trees.

I decided to take a break and rest on one of the scattered benches. I'd brought along a sandwich in case I got hungry, but I knew better than to feed any crumbs to the water fowl. Besides the various signs prohibiting that very activity, the birds often got aggressive in their begging. Many decided to stalk (or chase) those giving away food.

I gazed upon the water and wondered what lay beneath its dark surface. My dad had half-heartedly suggested fishing here once when I was a kid. He said they stocked a selection of trout or catfish in the lake, depending on the time of the year. Though not much of a fisherman, he'd told me he could get a special permit if I wanted to try fishing. I declined, especially after he'd described needing to place a wriggling worm on the hook. I'd just read *How to Eat Fried Worms* and had gotten disgusted at even the idea of bait.

A motion in my peripheral vision halted my reminiscing. Four figures slouched toward the manmade lake. They wore matching black leather jackets. When they turned their backs, I decided to creep up on them to get a closer look.

They faced the water and didn't notice my sneaking. As I drew near, I definitely spotted the "Fantastick Four" scripted on the backs of their jackets.

They seemed rather busy passing a paper bag back and forth. At first, I thought it might contain alcohol. Pretty soon, though, I realized my mistake as they stuck their hands in the bag and pulled out slices of bread.

They broke off huge pieces and tossed the bread chunks into the water. Some of them even started aiming for the heads of the ducks as they threw.

I couldn't stand seeing them do that to the animals, so I channeled my sister's strident teaching voice and said, "Stop that this minute, or I'll report you."

They froze. Then they slowly turned around.

Despite having my hands on my hips and using a wide-planted stance, the worried expressions on their faces changed to amusement. I wondered if it was my petite stature that had them convinced I was harmless. Or my fellow Asian face.

Not that they looked like authentic hoodlums, either. More like high school nerds who'd dressed up for an off-off-off-Broadway version of *Grease*.

One of them took a step toward me. The ringleader perhaps. He had slicked-back hair and clear chunky glasses. "Who are you?" he said. "The hall monitor?"

I frowned at the old-school reference. "You're not supposed to feed the birds—or hit them. Didn't you see the signs?"

Another Fantastick Four member made a wide-eyed, innocent face. "We're just feeding the local squirrels. But we have really bad aim." He pointed at something behind me. "Although I've never seen a white squirrel before."

Distracted, I turned around and spied Marshmallow's tail sticking out from behind a tree trunk.

The leader's voice rang out, and I turned my attention back to him. "Signs, schmigns," he said. "We make our own rules."

Irritated by his attitude, the words shot out of my mouth before I could reconsider: "Oh yeah, is that why you were trying to set off fireworks on Catalina?" Maybe I should've been more subtle.

One of his fellow goons startled. Was that a confirmation of their guilt?

"I have no idea what you're talking about," the ringleader said in a cool voice.

"There were witnesses at a local diner who saw you lugging around a suspicious duffel bag."

The four of them looked at one another and started whooping.

One member with a whiny voice piped up. "Maybe we did go to Catalina . . . but are you accusing us of having *luggage*?"

The ringleader gave the guy a small frown, maybe because his friend had semi-admitted to being on the island.

But it wasn't like any of them had confessed to any actual law-breaking. I stared at them for a long moment before I heard Marshmallow whispering to me, "Psst. You got to use leverage to make the 'crap-tastic four' squeal."

I thought back to the Reddit thread. "My boyfriend's a lawyer," I said. "Your jackets are a clear example of trademark infringement. But if you answer my questions, I'll let it slide."

Marshmallow gave a soft hiss in the distance. "That's what you came up with?"

The leader smirked. "We don't have to answer anything. Not without an attorney present. Who are you, anyway, asking us all this stuff?"

One of his buddies, perhaps trying to be helpful, added, "We did nothing wrong."

"How about 'breaking and entering'?" Marshmallow murmured.

I didn't know if they'd actually broken into the home, but I said, "Did you know that there was destruction of property from your smoke grenade?"

They seemed shocked, and I didn't clarify that I was talking about a small scorch mark.

I hurled my next words like they were my own detonation device. "There's footage of you leaving the scene of the crime with your very distinctive jackets." Then I pulled out Detective Brown's business card, making sure to cover up his name, and flashed the card before their eyes. I hoped they got an eyeful of the police department's flashy logo.

The Adam's apple of the leader bobbed up and down. "You're a cop?"

I continued, "I'm sure they'll find your fingerprints all over the explosive equipment you left behind. Fireworks are illegal on the island, as I'm sure you're aware of." I tilted my head at the leader and gave him a conspiratorial smile. "I could wipe your slate clean, though. Put in a good word for you."

The leader wrung his hands. "It wasn't our fault. The guy renting before us in our vacation house didn't leave like he was supposed to that morning, so we thought we'd give him a little scare. But then he called the cops, so we had to dip."

The others in the group nodded, and one even said, "We took the ferry back ASAP after that. Here, I'll show you."

A few moments later, and the guy extended his phone out for me to see the screen, which displayed a confirmation ticket for the *Catalina Flyer*.

Their story rang true to me. "Okay, I believe you guys," I said with a curt nod.

As I walked away, I heard the leader say, "Did she track us down all the way from Catalina?"

Leaning on the driver's side door of my car, I watched them huddle together for a few minutes. Then they started throwing bread at the ducks again. The four friends seemed like pranksters who enjoyed making small kinds of trouble. But ganging up on a duck, I thought, didn't mean they were capable of killing a man.

Marshmallow showed up at my Prius, and I said, "Couldn't follow my advice and stay put, huh?"

"Can't fault me for wanting to get a piece of the action," he said.

I wagged my finger at him but stifled any further scolding. He had given me the right motivational words to say to the group. Plus, I had to save my energy for getting through the rest of the evening.

•   •   •

Family Game Night was a longstanding tradition held at my parents' house. We met at least every few months depending on our schedules. I loved returning to my comfy childhood home with its fusion of décor that somehow worked together, like the brocaded silk throws, which were draped across long leather couches.

Dad gave me his signature bear hug when I arrived with Marshmallow, while Ma surreptitiously peered from the side to check out my left hand's ring finger.

She greeted me and examined me from head to toe. A worry crease wrinkled her forehead. As she steered me toward the laden dining table, she mumbled, "Gone down so much, too skinny."

Our lazy Susan was filled with patriotic treats done up with an Asian twist. I saw a tray of layered Jell-O in red, white, and blue; I bet the white layer came from almond gelatin. Sliced star fruit also spanned a nearby Corelle plate with flowered edges.

The doorbell chimed.

"Your sister," Dad said, "always ringing the bell out of courtesy."

Ma shuffled to the door and opened it.

Alice walked in and beamed at our familiar faces. First, she said hello to Ma and Dad. Then, she turned to me and winked. "Long time no see, Mimi."

Dad sat down at the dining table and proceeded to scoop some multi-colored Jell-O into a bowl for himself.

Ma swatted at his arm. "Save some for kids lah."

Dad made a big show of looking around the room. He even opened the front door again and peered outside. "We seem to be missing one." Turning to me, he said, "Where's that handsome fellow of yours?"

From one of the couches, where my cat had taken refuge, Marshmallow meowed. "Right over here."

Dad patted his stomach and said, "Josh always brings the greatest snacks to Family Game Night. I still dream of that *furikake* snack mix."

I'd actually been hoping against hope that he'd waltz through the door as well. But Josh liked being punctual, and it seemed he'd done a runner. I made an excuse for him. "Josh is busy tonight, so he can't make it. Lawyers, you know."

"July Fourth his off day, right?" Ma said as her eyes narrowed at me. Before she could start probing, though, my sister came to the rescue.

"Fine. Four players then." She marched over to the closet where we kept our board games. "Let me tell you our options so we can vote on the game."

She listed a few choices, and we ended up picking Sorry!. We played the competitive game with gusto.

My family members issued apologies while booting others back to the start position, and I couldn't help but be reminded that my own boyfriend still owed me an apology. It'd only take one simple word to make things okay again.

I stomped my red pawn around the board until Dad placed a firm hand on my shoulder. "Princess One, why don't you tell us about your Catalina trip?"

"Uneventful," I muttered. Besides the investigation part. Which I wasn't about to mention in front of my parents.

Dad relaxed his grip on me while Ma flashed me a questioning look.

"No bluff, Mimi. What stuff you do together?" Ma asked.

"Um . . . we saw some of the quaint houses around town and visited a few local businesses."

Dad beamed. "*Public* places. Excellent choices for a young couple."

From the corner of my eye, I noticed Alice trying very hard not to crack up.

"Good time, is it?" Ma said. "Too bad Josh not here for share his stories."

My sister piped up. "Your turn, Ma."

Ma flipped over the "4" card and moved backward four spaces. Seemed like a fair analogy of my dating life.

Trying to avoid more grilling from Ma and Dad, I changed the topic. "Enough about me, don't forget that Alice had an exciting time last night."

Ma's eyes glowed, and she leaned forward. "Speed date."

My sister covered her face and spoke through her hands. "It was a disaster. The superpowered theme meant everyone there wore a lot of Spandex, which I unfortunately can't unsee now. I had absolutely no chemistry with any of my partners."

Ma tapped the game board and said, "Like that ah. No worry, Alice. I join new Facebook group. All us from Perak. Many even have same Chinese background." Ma's hometown was located in Perak, a state in Malaysia, but as a Malaysian Chinese, Ma had often found herself in the minority while growing up. Over half of the people in the country had Malay heritage, after all. She once told me that she'd felt like a rambutan there—she'd looked like a strange sea urchin of a fruit among the other more typical produce.

Ma continued speaking. "Anyway, *sup sup sui*, very easy to find new connection."

I'm not sure if Ma meant a connection to her cultural roots or a new spin on how to make a love connection for my sister. Either way, Ma dreamily went about finishing the rest of the game.

Dad ended up winning Sorry!, and as if in celebration, a loud boom heralded his success as he collected the spare change jar as his prize. It sounded almost like thunderous applause and echoed in the air.

Marshmallow yowled from his perch. "Why do humans insist on making such a loud ruckus on this holiday?"

Alice pushed back her chair and tugged on my sleeve. Her excitement and rosy cheeks brought back fun childhood memories. "Let's go outside and see if we can spot the fireworks," she said.

My parents and I followed her out the door.

"I think it's right around the corner," she said, almost skipping on the pavement.

The rest of us stayed on the sidewalk, but Alice, being her impulsive self, stepped right into the middle of the road. She probably thought the cars' headlights would find her and drivers would swerve around her, as she tilted her face up to watch. Thank goodness the neighborhood was located on a residential street and didn't get much traffic.

A brilliant sparkle lit up the night sky. I sure hoped it had been launched from a nearby wide-open space. Since I stood close to my parents, I noticed when Ma squeezed my dad's hand under the cover of night. I startled. She usually avoided all public displays of affection.

A pang hit my heart. The Fourth of July. Independence Day. Somehow I felt like I'd been set loose from Josh, and I wasn't sure it was a freedom I really wanted.

CHAPTER

twelve

THE NEXT MORNING offered a welcome distraction from my morose thoughts about July Fourth and my newfound independence. A needle-thin owner and his Lhasa Apso showed up at Hollywoof, and the man started off with this ominous warning: "Beware of the ear hair."

I peeked into the doggie's ears and noticed tufts of hair populating the space and blocking his ear canals.

"You want me to trim these?" I asked.

"No." The thin man pinched his slender thumb and forefinger together. "Get rid of them by plucking each one out."

I bit my bottom lip. "Are you certain? Some vets don't suggest ear plucking."

"Mine does." The man waved away my concerns. "Maximilian here is prone to nasty ear infections, and the vet assured me increased air circulation could only help."

"If you're sure about it . . ."

"I am." He slid his cell phone out of his pocket. "Do you need me to call my vet so you can talk to her?"

I stammered. "Of course not. I believe you."

After making eye contact with Nicola at the register—I hoped she could somehow calm the man down while I worked—I began walking Maximilian to the grooming area. As I moved down the hallway, I could hear Nicola saying, "You know, there's a *Seinfeld* episode where Jerry tells George he only needs to worry about ear hair when there's a soft rustling sound . . ."

I heard the trail of the man's laughter right before we arrived in the back room. There, I examined Maximilian and made sure he had clean, dry ears to start with since I didn't want to aggravate anything. Then I hooked him to a grooming table and located the instruments I'd need to complete the task.

Instead of relying on my fingers to do the work, I preferred using hemostats. They looked sort of like long-handled scissors, but with blunt tips at the ends. First, though, I sprinkled a special powder on Max's ear hairs. This would make it easier to grip them to pull them out.

I took a deep breath and positioned the hemostats at the appropriate angle to grip the hair with an incisive tug. Confident plucking would ensure a pain-free experience for Maximilian.

It took a while to remove all the hair. At the end, I reinspected his ears. They looked clear and healthy. He also hadn't complained during the entire process, which I took as a positive sign.

When I brought Maximilian out front again, his owner and Nicola were in a deep conversation about their favorite *Seinfeld* episodes.

"All done," I said.

Nicola turned her head my way and jumped up from the bench where she'd been sitting and hurried to stand by the register.

The owner examined my handiwork and declared it "paw-sitively astounding." He then made his way over to Nicola, where I hoped he'd leave a considerable tip after all of my painstaking and detailed work.

Right after he left, I meant to ask Nicola if he'd been generous, but my phone rang. Josh? I checked the caller ID, and my heart sank a little. But it was someone else important.

I picked up. "Pixie?"

She sounded breathless over the phone. "Glad I caught you, Mimi. It's about the Catalina Chalets . . ."

My face flamed up. Oops. I'd never thanked her again after the Catalina trip. Or apologized for leaving the island early and making her pilot rearrange his schedule.

"Mimi, did you hear what I just said?"

"Um, no. Sorry, I just realized I never thanked you for the trip—and accommodating all the schedule changes."

"Never mind that." She blew out her breath. "There have been four in total. I'm not the only one of the Catalina Chalet owners."

The phone slipped in my grip, and I recovered it. "What? I don't understand."

"We'll be having a quick emergency meeting about it tomorrow."

"Can you explain it once again?"

A sharp yipping rose from her end. "Gelato, bad dog," she said. "Don't go near that power cord." She raised her voice. "I've gotta go, Mimi. I'll text you the details."

Then she hung up. I wondered what she'd learned about the other owners.

I shook my head to clear it. Well, I'd find out at the meeting she'd arranged. In the meantime, I busied myself with puttering around the shop, fixing crooked displays of collars and pooch pouches.

By noon, I looked forward to the shop's lunch closure and the chance to gobble down my Elvis sandwich. The peanut butter and banana combo happened to be one of my favorite comfort foods during stressful times. However, when I searched for my packed lunch, I couldn't find it anywhere. With a sinking feeling, I realized I must have left it on my kitchen counter.

Marshmallow sensed my agitation. "Who tugged on your whiskers?" he asked. "And why are you searching high and low?"

"Left my lunch at home," I mumbled.

Nicola, who'd opted to stay and eat in the store, said, "Go out and take a breather, then."

Marshmallow meowed in agreement. "I'll come with you. But I still don't get why missing a basic PB&J sandwich would be such a downer."

"It's PB&B," I whispered to him as we headed out the door. Even the warm sunshine didn't lift my spirits right then. My voiced had cracked a little over the letters because I couldn't help but remember the romantic date when Josh had carved a peanut butter and jelly sandwich into the shape of a heart for me.

After I started up my car, my hands seemed to have a mind of their own. I found myself on the highway traveling toward downtown Los Angeles without any recollection of doing so. As the traffic stalled on the 110, I drummed my fingers against the steering wheel.

"We can't keep on avoiding the topic," I said. "Josh and I are adults. We should be able to talk things through, right?" I waited for confirmation from my cat.

"Eh," he said. "Less talk, more action. Take things into your measly two paws."

"You're right, Marshmallow," I said.

He purred.

And that's how I found myself heading straight to Josh's office.

Standing outside his workplace, I again saw how the stolid building placed beside towering glass skyscrapers looked like a structural ugly duckling. After tucking Marshmallow inside my large Hello Kitty tote, we entered the cool lobby. (The building always ran the air-conditioning at full blast.)

"Insufferable trapped in here," my cat said. However, this would be the only way he could stay next to me undetected, so he soon piped down.

Near the staircase, I sought out what I'd secretly labeled as Josh's-and-my-bench. The seat even had a distinctive Charlie Chaplin statue resting on it. Josh and I had declared our official boyfriend-girlfriend status there, and the nook held a special place in my heart.

Josh would probably walk down the staircase soon enough, as he never bothered to pack lunch. While I waited for him to appear, I crossed and uncrossed my legs. Surely he'd be willing to talk things through? Maybe if I offered him some extra empathy, he'd soften up. We could then get things back on track. Why, Carl Rogers had based a whole thera-peutic model on active listening. There had to be a positive payoff for me if I followed the Rogerian way.

Marshmallow hissed from inside my tote. "Stop it with the whip-lash, Mimi."

I calmed down my fidgeting legs. Hearing footsteps pounding down the stairs, I wondered if it could be Josh. I looked up to see a giraffe-like man barreling down the stairs. I tried to shrink and curl up in my seat. It was Josh's loud-mouthed coworker, the guy who loved to make trouble for Josh.

I was so busy glaring at the man's back as he trotted through the lobby that I completely missed the *ding* of the elevator as its doors popped open. Only when the shadows crossed my path did I realize that a man and a woman were passing right by my hiding place.

At first, I thought they were a couple, what with their heads bent so close together. Then I noticed the man's familiar physique and signature floppy bangs. Josh. The breath whooshed out from me.

He nodded at what his female companion was saying, his bangs playing hide-and-seek with his sweet chocolate eyes.

I leaned in to hear the conversation better, but it all sounded like a secret code I couldn't quite crack. Some kind of legal mumbo jumbo.

Who was that woman? They'd already walked by me, so I couldn't see her face. My eyes took in her glossy blond hair, which swished down the length of her back. She also had on a sleek suit that accentuated her hourglass figure, and her short skirt revealed a lot of leg. A hint of vanilla lingered in her wake.

A few feet before the exit, I heard Josh say, "I agree, Gertrude."

My jaw dropped. "It can't be," I whispered. "That's the name of the new paralegal."

Marshmallow popped his head up. "What am I missing?"

We watched as Josh and Gertrude stepped outside, their strides in absolute sync. From an outsider's objective perspective, they actually made a striking couple.

My cat hissed. "'Paralegal,' you say? Para-lethal, more like."

I couldn't argue with his assessment, and I felt my heart wilt inside me.

CHAPTER

thirteen

PIXIE HAD ARRANGED for all the owners of the Catalina Chalets to meet at a local park, the midpoint commute location for most of the owners involved. She'd described the green space as "in need of a boost," but it appeared downright dumpy when I showed up there. Due to my nerves, I'd arrived early to the scene and got a good long look.

The park must have seen better days. Its field of yellowed grass appeared invaded by troublesome weeds. I could see dandelion puffballs all over the field. Trash choked the lawn: a sticky candy wrapper here, a glass bottle there. Thank goodness, I didn't see any children playing nearby. The rusted swings and splintering seesaw didn't appear kid-safe. At least the park offered some shade on bright days because I could see several sturdy trees with mighty trunks and fistfuls of leaves. Overgrown bushes also grew in patches, offering great foliage covering for playing hide-and-seek.

I was thankful we'd be meeting indoors at the park. Pixie had secured us a reservation for the community room. I figured it'd be inside the squat dirty brown building near the decrepit playground. As I walked toward the edifice, a man came from around the corner and peeked into the grimy window. He looked to be in his fifties with a smart dash of gray in his dark hair, and he wore a maroon sweater vest, khakis, and penny loafers.

He didn't notice me as I neared the door because he'd started checking his gold wristwatch.

"Excuse me," I asked him. "Are you here for the meeting?"

He turned to face me, and I noticed intelligent brown eyes assessing me behind tortoiseshell frames. "Yes. I'm Professor Villanueva, and you are..."

"Mimi Lee." I gave him my best honors student smile. "I'm a friend of Pixie St. James."

He nodded at the mention of her name.

To make small talk while we waited, I said, "Where do you teach, Professor?"

"University of California, Los Angeles."

UCLA. Hurrah. "Go Bruins." I pumped a fist in the air. "Which subject?"

"Public policy."

I scratched my head. "Where is that department located, exactly?"

"On the north side of campus, near Murphy Garden."

Oh, right. I remembered the rolling green lawn and the various metal sculptures dotting the landscape.

From my peripheral vision, a flash of movement caught my attention. I turned and watched a sleek black Tesla pull into the lot adjacent to the park. The driver glided into a specially marked space reserved for electric-only vehicles.

When he stepped out from the driver's side, his dark ensemble matched the color of his vehicle. He wore a black mock turtleneck with dark rinse jeans. If he felt hot on this warm summer day, he didn't show it. He had his dark hair gelled back, and I could fully see his square-shaped face as he marched toward us.

He could have been anywhere in age from twenty to forty. Like my sister often said, "Asian don't raisin."

The man met my curious gaze with a bold, unflinching stare. With that kind of intensity, he could've been evaluating me as a potential date or an interview prospect. Either way, I wasn't sure I'd passed his inspection.

Professor Villanueva introduced me to the stranger. "Mimi, meet Riku."

I scrunched my nose, wondering what his name meant.

As though he'd read my mind, Riku said, "It's Japanese for 'handsome.'"

"Oh." I bit the inside of my cheek. His dark brown eyes stayed on mine, and I couldn't tell if he'd been teasing me and joking about his name's origin or not.

Thankfully, Pixie showed up right then to unlock the door. A lifesaver.

"Just the three of us, huh?" Riku gave a pointed look at the main street. "She's late again."

"Well, she does have to drive all the way from Palos Verdes," Pixie said. "It's like the wilderness out there. Give her a break."

Pixie led the way inside the community room and flipped the light switch on. "Hopefully, she'll turn up sooner rather than later."

A table was already set out for us to use, but the folding chairs were still stacked against the wall. Pixie immediately went to retrieve one.

Meanwhile, Professor Villanueva stood back while directing me to help because he couldn't assist due to his "bad hip." Riku stood to the side, leaning against a wall, fixated on a slim phone in his hand.

Only when Pixie and I had set up the chairs did the men join us. Really? I blew out an angry breath and glared at them.

After we all sat down, Pixie explained to me how each of the other owners had a place on the island. She even brought out a folder with glossy images of their abodes. Professor Villanueva owned a mini Spanish villa while Riku's place looked like an alien house on the island with its S-shaped structure and glass walls.

The last picture Pixie pulled out was the same cottage Josh and I had seen being cleaned by Lavinia when we'd chatted with her. "This one," Pixie said, "belongs to—"

"*Me.*" A woman sailed through the door and practically sang out the word. Or maybe she'd floated across the threshold. The gliding movement, along with her big auburn hair and oversized flowing tunic, marked her as a vibrant personality.

She gave a brilliant smile to all, the huge grin making her laugh lines dance on her face. "I'm B-a-r-b-r-a. That's how you spell my name right."

"Barbra," I said. "Like the singer."

"Exactly." She settled into an empty chair. "Papa named me after Streisand herself."

Pixie cleared her voice. "Now that we're all settled, let's discuss the thefts."

I gasped. Is that what she was talking about on the phone? Professor Villanueva fidgeted with his glasses, Riku pressed his lips tight together, and Barbra patted at her wild hair.

After pulling out her phone, Pixie asked everyone to describe what had gone missing from their respective Catalina Chalet.

Professor Villanueva picked some lint off his sweater vest and mumbled, "Costume jewelry. I'm not comfortable sharing more in this public space."

Pixie nodded at him and tapped away on her phone. I bet she was logging the info into her Notes app. I'd have to ask her for the list later or hope that my memory would suffice.

Riku spoke next. Using a scathing tone, he said, "The robber stole the latest iteration of my top secret phablet."

I couldn't stop from asking, "What's a phablet?"

He stared at me with a nonplussed look on his face. "A phone tablet. Equals a 'phablet.'"

Well, okay. I didn't know all the techie terms in the world.

Barbra shifted in her chair, and her voice filled with plaintive sorrow. "I'm missing a customized painting from a renowned local artist. I don't know why my precious art piece would have been targeted." She sniffled.

"I'm really sorry, Barbra. As for me"—Pixie turned my way—"well, do you want to share about it, Mimi?"

"Sure," I said. "Pixie generously let me stay in her vacation home a few days ago. I noticed that she was missing a special headscarf from her display case of celebrity items. Turns out the renter before me, Dwayne, had trouble with a gang of minor hoodlums, but I'm not so sure they actually took the item. They did set off a smoke grenade in the house, though. The police were called in, but they ran off and weren't caught."

Riku's dark eyes probed mine. "Did you say the renter's name was Dwayne?"

"Yes, Dwayne A. vacated the house prior to me."

"A man with the initials 'D' and 'A' rented from me," Riku said.

The others nodded and babbled away. After some clarification, it turned out that all three owners had rented to a variation of the same name: Dwayne, Dwayne A., D.A., and D. Wayne.

Pixie raised her voice. "Should we alert the police to the discovery?"

Professor Villanueva's eyes widened. "No, I don't think so. Wait for the time being. This is all still conjecture."

Barbra sided with the professor.

Riku clenched his hand into a fist. "What we need is undeniable proof of Dwayne's involvement."

I raised my hand in the air like an eager schoolgirl. "I'd like to help. In fact, I've assisted the police on two very important cases before." They didn't need to know the details, that I'd been forced to do so because both Alice and I had been the prime suspects.

The Catalina Chalet owners looked at me with varying degrees of shock, admiration, and skepticism. The brief meeting had come to an end on a dramatic note.

Time being precious, a few of them (including Pixie) had to rush off to another prescheduled activity, but each of them agreed to be separately interviewed at their convenience. They all agreed to fill me in on the missing item and their interactions with "Dwayne," or rather, Davis Argo.

CHAPTER

fourteen

NOBODY ELSE COULD stay after the homeowners' meeting except for Barbra. "This may be an easy location for the others to get to, but I'm not driving all the way back here again to chat," she said to me. "Besides, I need to take a rest before getting back on the highway."

I noticed her shaking hands as we walked out of the community room. She must still be emotional about the theft that had happened on her property. To calm her down, I selected a wooden bench facing the sidewalk, where we couldn't see the eyesore of the rundown park. Plus, she'd receive the full warmth of the July sun shining down on her in this spot. Vitamin D was essential to good health, and sunshine boosted positive emotions—just ask anyone who'd ever suffered from seasonal affective disorder.

Barbra sat down on the bench with a drawn-out sigh.

"That stolen painting must have really hit you hard," I said.

She cast her eyes down to the ground, seeming very different from the woman who'd sailed through the door earlier. "It was a picture of my Buttercup."

"You mean, the yellow flower?"

"No. My horse. Buttercup. She died a few months ago. I couldn't bring myself to look at her portrait on the wall any longer. It was too painful, so I stashed it in my vacation home."

I made soft noises of comfort, which seemed to encourage Barbra to talk further.

"She was such a gentle horse. I rode her on every trail I could in PV. She lived a long, pampered life, but still, she was gone too soon."

My heart started aching for her. "The loss of an animal friend is rough."

She gripped the edge of the bench. "I just don't understand. I'd wrapped up the frame and everything. Stuck it in the corner of the bedroom closet. Who would have even known to look there?"

An inside job? I rubbed my chin. "Does anyone have access to the rental house besides you? Any of your family or friends?"

She shook her head. "Besides, everyone close to me knew I loved that painting for sentimental reasons. They wouldn't have wanted to emotionally destroy me like that. Not even for the value it could've fetched in the art world."

My ears perked up. "Who's the artist?"

"Astral. They have a small art studio in Venice. A rising star. Unfortunately, the studio is closed on the weekend, but you could check out their work on Monday."

I made a mental note to visit first thing Monday morning before I needed to open up Hollywoof.

Two young moms walked down the sidewalk, pushing their strollers. They sipped from travel coffee mugs and spoke to each other in voices that carried over to us on the wind:

"How about stopping here at the park?" one said.

"Uh-uh." The other mom eyed an overgrown bush—and even a bench—with disgust. "There have been reports of the homeless loitering overnight or even camping out on the lawn."

The pair of them moved away. I resumed my conversation with Barbra. "What do you know about this Dwayne fellow?"

"He rented under 'D. Wayne.' His profile picture should've given me pause." She shuddered.

"How's that?"

"He looked like a ruffian. I could tell even from the unfocused shot. He wasn't smiling one tiny bit. Not polished-looking, with hair in uncombed, crazy waves." I didn't dare to point out her own mass of hair.

"What made you eventually rent to him?" I asked.

She snorted. "Flattery. His sister remarked that my cottage looked like it came straight out of *The Secret Garden*, one of my favorite childhood books."

Stroking of the ego. It worked every time. But he'd mentioned . . . "His sister?"

"Yes, they were going to stay together for a weekend. Sibling bonding time."

Detective Brown had mentioned a sister. The worried woman who'd phoned Pixie to ask after Davis Argo's whereabouts.

I wondered if the detective had discovered any more leads. However, silence probably bode well. It meant he wasn't breathing down Pixie's neck. But it might help her case even more if I started tarnishing the image of the victim. After all, Barbra had just labeled the guy as a "ruffian."

"Remember any other details?" I asked her.

"I can't think of anything else," she said, as she rose up from the bench. "Thanks for letting me unload."

"But of course."

Barbra seemed in a better mood after having shared the information with me. I noticed she sashayed back to her car.

I stayed at the bench and dialed up Detective Brown.

He wasn't much for small talk, so I launched right in. "How's your investigation going?"

"I assume you mean the one into Pixie St. James."

I frowned. "No, the case is about Davis Argo, also known as 'Dwayne A.' You should be focused on the victim, not a fake suspect." I hated even associating Pixie with the investigation.

Detective Brown's deep voice rumbled back at me. "To be honest, I've gotten roped into other stuff because of July Fourth incidents."

"Right. That makes sense." I could imagine the holiday might lead to increased deaths, accidental or otherwise.

His voice took on a somber tone. "People don't have any sense. Running around everywhere, even celebrating with gunfire."

I softened my voice. "Sorry, Detective."

"It comes with the territory," he said.

Maybe I'd connected with him in some way because he added, "Okay, Miss Lee. I'll bite. What did you dig up?"

I stumbled over my next words in my excitement. "Davis was bad news. Who knows how many enemies he had?"

Detective Brown made me repeat my words at a slower pace. Then he said, "You're getting that info from what source?"

A little embellished lie slipped out. "Someone he rented from met him and told me he was a ruffian."

"How? Based on his appearance?" Detective Brown mumbled, "Though he seemed in awful shape behind that bush."

"What's that, Detective?"

He spoke in a louder voice. "I said, 'You sure don't beat around the bush.'"

That was not at all what he'd just revealed. And I wondered if he'd been thinking aloud or had purposely leaked that fact to me. Either way, it seemed like Davis's body had been found outdoors. Where exactly? I wondered.

Detective Brown hadn't given me much to go on. I bet Davis's next of kin had more details, though. And I knew Pixie had her number. I thanked the detective for his time and hung up.

After getting the digits from Pixie, I called up Davis's sister. All this call-making from the park made me feel like a literal benchwarmer.

"Hi, I'm Mimi Lee. A friend of Pixie St. James," I said.

"The vacation home owner." Her voice held a hint of distrust.

"Yes. You called up my friend when your brother was, um, missing." I kicked at a patch of bare earth on the ground and sent dirt flying. I couldn't bring myself to say that he'd been killed, but I added, "My condolences, Miss Argo."

"It's Dorris," she said. "Dorris Argo."

"That's a unique name."

She chuckled. "My parents wanted to name us after cities in this beautiful Golden State. They came up with Davis and Dorris." At least I'd broken the ice. Time to get into meatier topics.

"Look, I understand that you don't know me, but we're actually on the same side." I started walking around the field, feeling the dry grass crunch underneath my feet. "I want to know what really happened to Davis, too . . . and get Pixie's name off the suspects list."

Dorris didn't say anything for a few moments, and I wondered if she was digesting my previous words and evaluating my real intentions.

I continued strolling and searched for the fluffiest dandelion I could find in the park. After plucking it with care, I blew on its puffy head. Future apologies to the poor gardener.

Maybe my wish came true, though, because Dorris started talking again. "The authorities are very slow in finding any real answers," she said.

"I know what you mean, especially that Detective Brown." I remembered my own frustration with the detective when he'd failed to find the true culprit in his previous cases.

She snorted. "The only good thing about the man is that he likes cats."

"How do you know that?"

"There was some gray fur on his jacket when he interviewed me, and I asked him if he owned any pets."

"You're sharp, Dorris," I said. "If we could put our heads together, maybe we'd solve things even faster."

"Dole out some vigilante justice," she said. "I like the sound of that. Why don't we chat more at my place?"

Since I didn't have any plans for the weekend (no date with Josh, for sure), I agreed. And since it sounded like she liked animals, I asked if I could bring Marshmallow along on my visit. She acquiesced, and I found myself cheering on the inside. Three minds would be even better than two to get traction in this case.

CHAPTER

fifteen

DORRIS LIVED IN what might have been a luxurious gated apartment complex once but had gone downhill over the years. The security guard at his station lifted the barrier preventing me from entry after jotting down my car's make, model, and license plate number. But he never asked for my name. Go figure. Maybe everyone in Los Angeles was so attached to their vehicles, they became viable alternate IDs.

I drove past a small pond, which might have once held some koi fish. Now, the only living organism seemed to be the abundant algae floating in it.

Dorris's apartment was housed in one of the identical tall puke-colored buildings in the complex. I had to squint at the building numbers and circle the grounds twice before locating the correct address.

After scoring a close guest parking spot outside her building, Marshmallow and I approached the entrance. Noting the intercom on the wall,

I buzzed to be let in. Dorris answered right away and said, "The lock's broken. Come inside."

Thankfully, I didn't have to walk through any long winding hallways to find her door. She lived right near the entryway.

Seeing no bell to ring, I rapped on her door.

Dorris Argo opened it, and I did a quick double take. Maybe all that talk of vigilante justice had made me anticipate someone tougher.

Marshmallow pawed at my ankle. "Is it me, or does she remind you of a scarecrow?"

He'd hit the mark about her physical description. I took in her straw-colored hair, dull necklace, patchwork clothes, and stick-thin arms and legs. If she hadn't been holding on to the door, she might've gotten blown over by a passing breeze.

"Mimi?" she asked while also giving me the once-over. I hoped I'd pass her stranger-danger inspection because I knew I didn't have an intimidating presence. My petite frame and resting nice face had never once scared anyone.

She then glanced down and spotted Marshmallow lounging on the floor. He, at least, must have passed muster because she opened the door wider and beckoned us in.

The apartment was cluttered, but not absurdly so. I saw a few magazines lying around on the carpet, jackets slung over chair backs, and a horde of bobbleheads crowding the coffee table. Marshmallow went right up to one of the figurines and bopped it on the head to make it wobble.

Dorris sat down on one side of her dingy white sofa. I sat on the other end and immediately sank into the cushion. Guess she'd owned the thing for a while.

"Here, kitty," Dorris crooned to Marshmallow. He crept over, and she stroked his back.

"She's so skinny it feels like a feather's tickling me," he said.

I faced Davis's sister. "Again, I'm so sorry for your loss, Dorris."

She petted Marshmallow with a faster rhythm. "Davis always looked out for me. I sure miss him."

"Older brother?" I said. Sounded like Davis had filled the shoes of the usual big sibling protector role. I knew how that felt.

She swallowed hard. "Yep. Four years' difference."

"This might be hard for you," I said, "but what did the cops tell you about how he, uh, passed away?"

Her back stiffened.

Should I be pushing her so hard? But I didn't know how else I could introduce the subject.

Marshmallow purred. "Start slower, Mimi. Ask her about the time-line."

I gave Dorris a moment of silence before proceeding in a gentler voice. "Can you tell me in your own words what happened? From the moment you first thought he was missing . . . until later."

Sighing, she ran her fingers through her straw-like tresses and got her hand stuck there. She yanked her hand, pulling out a few strands by accident. "Davis had decided to visit Catalina for a couple of days."

I calculated backward in my head from my own July first arrival at the house. "Must have been . . . near the end of June?"

"Uh-huh." She fiddled with Marshmallow's ears, and he shook his head a little, but didn't leave her side. "Davis likes getting away from the city once in a while."

"I'm a little confused about the events," I said. "Did he go missing on the island?"

She furrowed her forehead. "I mean, he was supposed to come back on July first. I even debated on filing a missing persons report, but it hadn't been forty-eight hours yet."

"So you called Pixie instead," I said, "but she didn't recognize his name."

Her eyes filled with tears. "Yes, and Davis never came home."

I tried to shift closer to Dorris but sank farther into my cushion instead. "'Came home'?" I repeated. Was that a deliberate choice of wording on her part instead of "went home"?

She wiped away the wetness from her eyes with her slender fingers and then waved her hand around to indicate the apartment around her.

My heart seemed to skip a beat. "Did you two share this place?"

She pointed to the collection of bobblehead figures. "I just can't seem to put away any of his stuff."

I made a reassuring murmur. "Of course, that's totally understandable. It must have been such a shock, since he was so healthy. How could he have . . . slipped away?"

She jutted her chin out. "Well, I know he didn't drink himself to death. Which is what the cops first thought."

I raised my eyebrows at her.

"When they found him, the police also noticed an empty bottle of liquor. But he would have never been drinking that in the first place. Alcohol and his meds don't mix."

"He was on medication?" I asked. Maybe not so healthy then.

"It doesn't matter." Her fierce gaze met mine. "I'm sure it was foul play. I wished he didn't always feel the need to play big bro and had called me once he'd run into trouble and had to deal with some maniac killer."

"Don't blame yourself," I said. "There's not much you could have done when he was so far away in Catalina."

She blinked her granite eyes at me. "You don't know? He was found at a local park here in Los Angeles."

So that's why Detective Brown was handling the case. The death had happened on his turf. "A park? How strange."

Dorris took a deep breath. "Yeah, and not just any park. We used to go there as kids. I'd play on the swings while he hung out with his high school buddies."

"Geez. That's horrible." I couldn't imagine having sweet childhood memories become tainted with tragedy.

Her voice caught. "What's worse is that he was mistaken for a drunk at first. Nobody even bothered to report it to the police until later."

No wonder Davis had been considered "missing" for some time. "I'm so sorry," I said again, knowing my words would be ineffectual at providing solace.

She started crying and turned her face away from mine. "Can you give me a moment?"

"Sure." I stumbled down the hallway of the apartment. Noticing an empty bathroom, I darted inside to give Dorris more privacy.

I lingered in the bathroom, taking time to wash my hands with the eucalyptus mint–scented soap. There wasn't a window in the bathroom, so all I got was a view of my own face reflected from two angles— by the long rectangular mirror in front and a smaller side mirror.

Hmm, I wondered . . . I tugged on the side mirror. Lo and behold, it swung open to reveal a medicine cabinet. One that the Argos actually used for pills.

Dorris had mentioned her brother taking some sort of medication. What could it have been for? I noted the capped orange bottle on the shelf labeled with his name. Bingo. "Lopressor."

I heard Dorris calling for me. "You can come back now," she said.

I repeated the medication name in my head a few times in order to memorize it. I'd have to look it up after our meeting.

When I returned to the couch, Dorris appeared calmer, even though I noticed her red-rimmed eyes.

She kept petting Marshmallow, who lay across her lap, trying hard not to squirm.

He glanced at me. "I hope it was worth abandoning me in her clutches. Not only has Dorris practically swiped my fur off, but she's done it with *wet* hands."

From wiping her tears, no doubt. Not that it would matter much to Marshmallow. He hated his fur damp.

I decided to wrap up this conversation before he scratched her in defense. "Thanks for talking with me, Dorris. I'll be sure to let you know what I find out."

"Any time." She glanced down at Marshmallow. "I'm happy you brought your cat with you."

Marshmallow took that as his cue to leave. He scrambled off her lap.

After we got back to the privacy of my car, I filled Marshmallow in about the medicine I'd discovered.

"Look it up now," Marshmallow said. "Before you forget. Human minds are like sieves."

I typed in the medication name on my phone. "It's a beta-blocker," I said. "For heart conditions and to lower blood pressure."

"Interesting." He twitched his whiskers. "Do you think he drank even though he wasn't supposed to? At the park on the sly so his sister wouldn't know?"

I stared through the windshield at the apartment complex. "I'm not sure, but there are definitely secrets lurking in there. Davis rented the other Catalina Chalets, and the owners are all missing items from their vacation homes. Unlikely that's a coincidence."

Marshmallow bobbed his head in agreement. "So, what's the next step?"

"My trip to a local art studio early tomorrow morning might clear some things up," I said.

CHAPTER

sixteen

ASTRAL'S ART STUDIO was one of the glass storefronts on an industrial street in Venice. It sat between an artisan bakery and a furniture place that offered hand-carved teakwood tables. I'd walked up and down the street twice before finding the store. It didn't have any sign proclaiming "Astral's Art Studio." Instead, the business displayed a banner with moon and star symbols near the front entrance. I only found the store because my GPS pinpointed the exact location.

I walked in the door and noticed the back of someone sitting down at an easel. Besides the aquamarine smock, I could only make out a tangerine top. Plus the back of a half-shaved head.

"Excuse me?" I said, walking toward the artist. "I'm looking for Astral?"

The person rested their paintbrush on the palette beside them, and I noticed the painting on the easel for the first time. A giant tortoise took up the entire canvas.

"Well, you've found me." The artist turned around. Astral seemed almost like a watercolor of a person, with soft receding features. Even the eyebrows appeared as the barest arches of hair above light-colored eyes.

I must have been gaping because Astral tapped a foot against the polished floor and asked, "How exactly can I help you?"

"Er. That's a lovely tortoise," I said. Anything to ease the freeze rays from Astral's gaze. "So lifelike and large."

A closed-lip smile from Astral. "Of course. That's my specialty."

I peered around at the walls of the studio and discovered a pattern. Framed images of chickens, dogs, and even a pig greeted me. "You paint animals?" I asked.

"Affirmative. I'm a pet portraitist."

"Uh." I'd never heard of such a profession, even after all the chats with my grooming clients.

"Do you have a piece of art you'd like to commission?" Astral asked.

I shook my head. "Barbra mentioned your studio to me in passing, and I wanted to see it in person."

"Barbra?" Astral's pale eyelids fluttered. "I'm much better with the pet names . . ."

"She owns, or rather, owned a magnificent horse. Buttercup, as I recall."

"Yes. I remember the mare. I'd even added a matching flower garland around the horse's neck as a special touch."

I drew close to the painting in progress on the easel. Astral had somehow captured an action shot of a tortoise. Its pink tongue darted forth, attempting to eat a cabbage. I laughed. "You really do capture the spirit of the pet well."

Astral's head dipped. "I try my best." A pause. "And the high quality is reflected in my prices."

"I own a Persian cat myself," I said. "How much would it be to capture his likeness?" Not that Marshmallow needed anything else to boost his healthy ego. I just wondered about Astral's price for a pet portrait.

"My paintings start at eight grand and go up from there."

I almost fainted at the price. "Er, let me think about it some more."

Astral arched one shadowy eyebrow, probably knowing full well I couldn't pay the price and would never step into the studio again.

"Thanks for your time," I said.

Astral said, "Please give my condolences to Barbra." Even before seeing me nod, the artist had turned back to the canvas.

I exited the studio and reflected on the expensive pet portraits. Could someone have seen that painting of Barbra's, known about its value, and stolen it?

• • •

At Hollywoof, the first customer of the day turned out to be a man dressed up in a suit, complete with a folded handkerchief tucked into his breast pocket. He'd brought in Terry the terrier—"Get it?" the man said.

Marshmallow flicked his tail and turned to me. "Even you had the sense not to call me 'Catty,'" he said.

I nodded, but no matter the name, the terrier was adorable.

"A trim?" I asked.

"Hand stripping only," the man replied, before leaving to "make some essential phone calls" while I groomed his pet.

Nicola looked at me agog from where she was adjusting the spotlight to shine down just so on the cash register. "'Hand stripping,'" she repeated. "Is that like doing a wax . . . but on dogs?"

"Um, no."

"Because I wouldn't do that on a regular basis unless I had my pretty legs insured for a cool million like Taylor Swift."

"In grooming," I said, "hand stripping means I won't be using a razor on the little guy."

I brought Terry to the back room. Instead of using the clippers to remove only the top part of his coat, I'd be pulling his fur out from the roots.

Speaking to Terry in a calm voice, I said, "Don't worry. Hand stripping only sounds painful. You shouldn't feel a thing."

After sprinkling some stripping powder on Terry's body, I also put on finger gloves to better grip his fur. I made sure to work in sections, tugging in the direction of his hair growth. The fluffs of hair came out easily enough and reminded me of cotton balls as I placed them on the grooming table.

For his face, I made sure to not pull out too much beyond the back corner of his eyes. I also selected only the larger hairs near his eyebrows and along his muzzle to pluck. After my efforts, the hand stripping revealed a rich brown coat underneath his previously dull top layer.

I returned to the front room with the groomed terrier. "Ta-dah," I said to my small audience of Nicola and Marshmallow.

Marshmallow shrugged, but Nicola oohed. "That dog's got a brandnew fur coat," she said.

Grinning, I began parading Terry around the room. And that's how his owner found me—pretending to walk down a fashion runway with his terrier.

The man's eyes lit up, and he must have forgiven me for my silliness because he said, "Exactly what I was envisioning."

While the customer was paying for my excellent grooming skills, I heard my phone ring. The caller ID showed it was Pixie.

I hurried to take the call in the back room for privacy's sake. The rushing made me breathless when I answered. "Pixie?"

"Mimi, so glad I caught you. I just got off the phone with Detective Brown."

I groaned.

"Mm-hmm. Seems like he found another tie to me."

"What now?" I paced back and forth between the industrial-size steel sink and the grooming table.

"The reservation for the rec room at the local park was made under my name."

I thought back. "For the Catalina Chalets owners' meeting?"

"Yes." She gulped. "The park turns out to be where Davis Argo's body was found."

I shivered. He'd died on the same ground I'd walked through.

She continued, "He was half hidden by an overgrown bush. Police even thought he was homeless."

And drunk, according to his sister. I also recalled the snippet of conversation I'd heard between the stroller moms. They'd opted not to stop at the park as a pit stop because of reports of the homeless loitering at the park. Obviously the police had believed that rumor as well.

My voice came out in a squeak. "Pixie, this is important. How did you first hear about that park?"

She clicked her tongue. "After our first video call, we decided to meet up in person for clearer communication. So our Catalina Chalets group has met up there twice now. Someone suggested the place to me. We'd get free use of the space because they had connections."

"Do you remember who it was?" I held my breath. This could be a vital lead.

Pixie sighed. "I can't recall right now."

I frowned. "Nothing at all?"

"Well, I think it was one of the men who brought up the idea."

Uh-huh. That was something. And I'd be meeting with one of them soon for a lunch appointment: Riku.

CHAPTER

⇒ seventeen ⇐

RIKU WORKED IN Santa Monica. The beachfront city was known for its cool temperatures and hot sky-high rents. It had orderly streets with pretty blue signs, the numbers decreasing until they reached the golden sands and a festive pier with its giant Ferris wheel. Although urban, plenty of pedestrian crossings bisected major streets like Santa Monica Boulevard to create a more walkable city.

Riku's company didn't stop at one building but sprawled out across an entire campus. Beyond a picture-perfect green lawn, ideal for kicking a soccer ball or playing ultimate Frisbee, they also had a beach volleyball court. Maybe it didn't contain the fine sand of the actual beach nearby, but it was definitely a nice perk.

I entered the lobby of the mirrored building, all cool reflective blue panels from the outside. His office was located on the fifth floor, but he'd asked to meet on the ground level, where the cafeteria was located.

A security guard blinked at me standing there. Not wanting to get kicked out, I searched for Riku. Found him.

I sped over to where he was lounging in front of an archway to what must've been the eating area, given the number of people passing to and from there. That, along with the tantalizing smells drifting in the air.

Riku seemed so engrossed with his phone that he didn't even notice me sidle up next to him. He kept on scrolling.

"Hi, Riku," I said.

Only then did he glance my way and flash me a quick grin. He turned off the phone and pocketed it. "Glad you could join me for lunch," he said. "Pick up a plastic tray and check out all the food stations. I'll meet you at one of the registers after you decide on your grub."

I watched Riku step over to the fix-your-own-salad bar. He stood out against the crowd in his navy blue mock turtleneck and black jeans because the others swarming the cafeteria walked around in logoed T-shirts and shorts.

Assessing my options, my head swiveled between the three food choices before me: Create A Pizza, Chef Entrees, and The Teppan Grill. The lure of some grilled steak called to me.

After I received my tray of stir-fried veggies, noodles, and New York steak, I dashed over to Riku. I hoped he hadn't been waiting too long. He'd placed his tray down at the end of one of the checkout stations. I stared at the mound of overflowing greens on his plate. All vegetables. He didn't even have any salad dressing in sight.

Riku didn't bother to check out my food choice. "Use the credit from my account," he told the cashier, before he held out his badge for her to scan.

After a sharp beep confirmed his purchase, we moved to the dining area and selected a two-seater in the far back. I felt comfortable that no other patrons sat close enough to eavesdrop on our conversation.

At our table, I glanced around at the other seated employees. "Wow. Do all of these people work for you?"

"Nope. This workspace is shared." He held his fork aloft, brandishing it like a spear. "One day, though, I'll own the entire building." He stabbed his lettuce.

Ambitious guy. I picked up some noodles with my chopsticks. "Your products must be selling like wildfire then."

"My devices are absolutely top-notch."

"Mm-hmm." I took another bite. "You were saying the other day about your new phablet." I'd made sure to commit the term to memory so I could throw it around during our conversation.

"That's right." He placed his fork down, and his phone appeared in his hand like a slick magician's trick. "It's the lynchpin of my business plan. I call it Phoenix. Think of it as the Tesla of phablets: green energy meets stellar tech."

He proceeded to show me an image of the hybrid phone/tablet, and I made the requisite awed noises. To be honest, though, I couldn't tell much difference between the device with its sleek glass screen showcasing its pre-installed apps, and the other devices already out on the market. I doled out one true compliment: "I really like the fancy casing."

He nodded. "My brilliant idea. Gold exudes an aura of wealth. Like how the *Crazy Rich Asians* novel had that glittering cover."

I pointed at him with my chopsticks. "Do you have a lot of interested investors?"

Placing the phone on the table, he leaned back in his chair with a smug grin. "Plenty. They can't wait for Phoenix to launch. And I have pre-orders going up through the roof. We'll be sure to make IPO after that."

"IPO?" I knew it had something to do with stocks and was a big deal.

"Initial public offering," he said. "Everyone will want to snatch up my company's stocks, mark my words."

I picked up a piece of broccoli and chewed in contemplation. "So, you've already produced enough of these devices for people to clamor after them?"

He shifted in his seat. "Unfortunately not. The Phoenix in my Catalina home was the first working prototype."

"Oh, I'm sorry to hear that. And now it's gone? Can you build a new one?"

He used his fork to push around the salad on his plate. "I have my employees working around the clock on it."

"What a tough loss." I shook my head.

He stuffed a few pieces of lettuce into his mouth. Maybe he didn't know what to say in response.

Then Riku's phone started vibrating. He glanced at the screen. "Ah, I gotta go. I'm needed upstairs."

As he walked away, I called out to him. "I'll find the culprit. I've already solved two cases before."

I wondered if he'd heard me, or believed me. He didn't slow down his stride as he returned to work.

After finishing my stir-fry lunch, I stared at my empty soy sauce–splattered plate. Everything still led back to Davis Argo. But how had the man known which homes to steal from? And where had all the items gone?

CHAPTER
eighteen

AT DUSK, I met up with Professor Villanueva to gather more information. Thankfully, the man said he loved animals, so I didn't have to drop Marshmallow off at home before the appointed time.

The professor lived in Brentwood, a charming neighborhood close to the UCLA campus. His wide house sprawled across its large lot and was bordered by a bed of grass so green, the color looked painted on.

I rang the doorbell, and Professor Villanueva appeared in another of his dated sweater vests, this time in an argyle pattern, to let us in.

"Mimi, good to see you again. And what a fetching cat," Professor Villanueva said, leaning over to inspect Marshmallow in detail.

Marshmallow started purring, and the professor bent down. Before he could stroke Marshmallow's fur, my cat backed away. Maybe Marshmallow hadn't wanted the professor to mess with his precious fur?

I shrugged. "Sorry, Professor Villanueva. Cats, you know. They have a mind of their own."

Marshmallow twitched his nose repeatedly at me as we entered the house. I got only a fleeting impression of the dim interior since the professor led us straight through the open French doors into his expansive yard. I recalled briefly passing by dark heavy furniture while walking on polished hardwood floors.

Professor Villanueva's backyard was almost as unbelievable as his front landscape. Magical almost. A stately willow tree stood in the middle of the lawn, its green tendrils lazily sweeping the air as the wind blew. One corner of the yard held a row of rose bushes, each variety bursting with bright colors, although vibrant petals also littered the ground below the plants.

As we sat at a patio table under a vine-laden trellis, which cast down interlacing patterns of dark and light, I noticed a patch of brilliant flowers to my left. In blue and gold.

"Amazing," I said. "Those flowers match the Bruins colors perfectly."

"I know. It took my gardener and me multiple tries to get the hues exactly right." Professor Villanueva looked me in the eye. "By the way, do you still keep in touch with people at UCLA?"

"I emailed a few professors after graduation. We connect every now and then. Also"—I shuddered, remembering the disastrous date Ma had set me up with by using the connection—"I'm part of the alumni network."

From near my legs, Marshmallow yawned. "School spirit. Boring. Move on to some juicier topics."

Oh yeah. I'd better focus. Scooting my metal latticed patio chair closer to the professor, I said, "We should stay on task. I don't want to waste your time. What exactly was stolen from your vacation home?"

He placed a hand against his neck and rubbed it. "Costume jewelry, like I said at the meeting."

He sounded cagey. Was I being too intrusive somehow? I softened my tone. "I'm only asking because making a list of the missing items will really help me in solving the string of thefts. I think it's what the authorities would do as a first step."

"Yes, well." He clasped his hands in front of him on the patio table.

I decided to prod him for details. "Was the item something valuable?"

"To me." He cleared his throat, and his gaze landed on Marshmallow. "What kind of cat do you have there?"

"A Persian," I said. "Although he's a one-of-a-kind feline."

"Love the snow white fur," the professor said. "It reminds me of the powder I see when I go up to Big Bear in the winters to ski."

Why were we talking about my cat and snow? Perhaps he wanted to ease into the tougher conversation topics. Okay, I could do a few more minutes of small talk. "Do you own a pet, Professor?"

I glanced around the yard and tried to peek into the dark house. I hadn't noticed any food dishes or animal noises, but we'd rushed through the interior.

He shook his head. "No time while I'm teaching. I wouldn't be able to balance everything and give a pet my proper attention."

I figured we'd done enough chitchatting. Leaning in, I asked him, "Now if you could be more specific about the stolen item, I'm sure I could help you retrieve it." An empty promise, but he didn't have to know that.

Professor Villanueva clenched his hands together on the tabletop. "I'm sorry, Mimi. It's just too personal to share. I thought I could talk about it, but . . ."

I waited him out for a few beats, hoping he'd still tell me after my silent pressure tactic. Nope.

"Thanks for taking your time to drop by and for bringing your precious cat," he said.

Marshmallow hissed at him. "I can't believe he's kicking us out."

I shrugged. We were on the professor's private property, and I couldn't force him to let us stay in his home or to speak about things he didn't want to.

I left with a sharp sting of disappointment.

We settled in the car, and Marshmallow piped up. "That man's a liar."

"No doubt about it," I said, staring at the immense house with its dark rooms. "I wonder what secret he's keeping. After all, he'd been too willing to set up a meeting with me. But then to give me barely any info when I show up . . ."

"It's not just that," Marshmallow said. "He claimed he didn't have pets, but—"

"Did you see one?" A cat's eyes could probe the dark well.

"I smelled one on him. That's why I didn't want his mangy hands touching me. It could've been an old scent, but I still didn't want to be petted."

"What did you sense? A dog or a cat?" I asked.

"Some other type of animal, but I'm not certain which. I couldn't quite put my paw on it."

That's odd. Why would Professor Villanueva be hiding his pet from me?

CHAPTER
nineteen

NICOLA CALLED IN sick the next day and begged off work. Thankfully, it didn't seem like we had many appointments already scheduled. I bet I could handle the customers on my own.

The shop bell rang with a merry jingle at Hollywoof. By contrast, the owner and his accompanying basset hound couldn't have looked gloomier.

"I'm your ten-thirty appointment," the man said.

"Right." I studied my calendar and its accompanying notes. "Something about your dog excessively scratching?"

Marshmallow scooted away from the puppy and the owner. "It's not fleas, right?"

The melancholy owner turned to me. "Could you please take a look?"

I checked the dog's fur. No telltale signs of critters, but his skin did look pink and irritated. "Perhaps your dog has sensitive skin. Was he diagnosed with eczema by the vet?"

The man tugged at his earlobe. "Not that I know of, but I haven't taken him in a while."

"Hmm." I rubbed my chin. "I've got a soothing treatment that could help in the short run, but I'd also suggest a thorough physical exam."

"I'll try anything that might help him feel better," the owner said.

The man paced back and forth across the floor, threatening to scuff the golden stars with the doggie celebrity names. I asked him to sit down and watch the flick playing on the large screen as a distraction. The film was *Beethoven*, and I hoped it would settle the man.

I brought the basset to the back and secured him to a grooming table. He whimpered.

"Poor boy," I said, "but I think this might help." I selected a bottle of jojoba oil, known for its calming properties, even for humans. I started to rub it on his irritated hot spots. The dog seemed to enjoy the oil, either because of the extra massaging or due to the actual relief provided by the jojoba.

I also relaxed as I spread the oil. It helped me to release my worries and free my thinking as well.

I'd investigated all four robbery incidents connected to the owners of the Catalina Chalets: Pixie with the Marilyn Monroe headscarf, Barbra and her beloved pet portrait, Riku with his phablet, and Professor Villanueva with his mysterious jewelry. All the objects could be worth a lot, though I couldn't really tell with the professor's secret item. He'd called it "costume jewelry," so why would it be stolen?

Marshmallow broke into my thoughts when he popped into the grooming area. "What's that burnt smell?" he said. "Kind of like a campfire?"

The basset looked with doleful eyes at Marshmallow lingering in the doorway but didn't even bark in alarm.

I sniffed the air. "I don't smell a thing, but you're probably talking about the jojoba oil."

"Mr. Glum is still moping out there, and I couldn't handle his pouting anymore," Marshmallow said. "But what's going on with you, pussycat? You look downtrodden, too."

"It's this frustrating murder case," I said. "I'm not making any headway on it."

Marshmallow licked his paw as I proceeded to recap the different thefts.

"I wish they had installed nanny cams in their places," I said. "Or that I had some sort of eyewitness to the crimes."

"Or cat-witness," Marshmallow said. "Human bystanders are known to be unreliable. Just ask any judge."

I reflected on his remark. "Agreed. The eyewitness would have to be somebody observant and unbiased, a person who'd been at the scene of each crime."

Marshmallow softly padded toward me. I'd finished with the basset by now, and he didn't react to my stealthy cat coming closer. The dog lay there, relaxed.

"You need someone silent like a cat," Marshmallow said. "A person who others don't even notice because they're in the background so often."

I caught his drift and murmured, "What about Lavinia?" She had been inside every house and could have noticed key evidence left behind in the other Catalina Chalets.

"Cats and cleaners," he said. "We're both frequently dismissed, but often in the know about oh-so-many things."

I already had Lavinia's number from before, so it'd be easy enough to make a quick phone call to her during break time. First, though, I had to return the basset to his doleful owner.

After that, I received a huge delivery of extra supplies. I unboxed the items, leaving out the empty cardboard boxes, and Marshmallow pounced on them at once. Well, better he claw those than the pleather benches.

I ended up finally phoning Lavinia around noon, when I knew that the shop would be quiet.

Marshmallow pushed around a large box as the call went through. I switched to speakerphone, so he could listen to the conversation.

I introduced myself again to Lavinia, referring to how she'd met Josh—my heart felt pinched as I said his name—and me at Catalina.

"Yes, I remember you two," she said. Her "lovebirds" comment floated back into my mind.

I picked at the cuticle on my thumb. "Right. Anyway, you were really helpful when you highlighted the junk left behind on the patio of the house that we were renting. The bag turned out to hold some dangerous fireworks."

She gasped. "Oh dear."

"If you hadn't told me, who knows what damage might have occurred?"

"Uh-huh," she said and tutted. "Like the Great Fire of 1915. Almost burned down Avalon, except we were saved by blessed nature when the wind shifted."

I looked over at Marshmallow, and he nodded at me. I'd buttered Lavinia up enough. She felt like a heroine now. Time to swoop in on some incriminating details.

"I thought you could help me with another matter," I said. "Stuff has gone missing from all of the Catalina Chalets. I know you and your crew are honorable and impeccable in your cleaning efforts." I made sure not to cast any suspicion on her. "Did you notice anything off in the homes owned by Professor Villanueva, Riku, and Barbra?"

She made a clicking noise with her tongue. "Can't say that I do, offhand."

Marshmallow batted at the box closest to him in frustration.

"That's too bad." My voice quivered. "I really wanted to help Pixie out."

"Pixie St. James? How is she involved?"

I'd asked Lavinia at our first meeting in a broad manner if she'd seen anything amiss in the living room. Now I had to be more direct. "A headscarf in her glass cabinet display went missing," I said.

"But that can't be."

"What makes you say that, Lavinia?"

"Well, before your arrival, my team cleaned the house, of course. I personally Windexed the display case myself. It was locked up tight. I would've noticed if the door had been wide open or the lock had been tampered with." She paused. "It's a real shame I didn't bother double-checking the contents inside, though."

"Not your fault," I said. Identifying missing items wasn't a part of Lavinia's job description. And who would have really scrutinized and itemized a curio case? Except for my intelligent cat. I glanced at Marshmallow now. He'd tucked himself inside the smallest of the boxes. How had he managed to squeeze into such a tight space?

"I'm sorry I couldn't be of more help," Lavinia said, her voice dripping with apology.

"Actually, I think you've been of great assistance," I said and reassured her once more before I hung up.

And she had. I moved over to the box holding Marshmallow and closed the flaps over his head.

He popped up like a feline jack-in-the-box. "Hey, why are you trapping me in here?"

"To test out a theory." How did a cat—or a scarf, for that matter—escape from a locked box?

Lavinia had sworn the case had been closed, the lock untampered with. There was really only one conclusion after that observation, but I'd been concentrating so hard on Davis having ties with the Catalina homes that I'd glossed over a key aspect of the headscarf disappearance. The theft had been an inside job.

I texted Pixie, who confirmed my suspicion. She wasn't the only one with a key to that glass cabinet. She'd passed on a copy to her unscrupulous property manager, Lloyd.

CHAPTER
≈ twenty ≈

WANTED TO SEE Lloyd face-to-face because, according to an old psychology study, ninety percent of communication is nonverbal. In person, maybe he'd give away something vital.

My conversation with Lavinia hadn't taken too long, so I used my lunch hour to also call up Pixie and ask her to schedule the meeting with Lloyd. He couldn't say no to his boss, right?

She managed to have him clear his schedule come Saturday morning, and I was ready to fly to the island again (courtesy of Pixie) to do my in-person snooping.

Preparing to meet with Lloyd in his tight office space in the back of his brother's career placement center reminded me of Josh. But what didn't?

If only I could turn back time, before we'd gone on the trip and somehow rocked the equilibrium in our relationship.

Even though our telepathic communication went only one way, I swore Marshmallow could read my mind sometimes. "Call him up already," he said.

I took my cat's urging as a sign.

"Hey, Josh," I said when he picked up.

"Mimi." He said my name in a detached tone, almost bored, and Marshmallow arched his back in indignation.

"Um, I was wondering if you were free on Saturday. I'm flying out to Catalina again..." I'd hoped for some sign of excitement on his end, but all I got was silence. How I wished I could see his face through the phone.

He hemmed and hawed. "I'm actually busy this weekend."

"Oh." My voice shriveled up.

"But, tell you what, we have a mixer tomorrow evening at the office. Would you like to come?"

My brow furrowed. "I thought you hated going to those stuffy things."

"Usually, but this one's important. Can you make it?"

I bit my bottom lip. "Of course. I'll be there." He couldn't complain that I wasn't supportive of his career if I put forth my best effort to join him at a work event, right?

"I'll text you the details soon."

After we hung up, I made a face at Marshmallow. "Well, that didn't go like I'd planned, but at least Josh and I are still meeting up."

Marshmallow blinked at me. "What exactly were you expecting, Mimi?"

A montage of sappy rom-com film endings flashed before my eyes. "What happened to all that love and support you gave me before?" I asked.

Marshmallow sat on his haunches. "Huh?"

"You told me to call him."

"Um, I meant a different *him*. For you to speak with Detective Brown," he said. "About your new findings."

Whoops. Guess I'd taken Marshmallow's suggestion my own way, to cater to my own heart.

"Never mind," Marshmallow said. "You don't have to call him anymore."

"That was a good idea, though—I probably should."

"Doesn't matter. Detective Brown's at the door right now. You don't have to talk to him over the phone."

"What?" I swiveled toward the entrance of Hollywoof and noticed the detective peering through the plate-glass window.

He caught me looking at him and motioned for me to unlock the business with his free hand. The other held up a takeout bag. I hurried to comply and opened the door wide.

"Detective?" I said. "What are you doing here?"

A loud purr attracted my attention, and I noticed Nimbus sitting near his feet.

"I'm not sure if you're aware, Detective, but cats don't really need baths."

"Oh, I happened to be nearby," Detective Brown said, "and thought we could chat during your lunch break."

"Okay . . ." I said slowly and let them enter the shop.

He lifted his to-go bag. "Lunch is on me."

When I realized the takeout was from Tommy's, I knew I'd succumb, even though I'd already planned to eat a healthy kale salad for today.

I gestured to the waiting area. As he sat on one of the benches and took out two wrapped burgers, I salivated. Chili scented the air.

Mmm. I hadn't eaten one of their famous chili burgers in a long time. I hoped the sauce wouldn't stain the cream-colored benches, but even if that happened, it'd be worth it.

"Enjoy," Detective Brown said, handing one of the burgers over to me.

Once he'd distributed the food bribe, the detective got down to business, as I knew he would. "So, you're good friends with Miss St. James, right? Would you say you know a lot about her?"

What info was he fishing for now? I gave him a slow nod as I unwrapped my burger.

"She's a single woman, and I wonder if she feels unsafe in these parts." He waved his hand around.

Um, was he referring to the super dangerous beach scene? Or the crime-ridden upscale golden Hollywood Hills area where she lived? I stifled my laughter by biting into my burger.

He didn't unwrap his own chili burger, but played with the wax paper, crinkling it. "Well, did she take any classes to protect herself? Martial arts, maybe? That sort of thing."

Had Davis Argo been attacked with a bo staff or something? Maybe I could lay the detective's suspicion to rest. "She only took a self-defense class once. The kind where they teach you to jab at the eyes or knee a man's family jewels."

Even while he winced, the detective's ice blue eyes glittered. "Interesting. Did she carry a weapon to protect her? Club? Mace? Taser? Anything like that."

"Uh, no." But my reply came out in a questioning tone. I scrambled to explain myself. "I mean, who really knows what a woman carries around with her? Haven't you heard of that baby shower game where attendees dig into their purses as a kind of scavenger hunt? Surprising things can surface from the depths of a woman's bag."

Detective Brown unwrapped his burger and starting eating with glee, almost smacking his lips in delight as he chewed. I watched his sudden joy with growing unease. My own stomach began twisting in anxiety. Had my comments somehow provided ammunition against Pixie?

I fixed my gaze on the cats for a moment to calm myself down. Their animated purrs to each other re-centered me. I still could turn the tables around in this conversation.

"Detective Brown," I said. "I'm sure you're acting with due diligence in interviewing all the potential suspects in this case. Let me tell you something. Pixie's property manager is really fishy."

The detective cocked his head at me. "I'm sure you're about to share one of your wild scenarios."

Taking that as permission to speak, I proceeded to tell him about the thefts at each of the Catalina Chalets. And how the loss of the famous headscarf at Pixie's rental home had been an inside job.

He finished his burger and scrunched up the wax paper into a tight ball. "Miss Lee, you can't go around accusing people of different crimes. First off, how do you even know the items were stolen? Maybe they were misplaced—that professor wouldn't even tell you what item of his went 'missing.'"

After taking a deep breath, he continued, "And even if your theory did hold water, how is a shifty property manager stealing something related to the same guy murdering his own rentee?"

"I don't know," I said, squaring my shoulders. "But I intend to find out."

Detective Brown gave me a warning look. "While you already took it upon yourself to investigate two of my other cases, don't meddle with this one."

Feeling a growing frustration, I lost my appetite and wrapped up my burger to save for later.

Detective Brown drummed his fingers against his knee. "One other thing. Miss St. James also has the key. Couldn't she have unlocked the cabinet herself?"

I spluttered, "Excuse me? I'm not following you."

"Maybe she staged the theft."

"And why would she do that?"

"So that when the victim's body turned up, suspicion would be cast away from her."

I huffed. "Ridiculous."

He raised his eyebrows at me. "How well do you really know your friend, Miss Lee?"

I felt my face redden. "My lunch break is over," I said, practically pushing him out the door of my shop.

CHAPTER

twenty-one

STOMPED AROUND THE store in frustration and shoved the remaining half-eaten Tommy's chili burger into the small fridge in the back. How could I have botched up the conversation so badly?

When I returned to the front, seething, Marshmallow crept away from me. "Watch that you don't crush my tail while you're fuming."

"Sorry," I said, shaking my head. "I just can't believe I made Pixie's situation even worse. And I didn't even get any good intel from him."

Marshmallow put a paw up. "Didn't you, though?"

"If only . . ." However, I stopped with my rage stepping and stared at him. "Well, the detective did mention something about self-defense. If I could narrow down what he meant by that, maybe I could figure out the means of the murder."

"Why don't you ask the cat?" Marshmallow said, curling up in his usual napping spot.

I tilted my head at him. "You know the answer?"

He twitched his nose at me. "Remember how I said that cats make good eyewitnesses . . . Kittens do, too."

I slapped my palm against my forehead. "Nimbus."

"Uh-huh. I taught her well."

Remembering the cats' animated interaction during my discussion with Detective Brown, I said, "She heard something?"

"Saw something." Marshmallow licked his paw. "The detective just happened to be cuddling her while reading the autopsy report."

"Did she see the cause of death listed?"

Marshmallow squinted his eyes at me.

"Oh, right." I ran my fingers through my hair. "She can't read, not like you. So no help there."

"Au contraire," Marshmallow said. "Nimbus peeked at the accompanying photos."

My questions came out in a flurry. "Did she see bruises?" I asked. "Or maybe a pink ring around the neck?" I shivered, recalling how I'd been nearly strangled before due to my nosy sleuthing.

"Red markings, yes," Marshmallow said. "Near the chest."

Hmm. I counted off the weapons Detective Brown had mentioned on my fingers: club, mace, Taser. Which could he have been homing in on?

I pondered for a few moments. Then I had to file my questioning away when I received an SOS text from my sister.

Apparently, Ma hadn't been satisfied with the speed dating flop. She thought the problem was a lack of strong candidates. By participating in her online Malaysian forum, Ma had lurked on the threads and found the "perfect" match for Alice. But *his* mom wanted to vet my sister in person, and Alice asked me to come for support.

We found ourselves in front of an impressive building a few hours later. The bronze exterior almost shimmered in the sunset rays. A bio-tech company.

I pulled open the heavy glass door to the building, and we headed toward the elevator bank.

"Dr. Wu," Alice murmured, checking the building directory. "Unit 888."

Eight-eight-eight. It sounded like the word for "fortune" times three. I pressed the up button, and the elevator slid open with a whisper.

On the eighth floor, Alice said, "Here goes nothing." We wandered down the hallway until we located the right door. Alice knocked.

No answer, but the door was open a crack. She knocked some more and managed to widen the gap further.

"Hello?" My sister's voice sounded tentative, and she looked at me for help. The lights in the office were on.

Figuring somebody must be around, I peeked inside and found a tiny office taken over by a huge oak desk. A high-backed leather chair behind the desk was turned away from me and faced the broad window, which overlooked the busy major street outside.

I walked into the office with feigned confidence. "Dr. Wu," I said.

"Yes," a sharp female voice answered back.

The leather chair swiveled around, and I saw a woman in her fifties, staring at me with shrewd, narrowed eyes. Everything about her face appeared hawkish, from her searing predator look to her pointed beak of a nose.

"Alice, my sister, has a scheduled meeting with you." I beckoned my sister in from the hallway.

Despite Alice's sweet hello, complete with her using the honorific title of "Auntie" to the woman, Dr. Wu didn't crack a smile. This woman's dour mood screamed total judgment and Tiger Mama.

I crossed my arms over my chest, ready for the oncoming inquisition.

Dr. Wu acknowledged my battle stance with an incline of her head.

"My son can't date just any girl off the street," she said, addressing Alice. "I have a few simple questions for you."

Alice nodded and slipped her hand in mine. It felt like we were standing before a Sphinx, trying to earn our entry into somewhere important.

"Number one," Dr. Wu said. "What is your job title, Alice Lee?"

Before she could answer, I replied. "She's an instructor." That sounded pretty good to my ears.

My sister squeezed my hand, held her head up high, and said, "I'm a kindergarten teacher."

"Interesting," Dr. Wu said. "Your mother put down, 'Professor of Educational Development.'"

I found myself nodding at the title. Not a bad spin on things.

"A lie," Dr. Wu said, her nostrils flaring a bit.

"Er, what's the second question?" I said. Maybe we could redeem Alice's standing with the next answer.

"How many languages can you speak?" she asked.

My sister bit the tip of her fingernail before she answered. "English only," she said. Guess the Spanish she'd taken in high school hadn't made the cut.

"That's what I figured." Dr. Wu settled back in her chair, the disdain dripping from her voice. She stared us down. "Last question. Can you translate 'Mempersiasuikan'?"

My sister and I looked at each other, lost. What language was the woman even speaking?

As though we'd said it out loud, Dr. Wu said. "'Memper' is Malay;

'Siasui' is Hokkien; and 'Kan' is Malay. Basically, the phrase means 'to be a disgrace.'"

I gulped.

"It's Manglish." Dr. Wu's voice turned sweet as saccharine. "Don't you recognize the term?"

Alice scrunched up her nose. "Ma never taught us that."

"Exactly." Dr. Wu positioned her hands on the gleaming desk. "You two have received very watered-down roots. Your mother can't even use true Manglish with you because you wouldn't be able to understand it. She told me she picks and chooses her words, constructing everything in a more 'American' way in order for you to understand."

Alice's cheeks turned pink. I also felt my face flaming up, but while my sister probably suffered from shame, my fiery heat came from anger.

"That will be all. Thank you for coming," Dr. Wu said, shooing us in the direction of the open door.

In the hallway, as we waited for the elevator to come, I whispered, "What a horrible woman. Imagine if you did actually date her son, you'd have to practically grovel and ingratiate yourself with her."

"What if she's right about us, Mimi?" Alice said, twisting her hands. "We're too, like, whitewashed."

"Excuse me?" I placed my hands against my hips.

The elevator arrived, and we stepped inside.

"Did you hear what she called us at the very end?" Alice asked.

My hand stilled before the elevator panel. "She said something else negative after pushing us out the door?" Maybe my ears had blocked off everything after her thorough tongue lashing.

"Dr. Wu called us 'jook sing' right as we walked off."

I'd heard that term before. It meant "hollow bamboo." I jabbed at the down button to go to the first floor.

Jook sing. An Asian American with no substance. Other words floated into my mind: banana, Twinkie. The taunting wasn't anything new, but I looked over at my baby sister.

She'd started rubbing her eyes, as though to prevent tearing up. I placed my arm around her as we rode down the elevator. I observed the pair of us in the mirrored wall: Black hair, light brown eyes. Hapa. Half-half. Never whole, and never enough.

I wondered if other people saw me the same way as Dr. Wu. An inadequate daughter. A subpar girlfriend. Maybe even a failure of a friend—especially to Pixie, given how this murder case was shaping up.

CHAPTER

twenty-two

THERE WAS ONE job I knew I could do confidently. When I showed up at Hollywoof the next day after the run-in with the Tiger Mama, I gazed at the marquee sign outside the shop and drank in my store's motto: "Where we treat your pets like stars." Unlike my misgivings about my identity or about my relationships, I knew I gave top-quality grooming service.

I enjoyed shampooing pooches. Something about transforming a dog from dirty to clean through a simple wash made me feel proud. Too bad I didn't feel the same way about piles of dirty dishes and clothes.

I had unlocked the shop and even propped the door open to catch the eyes of wandering pedestrians when I saw Nicola arrive for work. Her appearance seemed normal, but she did move around slower than usual. "Are you feeling better today?" I asked.

"Thankfully," she said, touching her stomach. "It was one of those quick bugs."

"Sorry to hear. Still, take it easy."

"Okay," she said, pulling out a glossy gossip magazine from her bag and sitting behind the register. She opened up the magazine but paused to peek at me. "Did I miss anything in the past twenty-four hours?"

I chortled. "A nosy detective came by."

"Uh-oh." She frowned at me.

"Tell me about it, but I'll get him off my back soon. In fact, I'm going to poke around Catalina this weekend for clues."

"You are? When?"

"Flying out on Saturday morning." For fun, I added, "In a private plane."

She jabbed at the cover of her magazine. "You're just like one of these celebrities, Mimi. Jetting around everywhere."

I laughed her off. But it was true. Not many people got to visit Catalina on a whim. Or even regularly. That required extra dough.

Wait a minute. Then how had Davis Argo managed to rent so many homes? What had been the guy's profession anyway? I didn't think his sister had ever said.

I placed a quick phone call to Dorris, but it went straight to voice mail. After leaving her a message to return my call, I turned my attention to a customer who'd walked in.

A simple wash-and-dry client. Exactly what I needed to clear my head.

In the grooming area, I breathed in the lavender scent of the shampoo. I reflected more on my troubled thoughts about identity as I washed the dog. Maybe I wasn't such a "hollow bamboo" and was worthwhile after all.

My parents were proud of me and Hollywoof's success. Plus, I was making some headway in the case; I'd definitely shake down Lloyd on

Saturday. And I'd be showing up at the social mixer tonight at Josh's law firm to set things straight—for him and Gertrude.

I dried the pooch up. He wasn't the only happy camper when we returned to the front room.

But my mood soured over the next few hours as I waited for Dorris to return my call. When she finally did around five, I nearly leaped at my phone to grab it.

"Thanks for calling me back," I said, biting my tongue from saying anything snippy like, "It took you long enough."

"Sorry. I must have missed your call earlier while I was at work. I don't have a cell phone, only my home line."

Guess there were some people who still hadn't embraced the digital age yet. "I was just curious, Dorris. What did your brother do for work precisely?"

She coughed a little. "Come again?"

Guess that question had hit her out of the blue. Or maybe it was still really hard for her to talk about anything related to her brother because it made her grief fresh. But I figured it was better than asking Dorris outright how much money he made. "His job info would help with the investigation."

"Really?" Skepticism crept into her tone. "Tell me what steps you're taking to truly follow up on my brother's death."

"I'd be happy to," I said. I gave her a cursory summary of my previous interviews and told her about my impending trip. "I'm sure there's more to come."

She sighed. "When is the soonest you'll be able to share what you learn from Catalina Island with me?"

"How about Monday morning?" I said.

"Okay. I get a lunch break from my shift at one." She gave me her workplace details, and we hung up. I made sure to put the meeting on my calendar app, along with a reminder alarm.

Done. It'd be a useful meeting for the both of us. I bet I could also extract more details about her brother when meeting with her.

Now to attend another kind of info-gathering event . . . I checked the time and waved goodbye to Nicola. I'd need to rush home to change into something less fur-covered before Josh's work mixer.

• • •

I selected my go-to dress, a little black number I wore on all formal occasions. Since Josh worked downtown, I made sure to leave buffer time to travel there, but I still hit traffic.

After traveling on the 110 at a snail's pace and paying for an expensive spot in a downtown parking lot, I finally entered the familiar sandstone building.

The lobby remained as frigid as ever when I entered and made my way over to the elevator. I got off on the fifth floor and headed to the heavy wooden doors of the law firm. Before walking in, I took a moment to admire the bronze plaque on the wall, imprinted with the illustrious names of Murphy, Sullivan, and Goodwin.

I opened the door and walked past the empty reception desk to the open office area. The straight rows of desks looked the same as before. I took a quick peek at Josh's desk: all stacks of folders and a half-empty glass jar of fortune cookies. Guess the party wasn't in this tight space. It would've been too hard to move around the various desks with their tall hutches.

A cheer sounded from down a side hallway, and I followed the noise. I knew that the offices for the senior partners were hidden in the back, but I'd never checked out this part of the law firm before. Passing by closed doors, I finally found a room streaming with brilliant fluorescent light.

Applause sounded from inside what looked clearly like a conference room that had been repurposed into a makeshift party place. A group of about three dozen people stood watching an older gentleman with a shiny bald head speak. I crept inside and joined the onlookers.

"Five years? I can't believe it." The man wiped a mock tear away from his eye. "Couldn't have made it this far without these two fellas. Sullivan and Goodwin, come on up."

Two men detached themselves from the group. One, in contrast to the speaker, had a full head of hair and a thick beard just ripe for shaving; the other looked a lot like a dead ringer for Woody Harrelson. They went and stood next to the first man, who must have been Murphy (the other member of the trio), and beamed.

People whistled and cheered before Murphy spoke again. "A big thank-you to all our hardworking employees as well, who make this law firm spectacular. So without further ado, let's celebrate with cake."

Everyone clapped and then split into smaller groups. The partners started milling around the room. The only two lone rangers I saw there were the middle-aged receptionist, who appeared to be at the conference table slicing a large chocolate cake, and Josh's irritating coworker, who'd labeled me a distraction when we first met by saying to Josh, "Bras before bruhs." It was no wonder *he'd* been left all by his lonesome.

I spotted Josh now speaking with one of the partners, the bearded one. Josh tossed the man's name around, and I realized the partner was the fortuitously named Goodwin. As I drew closer, I realized they were having an animated conversation about estate law.

Josh must have seen me in his peripheral vision or sensed my presence somehow because he pivoted toward me all of a sudden. He introduced me to his boss as "my girlfriend, Mimi Lee." I perked up at the official title and offered up a dazzling smile to the both of them. Mr. Goodwin barely acknowledged my presence.

A cloud of vanilla floated my way. Gertrude appeared a moment later, turning our trio into a quartet.

"Gertrude dear," Mr. Goodwin said, noticing *her* presence. "I've heard a lot of good things about your work."

"Thank you, sir." I noticed that Gertrude had dressed up in a sophisticated dove gray suit, and I felt embarrassed by my obvious cocktail number.

She didn't say hello to me but continued to focus on the senior partner. "It's my pleasure to work here. And everyone has been so welcoming." She placed a gentle hand on Mr. Goodwin's arm. "Thank you for hiring me on."

Mr. Goodwin's voice beamed with pride. "Sounds like you're an excellent addition to the team."

Josh piped up. "She's been stellar, even doing double duty when I missed that filing deadline."

Gertrude lowered her gaze. I marveled at her impressive fringed eyelashes (almost like a doll's) and wondered if they were fake.

"I can't believe I submitted the materials on the wrong date," Josh said. He mussed his hair with his hand. "My fault that I put the wrong deadline on the Post-it note."

I longed to smooth down his hair but resisted the urge to do so in this business setting.

Josh tilted his head at me. "My girlfriend keeps on telling me to use some sort of electronic calendar or reminder system. No matter how many times she tells me, though, I always forget."

I bit my lip. Did I sound like a nag to his colleagues? The old ball and chain, even though I'd only wanted to help Josh out. He needed to be more efficient, instead of losing his sticky notes everywhere. They fluttered away in his apartment or stuck onto random places in his car. I'd advised him to at least take a photo of all his Post-its once he'd written them to keep track of everything. He rarely listened, and I'd had to sneakily use his phone to take snapshots just last month.

I tuned back into the conversation and heard Gertrude waving away more compliments. "It was nothing," she said.

"You really saved me." Josh flashed his brilliant dimpled grin at her.

I did a sharp intake of my breath, when Gertrude responded to his gesture with her own sweet smile. That, coupled with the lustrous blond hair haloed around her head, made her look like an angel.

The two men moved closer together and continued their previous legal discussion. Gertrude tried to interject and impose her opinions at a few points. They nodded at her, but Mr. Goodwin usually steamrolled over her thoughts by saying a disinterested "that's nice" and leaning in toward Josh to ask, "What do you think about that?"

My own eyes were starting to glaze over with the endless confusing terminology. Gertrude must have picked up on my boredom because she tugged on my elbow and moved us a few feet away.

"So, how long have you and Josh been dating?" she asked.

"Not quite a year."

Her gaze slid to the naked ring finger on my left hand.

I hid my hands behind my back. "What about you, Gertrude?"

"My friends call me Trudie," she murmured. Her head inclined toward Josh.

"Yeah," I said. "When I first heard your name, I pictured you differently. Gertrude does sound a bit old school."

She stiffened. "It's a family tradition to pass the name down. It went from my great-grandma to my nana to my mom and now to me."

Whoops. "Sorry, I didn't mean to say anything offensive about your family." I shifted my weight from foot to foot. Respect for customs and elders meant a lot to me.

"It's fine," she said. "As for your original question, I'm still single and looking for the right man."

"It might take some time," I said. Goodness knows how Ma tried to hurry things on my end, but sometimes opportunities couldn't be forced.

"You're lucky," Gertrude said. "Josh is a real catch."

"Uh . . ." I hated categorizing men like that, as though they were supposed to be some sort of prey.

"He's a rising star in the firm," she said, staring at Josh's back with a weird intensity, as though calculating his future net worth.

I gave her an awkward smile that she probably didn't even see. "Well, it's been nice chatting with you." I didn't want to go any further along with her line of thinking. "I'm kind of hungry, so I think I'll grab a slice of cake."

I sidled up to the conference table, looking over the selection. Which slice should I pick?

The bald-headed Mr. Murphy and Bras before Bruhs also approached the table. The senior partner said, "You've got to mingle, son. Show you care about your colleagues if you want to move up."

I almost laughed out loud. Good luck changing the spots on that one, I thought.

Grabbing two forks, I opted for a huge slice of cake to share. I wove my way back to Josh with the dessert. When I showed him the plate, his eyes glittered.

We took turns eating the cake, and I felt comforted by this small shared food experience. The cake eating seemed to indicate that we were trying to build a bridge back to our previous connection.

When we finished with the cake, I wandered over to a nearby trash can to deposit the used plate. As I did so, I felt the hairs on the back of my neck rise. I turned to see Gertrude watching me.

Her mouth was pursed, but she smoothed out her lips when she caught me looking. Gertrude swiveled her head to look elsewhere, as though she'd been merely scanning the room, but I had the feeling she'd been staring at me, in a calculating manner, for quite a while.

CHAPTER

twenty-three

ON THE FLIGHT to Catalina, as I traveled away from Los Angeles, I decided to leave behind my personal drama. Josh and I had made a shaky reconnection at the mixer, but we hadn't gotten a chance to really talk things through at the social event. Also, I wasn't quite sure about that para-lethal, but I knew I needed my wits about me to deal with Lloyd, the shady property manager.

Back in the quaint Avalon downtown, I barged into The Job Joint. I hurried over to the back room that served as Lloyd's office and swung the door open without knocking on it.

"Mimi," he said, not bothering to get up from his chair behind the cluttered desk. "How lovely of you to take a day trip to the island."

"Cut the chitchat," I said. "I'm here about the missing headscarf."

He gave me a puzzled look.

"The one taken from Pixie's home—stolen despite being stored in a locked glass case." I glared at him.

"Ah." He sat back and twiddled his thumbs.

"Did you ever end up filing that police report after I told you about it that first time?"

He gestured to the papers sprawled all over his desk. "I've been busy, can't you tell?"

I gave a loud exhale. "How do you explain away this new fact? Only you and Pixie had keys to the cabinet, and I'm sure Pixie didn't steal from herself."

Lloyd put his hands up in a "stop" gesture. "I'm not sure I like what you're implying."

"Where is that headscarf?" I asked, getting close up to Lloyd. At least with him seated, my five-foot frame might be semi-intimidating.

"I truly don't know, Mimi," he said. "And there's no reason for me to lie to you."

"Oh, really?" I snorted. "Avoiding jail time is a great motivator for dodging the truth."

"What about that Davis fellow?" Lloyd said. "He seemed like a sketchy guy to me and to Pixie. That's why she told him to vacate on pain of death—"

"How do you know about that letter?" The one Pixie had never laid eyes on herself.

Lloyd reached behind to rub the back of his neck, and I noticed the faint yellow armpit stain on his seersucker suit. Ick. I hoped he wasn't wearing the same outfit he'd had on the last time I'd seen him.

"Gotcha," I said. "And, by the way, 'on pain of death' isn't really a common phrase. But how did you get her signature?"

He snuck a peek to the corner where the copy machine lay.

I gasped. "You copied her signature from somewhere and spliced it with your typed note. That's forgery."

He shuffled some papers on his desk. "Nah, it's not so bad. I really was trying to do my job. I needed some extra authority to make Davis vacate the rental home on time."

"Lloyd"—I slapped my hand on his desk—"you've got to tell the police it was forged."

"I don't think that would help." He pinched a dead leaf off the desultory plant I'd seen before on the tabletop. "There's no need to rock the boat."

I straightened up and put some steel into my voice. "You don't get it. Pixie is in a bad spot because of your letter. A homicide detective is breathing down her neck because of its threatening contents. He calls it a motive for murder."

Lloyd sat frozen at his desk.

I retrieved Detective Brown's business card from my purse and placed it on the desk. "Call him, and make things better. Right now."

Lloyd roused himself and took out his cell phone.

I tapped my toe against the floor as he dialed the digits.

He waited, frowned, and then proceeded to leave a message. It was short and sweet: "Lloyd Webster here. I wrote that threatening note to Mr. Argo, Detective, not Pixie St. James." While the faked letter wouldn't totally exonerate Pixie in Detective Brown's eyes, at least it was a start to proving her innocence.

I cleared my throat. "Actually, I have one other ask of you."

He dragged a palm across his face. "What more do you want?"

"I need to see the house again. Pixie told me that new tenants aren't due to arrive until later this afternoon, so I have time to visit it."

He nodded and searched through the messy piles on his desk before locating a silver key. "Here you go. Have at it."

"You misunderstood me." I pointed at him. "I want you to walk me through the place."

He blustered. "But I have tons of paperwork to do."

"If I recall properly, our meeting was scheduled to be two hours long. You have plenty of time to go there and come back."

He groaned but stood up. His chair creaked from the shifting of his weight. "Fine, but I better be back within an hour."

Even though Lloyd owned a beat-up sedan, I called for a cab to take us over to Pixie's rental house. It felt safer that way, not being alone with him controlling the car. I paid the driver extra to wait for us outside while we did a quick walk-through.

The vacation home looked the same as before. I hoped that as we walked through it, I could spot some more clues or Lloyd would incriminate himself. Before crossing the threshold, I made sure to have my cell phone on hand and Detective Brown's number at the ready to dial.

The house appeared neat and tidy on the inside as well. The lingering smell of lemon adorned the air.

I paused before the glass case and pointed at the lock. "Does it look tampered with to you?" I carefully watched Lloyd's reaction. Although he'd pinned the blame on Davis, I wasn't sure if I believed him or not.

We both examined the lock. No scratch marks or anything that showed brute force.

He tugged on the lock, and it didn't budge. "Shut tight. But a man like Davis, he could have picked it and locked the case again."

It still didn't make sense why Davis hadn't taken all the items from the display. Surely, the whole lot would have been valuable, given the celebrities paired with them. I checked the contents again, but no other items were gone, and I let out a small sigh. Still suspicious of Lloyd, as we continued exploring the rest of the house, I made sure to have him walk in front of me. That way he wouldn't be able to surprise me with any sudden actions.

In the living room, I again admired the chandelier and the bright yellow furniture. The fluffy carpeting. Striped zebra rug.

We checked out the other rooms, and the last one we entered was the bedroom I'd slept in during my lonely night. I remembered staring dazed at the faded wallpaper stamped with large leaf prints, and also at the framed artwork on the wall, like the photo of the iconic Casino when it was actually used as a ballroom.

Then I noticed something strange. Maybe I'd been too distracted to see it during my previous stay. Or perhaps my eyes had glossed over the faded area because it blended in with the rest of the wallpaper. I stepped closer to the wall and cocked my head.

Yes. Right there. A spot where a painting might have been hung. I could even see its outline. I beckoned to Lloyd. "What used to be up there?"

"Where? I don't see anything."

"Over here. Let me show you." Moving my finger in the air next to the wall, I traced the missing rectangular frame.

"I never noticed that before." Lloyd looked around the room. "Maybe it got moved? Put on a dresser or something."

Nope. I didn't spy many knickknacks, much less anything resembling a framed picture lying around.

"Pixie might've wanted to redecorate," he said. Maybe, but she'd already hired an interior designer to have everything just so.

I held up two fingers. "There's also the possibility that multiple items went missing from this house."

Lloyd shuffled away from me, tripping over his own feet. He wobbled.

"You okay there?" I asked.

He regained his footing. "Fine. Just a little low blood sugar. Happens to me sometimes."

Lloyd walked out the front of the house and took a breather in the sunshine. After he'd collected himself, we got into the waiting cab to return to the Catalina Chalets office. On the ride back, he stared out the side window at the road, while I examined his profile.

I knew he was hiding something, maybe a lot of things. How could there have been two items gone from the same house, and what was the tie between them?

CHAPTER

twenty-four

AFTER MY QUICK day trip to Catalina, I returned to my apartment complex with questions still buzzing in my head about the missing items from Pixie's rental home. It couldn't be coincidence that two items had disappeared; I bet they'd both been stolen.

When I opened my door, I found Marshmallow staring up at me. Had he been waiting for me to come home, all this time listening for the key to turn in the lock?

"Mimi, you're bac—" His ears flattened, and he stared beyond me to the inner courtyard.

"What is it?" I turned around and noticed a bushy tail waving behind one of the potted ferns on the artificial turf.

"Uh-uh. I don't want any surprise squirrel presents on the doorstep."

I walked in and literally closed the door on his predator instincts and the large rodent temptation outside.

"Okay, sharp eyes," I said to him. "I have a question for you."

"Ask away, Mimi. But feed me first."

Ah. No wonder he'd been waiting right by the door for me.

I shuffled off to the kitchen and retrieved his dish, filling it to the brim.

He darted to the food and started devouring it.

"Here's what I want to know, Marshmallow. I'm sure you remember the Catalina house."

Turning his head, he gazed at me while eating.

"When I revisited the house today, I noticed that in one of the bedrooms—the one we slept in actually—a picture frame or some sort of artwork was gone. I mean, there was a faded outline where something rectangular had been tacked onto the wall."

"I remember that," Marshmallow said. "Couldn't help but notice. Nothing else to look at besides those old photographs while crooning you to sleep."

I thought back over his comments about the missing picture. So I hadn't been making things up. My mind snagged on his previous wording. "Did you say 'photos,' Marshmallow?"

My cat finished the food in his bowl and licked it clean. "Yeah. All those framed black and whites on the walls."

I crouched down and looked him in the eye. "What kind of pictures?"

"Boring ancient stuff. Like a huge ballroom with folks twirling around."

The Casino in its heyday, the photo I'd remembered. "What else?"

"Pictures of people." He yawned. "All wearing old-fashioned clothes."

Period pieces from bygone days. I paced around the kitchen floor. If only I knew what the missing photograph had featured.

Someone knew the missing link, and I intended to find out the connection. I sat down at my kitchen table, my fingers flying over the phone, and dialed Pixie.

When she answered, I said, "Thanks again for the flight. I'm back safe and sound. While on the island, I took a look around your rental place. I'm curious . . . do you remember the photos that were hanging in the bedroom with the queen-size poster bed?"

Pixie chortled. "Of course not. That's the decorator's job."

"Could you give me their number?" I asked.

"You want to chat with her? I know you're off tomorrow, and I bet she'd love to have afternoon tea together. I'll make some calls."

Ten minutes after she hung up with me, she sent me a reservation confirmation for two at Royal-Tea Only.

· · ·

Royal-Tea Only was a great place to have an intimate conversation. The cozy tables covered in lace tablecloths were distanced apart for privacy. Beyond that, giant potted fig plants and rice paper folding screens shielded diners from wandering eyes. Even the gurgling water fountain feature in the middle of the room made conversations impossible to overhear.

As I stood admiring the room, an Asian woman came up and extended her hand to me. "I'm Lissa," she said as we shook hands.

I loved how her caramel wavy hair played against her darker skin nicely. I wish I had the guts to make my black hair more honey in color. "Thanks for meeting with me," I said.

"No problem. Pixie and I are old friends. Besides"—she tossed her caramel hair—"I couldn't pass up an offer on tea. I'm a complete Anglophile."

She beckoned me to follow her, and we selected a small two-seater table hidden by a display of fine porcelain teapots, the accompanying saucers and cups stacked in a solid pyramid structure. I made sure to sit in the chair opposite from them, lest I knock everything over through sheer clumsiness.

The server came by as soon as we sat, assuring us that the tea service for two would be out shortly. Despite the preset menu, we did have the option of choosing our tea from a list that boasted over ten pages of selections. Lissa went with the Assam, while I chose a guava tea.

While we waited for our order to arrive, Lissa placed her hands on the fine lace tablecloth and smiled at me. "Pixie mentioned you wanted to talk about the Catalina house I decorated."

I'd start in on a general topic and then whittle down to the fine details. "Yes, I really like the Art Deco style you created."

"It was such a fun home to work on." Her brown eyes twinkled at me as she described the overstuffed furniture she found, and the touches of pizzazz, like the sunburst mirror.

Our drinks arrived in individual pots along with delicate porcelain teacups, but we waited to make sure the tea fully steeped.

"I really like the leaf print wallpaper in one of the bedrooms," I said.

"That was there from before. I kept a lot of the original features, although I did have to fill in some chips on the checkered bathroom floor."

We poured out our tea. I took mine plain, but Lissa made sure to add milk and sugar to her cup.

I drank my guava tea, loving the hint of the tropics rising up from the steam to greet me. "What about the artwork?"

"There were a lot of pictures and paintings already in that house. I kept them all." She sipped her tea and closed her eyes in pleasure.

"Even those photos in the room with the poster bed?"

She opened her eyes and tapped her lip with a finger. "Let me think…"

"One black-and-white shot featured the Casino in its heyday."

"Ahh, you must mean the historical-themed room. It had pictures of life on the island from the glory days. Even a few celebrities posed in those photos."

I paused in my tea drinking and focused on the conversation. "Like whom?"

"The Chicago Cubs, who used to train there. Humphrey Bogart. Marilyn Monroe."

Marilyn again. I gripped the edge of the soft tablecloth in my hand. "Are you sure about those names?"

Her eyes scrunched up. "I'm pretty confident those were the bigwigs, but I also keep an online portfolio of my work."

I waited until she'd found the right links on her phone. She then showed me an image of the bedroom and scrolled through the framed photos on the wall.

"Stop," I said, and she paused on the monochrome picture of Marilyn. In it, a headscarf pulled back her brown hair, so you could see her beautiful young face and dazzling smile.

"Confident and absolutely gorgeous," Lissa said.

"Agreed." How could it be a coincidence that this particular photo and the headscarf had gone missing at the same time? "Do you have pictures of the living room as well?"

She went through shots of the sunny yellow furniture and the zebra rug.

"Let me see that pic with the glass display case." Thankfully, that had been around when Lissa had taken her photos. "Can you zoom in on it?"

"Okay. Here, take a closer look." She handed me her phone.

Even though the photo on the bedroom wall had been a black-and-white shot, I realized that the headscarf in the case looked like the same one Marilyn had been wearing in the framed print. A combo steal, quite literally.

Our food came served in an elegant tiered tray: an assortment of mouth-watering finger sandwiches and scones. Lissa oohed over the clotted cream and fresh marmalade that accompanied the meal.

Everything looked so delicious. I tried nibbling at a cucumber sandwich, but with my growing sense of unease, I knew I wouldn't be able to appreciate the snacks.

twenty-five

BACK HOME AFTER the Royal-Tea Only rendezvous with Lissa, I made sure to catch Marshmallow up on the latest happenings. We sat on my lime green futon as I revealed the news about the "combo steal." Well, I sat on the couch, while Marshmallow paced back and forth, using my lap as a bridge to walk from one side to the other. I didn't even chide him for leaving white fur on the fabric because I knew he was deep in thought.

He stopped suddenly, arched his back, and stared at me. "'Combo steal,' huh? What about a combo deal?"

"Translation, please."

Marshmallow stretched out across my lap and purred. "It's a two-for-one steal of a deal: headscarf plus matching photo."

I stroked behind his ears. "That's so true. Whoever purr-loined them both can set double the price."

He groaned. "Stop it with the bad puns, Mimi."

"Sorry." I giggled. "I couldn't help myself."

"On to more serious digging." He sprung off my lap. "You should browse online to see if the items are for sale somewhere."

Good idea. I pulled out my phone, and we put our heads together to go through all the listings on the Internet.

We searched until my eyes got bleary, and even Marshmallow seemed to experience screen fatigue by taking a break and curling up on the futon beside me.

"There's nothing online," I said.

"Well, we did find the auction listing for the headscarf, when Pixie originally bid on it," he said.

"I don't think the fact that it was 'worn by Marilyn Monroe' and was 'in very good condition' is crucial to our investigation."

Marshmallow laid his head on his paws and looked up at me. "Maybe the thief is waiting for a better moment to advertise the headscarf. When the heat dies down."

It made sense. Selling when it'd just been stolen wasn't the best timing. It might be too identifiable, but as the days passed, there might be a better opportunity. I raised my eyebrows at my cat. "Then again, wouldn't it be great to get rid of the evidence now? Plus, selling two items together might not be as big of a red flag."

"Who are you pegging for the theft?" he asked.

"I think Lloyd's our man. What with that forged note, I don't trust him one bit. Plus, he had the key to the cabinet."

Marshmallow tilted his head. "How about Davis a.k.a. Dwayne? He's been on the scene of the crime at each rental."

"Possibly . . ."

"Besides," Marshmallow said, "dead men can't hawk their wares, so that would explain the lack of listings."

I coughed. "You couldn't have put that any gentler?"

"I tell it like I see it, sweetheart."

"Well, maybe I'll get some info on him when I visit his sister to-morrow," I said.

"Way to work it, Mimi." He put his paw up, and I high-fived it.

• • •

Dorris Argo worked at What's In Store, a public storage facility, as I found out on my lunch break the next day.

What's In Store was painted in the bright eye-catching colors of Halloween: a dark black coupled with pumpkin orange. Inside, I found Davis's sister seated behind the front counter, smacking some gum. The small cluttered room almost made me feel claustrophobic, and I did my best not to bump into the stacked cardboard boxes or the rolls of pack-ing tape up for sale around me.

Dorris blew out a few bubbles with her gum at me before her vacant stare fled, and recognition took hold. "Mimi," she said, yanking out the wad of gum and making it disappear—hopefully, into a trash can and not conveniently stuck underneath the counter.

I pretended not to notice how she'd reached into her mouth and extracted the gum. I'd definitely skip on the hand shaking this time around. "Hi, Dorris. So this is where you work. How long have you been here?"

"Since after high school graduation." She reached behind her and retrieved a grease-blotched bag. "Perfect timing. I can take my lunch break."

I wondered if I'd have to stand here watching her eat a corn dog as a deep-fried batter smell permeated the air.

But she dispelled that queasy notion. "Can we walk and talk?" Dorris asked. "The manager hates me eating inside the building."

Yes, it sounded like an excellent idea to go outside for a breather and get to stretch my legs. Since she was the only one on site, though, Dorris couldn't go for a quick walk around the block. Instead, we both ended up in the sunshine in the gated area of What's In Store. Customers who wanted to access their storage units could drive on through once they entered the correct digits in the code box out front.

Each garage door of every storage unit, painted in the facility's signature bright orange, looked identical to the one next to it. None of them were open, and no customers lingered in the area.

"Where is everyone?" I asked. "No clients this afternoon?"

Dorris shrugged and bit into the top of her corn dog. "It's real quiet here on most days. Once people store their stuff, they hardly check on it. Too busy with remodeling their homes or moving or whatever it is that made them lock up their things in the first place."

"Out of sight, out of mind," I said, as we started strolling the perimeter. The route would take us in a circle past all of the closed orange doors. "Seems like a low-key kind of job. What about your brother? Where did he work?"

Dorris chewed on her corn dog, reaching the halfway mark. "He's a cameraman for a YouTube show, but his boss didn't appreciate him very much. Called my brother 'flaky.' Oh, I mean, he *was* a cameraman."

I wrung my hands. "Again, I'm sorry for your loss."

She turned her head to look at me. Her face hardened. "So, tell me, Mimi. Did you get any new information on what may have happened to Davis?"

I scrutinized her face, but she busied herself with her food again, so it made it hard for me to track her emotions. "Did he ever mention someone named Lloyd to you?"

Dorris had been about to eat her corn dog. By accident, she bit down hard on her own lip. "Ouch!"

A drop of blood emerged, and I rummaged in my purse to hand her a clean tissue.

She took it and blotted her lip.

With all our ambling, we'd already circled around and ended up at the front again.

She let me back into the cramped business. "What about this Lloyd person?"

"He was the manager of the place Davis stayed at in Catalina. And he'd written a note to Davis for him to vacate the property 'on pain of death.'"

Dorris gasped.

I crossed my arms over my chest. "Interesting choice of words, right?"

She gulped hard and let her corn dog drop onto the counter, but she didn't seem to notice. In a strangled voice, Dorris said, "Thanks for the info, Mimi. Now I'd better get back to work."

I turned around and exited What's In Store. At the front door, though, I paused. Peeking through the glass, I spied Dorris sitting behind the counter with her chin propped against her hand, deep in thought.

CHAPTER

twenty-six

W HEN I RETURNED to Hollywoof after my trip to What's In Store, I was in for a treat. There, waiting for the doors of my shop to open, were two of my favorite people in the world, Henry and Shirl. I'd met them separately during my first case last year, but the two elderly neighbors had started dating, and I loved seeing them as a couple.

Henry, leaning on his cane, wore his usual polished ensemble, a shirt and suspenders combo accessorized with a newsboy cap. Shirl, on the other hand, adored more comfortable attire, as her baggy sweatshirt and elastic pants attested. They both stood there, smiling at me, with a dog near their feet.

"It's been too long," Henry said.

"Agreed." I gave them both hugs and ushered them into the shop.

The bell tinkled merrily as we walked in, and Nicola looked up. Seeing that I had things under control, she smiled at us.

"As you can see," Henry said, "we now have three in our family."

Marshmallow arched his back. "You didn't get a cat?!"

Shirl stepped over to Marshmallow and crouched down to his level. "Don't be cross with me. I couldn't find a cat half as brilliant as you, Emperor." She had used her majestic nickname for him. After Shirl explained her reasoning, Marshmallow settled down, even allowing her to pet him.

However, I wrinkled my nose at Shirl. "But I thought you preferred cats."

She jingled her medical bracelet at me, with a cat paw marking on it as a personalized design. "I do, but I find that you have to compromise as a couple. He wanted a dog. I wanted a cat. We went for a—"

"Basenji," I said, checking out the reddish dog before me. The canine breed had a distinctive tail that curled up.

Henry thumped his cane a little. "This pup is the best. We call him Boss. Because, basically, he's in charge."

"A Basenji is a good compromise," I said. "He's the most catlike canine you could have found."

Shirl tapped her ears, which she'd often labeled as sensitive. "Barkless, some people say of the breed."

"And he even grooms himself," Henry added.

I scratched my neck. "Yeah, he doesn't really need a bath unless he decides to play in the mud. I'm not sure how much help I can be for you today."

"When we got this little guy, Shirl and I remembered that you ran a pet grooming shop and decided to visit," Henry said. "Boss does need his nails trimmed, and we can catch up in the meantime."

"That would be lovely. Why don't you have a seat, and I'll be right back with the proper tools," I said.

After a short sprint to the back room, I returned and sat beside Shirl and Henry on a pleather bench. While I worked on Boss, we caught one another up on life. Shirl and Henry continued to live as next-door neighbors and saw each other every day. They, however, didn't want to give up their respective houses because as Shirl put it: "A lady must maintain an air of mystery."

I also updated them on my life, including my pride over the growing business and how I'd found a cute stray kitty last February, who a cop had now adopted. They asked after Josh, and I decided to paint my dating relationship in broad, optimistic strokes.

I'd finished with the trimming and moved to polishing the nails. I spoke up to talk over the whirring of the nail grinder. "Are you still watching those YouTube shows?"

"Of course," Shirl said. "Only I've diversified the content I watch. Not just cat tricks anymore."

Henry chuckled, placing a loving hand on top of Shirl's. "I've got her hooked on this show called *One Man's Junk*."

I had no idea what he was talking about, but I'd buffed the nails by then and showed them the finished product.

"Beautiful," Henry said.

"Lovely, and it was good to see you again," Shirl added.

I tried to give away the service for free, but they insisted on paying. In return, I threw in a free doggie pouch my friend Indira had made. "These carriers are designed with eco-friendly colors and materials," I said.

They thanked me and waved, promising to come back if they needed any other doggie supplies or possibly for infrequent baths for Boss.

I turned to Nicola at the register, who watched them with a soft smile playing across her lips. She was a sucker for love stories.

"Do you know anything about that show Henry mentioned?" I said. "What was the name of it again?"

"*One Man's* . . . something? I haven't heard of it before, but I can research it later. Maybe I can be a lead on the show." Nicola always had dreams of making it big in the TV or film industry one day.

After Henry and Shirl, I couldn't stop thinking about how cute they were as a couple. They were neighbors, like Josh and me, and obviously adored each other. They'd even picked out a dog together. Shirl had mentioned compromise. Is that what Josh and I needed to do to thoroughly reconnect?

Figuring we could at least meet up to discuss things, I texted him to see if he'd be free for dinner at his place. He responded with a quick happy face emoji, which I took as a good sign. Not feeling inspired to cook, especially given my lack of talent in the kitchen, I told him I'd pick up Chinese food and drop by after work.

The hours dragged by despite occupying myself with foaming suds and wet fur. Unwilling to wait any longer, I decided to leave early to account for the extra time I'd need to spend picking up the food.

I drove to Wok On and ordered several dishes there. They had this orange chicken dish that Josh loved. Thankfully I didn't run into the delivery guy who'd been an awkward blind date setup from Ma in the past. I even got the food faster than expected. As an extra peace offering, I made sure to snag a dozen fortune cookies for Josh, who loved to snack on them, especially when under stress.

Due to the quick restaurant service, Marshmallow and I arrived early to the courtyard of Seaview Apartments. I juggled the plastic takeout bags in my arms with difficulty. Flustered, I said, "If you only had arms to help me, Marshmallow."

"You forget who's the real boss in our household," he replied, his tail up, as he padded along beside me.

"Whatever. At least it's a short walk." I glanced at Josh's apartment door but stopped mid-stride.

Somebody was at his door. A blond someone. Though she wore a conservative pant suit, I could see the lacquered red soles of her stilettos. Was this visit for business, or pleasure?

She adjusted her hair so that it lay over her shoulders in glossy waves before knocking on his door.

Josh opened it. I could see his wide smile before she blocked it from view with her shiny head of hair.

"Is that the para-lethal?" Marshmallow said. "Let me take care of this." He moved forward in a stealth attack.

I followed him at a slower pace, almost in disbelief at the scene before me. As I crept forward, I could hear their voices better. For the life of me, though, I couldn't make out any of their words with all the blood rushing to my head.

Marshmallow stopped right next to Gertrude's long legs, unsheathed his claws, and scratched at one of her shiny precious shoes. Whether they were real Louboutins or knockoffs, I knew she wouldn't be wearing them again anytime soon.

"Ugh, you filthy beast." Gertrude made to kick at my cat, but I called out her name, and she startled.

She spun around, an impressive feat, given her high heels. "Mimi? What are you doing here? Aren't you still working?"

Marshmallow slitted his eyes. "That minx knows your schedule."

Probably to make sure I was out of the way so she could visit Josh while I wasn't around. I arched an eyebrow at her. "I could ask you the same thing. Why are you at Seaview?"

She tittered. "I'm here to help Josh with his workload."

I glanced at Josh, and he frowned.

His forehead creased. "But I didn't ask you to come, Trudie."

Uh-oh. He was already on a nickname basis with her, but I knew she didn't want to be just *friends* with him. I kept my eyes leveled at my boyfriend as I said, "I guess you didn't realize, Gertrude, but Josh and I live here together." In the complex. So, really, it was only a tiny white lie.

Josh's eyes widened a little, and Gertrude teetered on her heels. "No. I didn't realize that," she said.

"We were just about to have dinner together." I lifted up the takeout bags.

"Um, sorry to disturb," she mumbled as she swept past us.

Good riddance. I watched her go with satisfaction.

"Way to let your inner lioness out," Marshmallow said.

I smiled at him.

Then I turned to face Josh. "What was that all about?"

He put his hands up. "Honestly, I'm not sure."

"How does she know where you live?" I tried to keep my tone light and innocently curious. "Has she been here before?"

"Nope. We've always met at a café or something, and I know I didn't give her my contact info." He scratched his head. "Hmm. But we do have a staff directory for our law firm. I have it somewhere in the apartment. Why don't you come on in?"

Marshmallow and I entered his tidy place, all white walls and stacked dishes. While he rummaged in his bedroom for the directory, I placed the food down on his unique dining table.

"Found it," his muffled voice said before he sprang out with a copy of the paper directory in his hands.

I took the spiral notebook from him and flipped through the pages. One header read, "Associates," and my eyes flicked over the list of names: Akana, Brewer, Garcia, Murphy, Sorenson. He did have his address listed there, right along with his email and cell phone.

"Yeah, I guess she could've gotten your details from this," I said.

His tense shoulders relaxed.

I continued, "Gertrude seems to have poor work boundaries."

"I think she's just overly eager and wants to move up in the ranks."

By any means necessary, I thought, but I kept quiet. I didn't want to make things worse for us. Besides, he had agreed to send her packing in the end.

Josh went over to his kitchen to grab us some clean plates. "Let's have a proper meal together instead of using the takeout containers to eat from."

"Fine by me. Your dishes to wash," I said.

He gave a chuckle, and my heart hitched. I'd missed the sound of his laughter.

Dinner went well, as we shared the orange chicken, sautéed garlic string beans, and mounds of white rice. We stayed on safe topics to talk about, so no mention of Gertrude. I decided to tell Josh about seeing Henry and Shirl at the shop. He'd also met them before and liked the couple.

Later, when we'd moved on to the fortune cookies part of the meal, I thought we were out of harm's way. I counted out the dozen wrapped goodies for him.

"Thanks for thinking of me," Josh said. "I'll save some to replenish the collection in my jar."

Time for the tough part of the evening. "We need to really talk about things," I said, pushing aside a saucy takeout container. "You know, discuss what went on back at the island."

"Oh. Catalina." He pushed the bangs away from his eyes.

I took a paper napkin and started folding it into little squares. "You sure had a lot of work to do during that trip."

"There was a missed deadline. It was essential for me to fix my mistake." He grabbed a fortune cookie from the pile and pulled open the wrapper. "Anyway, you had Marshmallow for company."

"But he's a cat."

Marshmallow rose up from his haunches. "Excuse me? Is that an insult?"

"Just shut up," I mumbled.

Josh's head jerked back, as though I'd slapped him in the face.

"I didn't mean you," I said quickly.

His voice turned cold. "Really?"

I'd never told him to shut up before. And I didn't think explaining about my talking cat was going to resolve matters at this point.

He crushed the fortune cookie in his hand. It broke into multiple shards, and he didn't even bother to read the slip of paper. "You know, going on that short trip was a lot of pressure for me. I had to clear my schedule, move a lot of things around."

My voice pitched higher. "I thought you wanted to go. Why'd you agree if it was such a *hassle* for you?"

"You asked me to."

"I get it." I unfolded the napkin and started ripping it up. "You felt guilty. Went only because you thought you had to for boyfriend duty."

His breathing grew more rapid. "Whoa. That's not what I said, Mimi."

I clenched my jaw. "You didn't have to. I'm, like, a certified mind reader."

Snapping my fingers at Marshmallow as a signal for him to follow me, I stormed out of Josh's apartment. I strode clear across the court- yard and holed up in my apartment, locking the door up tight.

Inside my home, I paced around. No wonder my parents had never argued. Look at what all this heart-to-heart talking did. It exposed all the fault lines in our relationship, like an earthquake ready to rock the ground and collapse everything we'd ever built together.

Josh tried calling me a few times and even knocking on the door, but I didn't answer. What would I even say to him?

I wanted to calm down somehow, eventually read a book or watch a show to redeem the evening, but I couldn't stop fuming.

"Do not stomp on me," Marshmallow warned. He jumped up onto the dining table as a safe perch. I didn't care enough to reprimand him for lying across its surface.

My phone trilled during my third loop around the apartment. Maybe I could block his number temporarily.

When I checked the display, though, I didn't recognize the caller ID. Could it be spam? But the last time Pixie had assumed that, it'd been an important call from Dorris.

I picked up.

"Oh, thank the heavens," a woman said. "Pixie gave me your number, but I wasn't sure you'd answer my call."

"Er, who is this?"

"Sorry, this is Barbra. One of the Catalina Chalet owners. Do you remember?"

"Of course." I wondered if she'd forgotten to give me a key piece of information during our interview at the park. "Did you remember something?"

"I wanted to tell you about a new development. I got my painting back." Her voice almost squealed with excitement.

"The horse portrait?"

"Yes, Buttercup's likeness, as painted by Astral. I placed a Google alert about it, and the portrait turned up on the Amazing Online Bargain website." She clucked her tongue in dismay. I wondered if she thought it'd surface on something more like the Sotheby's auction site.

"Did you track down the seller?" I asked.

"No, but once I reported it as stolen, it was returned to me."

I wondered what details I was missing about the situation while Marshmallow gestured outside with his paw. "It'll be good for us both to get some fresh air instead of you pacing up a storm in here. Maybe we could interrogate Barbra at her place?"

A change of scene and distraction could help settle me down. "Do you mind if I dropped by your home tonight to see your painting?" Plus, maybe I could find some clues the thief left behind by seeing the portrait up close.

"But of course! Why didn't I think of that earlier? I'd love to show you the painting."

Marshmallow looked at me with pleading eyes.

"Um, can I bring my cat along? He's got a bit of separation anxiety." Not very catlike behavior, but it was the only excuse I could come up with on such short notice.

As though affronted by my comment, Marshmallow bristled his fur.

"The poor dear. Yes, please bring him along." Barbra rattled off her address to me. "Make sure you leave now, though. There are no street-lights in the area, so when it gets really dark, it makes for unsafe driving conditions."

"Will do," I said, grateful for summertime, when the sun set much later during the day.

• • •

Barbra wasn't kidding when she said the streets would be hard to drive without adequate lighting. I curved my way around a road so close to the water's edge that I both marveled at the blue expanse while worrying that I'd tip over into the coast. She herself didn't live right on the peninsula edge, but farther up a twisting road. I had to park on an incline and turn my wheels against the curb to brace my car against sliding.

At her front door, when I turned around and peered back, I could see the Pacific Ocean winking at me in the distance. I rang the doorbell, which chimed out a happy melody. Barbra soon greeted Marshmallow and me but continued blocking the doorway. Instead of inviting us inside the house, she said, "Let's walk over to my office."

We followed Barbra around the side of the house. She paused for a moment on the hill. Her teal tunic billowed around her legs in the soft breeze as she gestured. "Do you see my stable down there?"

I could spy the outline of a brown building below us and nodded.

"Come this way," she said, kicking up a few pebbles on the dirt road as she traveled to a small office structure. She pulled open the sliding door and ushered us inside.

Larger than a shed but smaller than the main house, I admired the purpling sunset sky through its large glass windows. The soft colors illuminated the all-white furniture: bookcase, table, and armchairs.

Barbra noticed me checking out the space and said, "You know, white furniture always makes a space look bigger."

Marshmallow fluffed out his fur. "What a coincidence. That's what the color does to my body."

"So this is your office?" I asked. "Do you telecommute?"

She smiled at me. "I get to work here from time to time when I'm not showing homes. I'm a real estate agent."

No wonder she could afford living in luxurious PV. I admired the gilded framed artwork on the walls. She seemed to enjoy landscape paintings. Except for one side of the office, which featured a hook with a bridle hanging from it. Next to the riding equipment, I noticed a realistic painting of a bay horse with one hoof lifted in the air. A garland was strung around the animal's neck.

Barbra confirmed my educated guess. "That's Buttercup," she said. "All I have left of her presence now."

"Nope." Marshmallow sniffed the air. "I can still smell horse in here. Blech."

"I'm glad you got that portrait back. Pets are so precious." I made sure to spend a lot of time admiring the painting and the horse it depicted. Unfortunately, since she'd already hung up the artwork again, I bet she'd erased any fingerprint evidence.

Barbra gazed out the glass door toward the stable. "I never wanted any other type of animal in my life. As I say to all my friends, 'Equine is divine.'"

"I have a few questions for you," I said.

"I'll try to answer them the best I can."

I sat in one of the white armchairs while Barbra sat at her desk and faced me. Meanwhile, Marshmallow prowled the space, slinking across the floor.

"What was the name of the seller who had the painting?" I asked.

She moved around a few stray paper clips on her desk. "I don't recall. The information got taken down pretty quickly."

I clasped my hands together. "But we could locate the seller. Maybe contact Amazing Online Bargain."

Barbra pointed to Buttercup's portrait. "Why bother? It's here safe and sound now."

My heart sank. I wanted her to pin down the seller, but I wasn't sure I could change her mind. "What if another theft happens?"

"No chance of that. I'm keeping this painting here, locked up tight under my security system. Not stashed away in a closet."

"How did someone even stumble on your painting if it was hidden?" I asked.

"I don't know." She started making a chain from the paper clips. "I even made sure to put it in the very back and asked Lloyd to place some cardboard boxes to block it from view."

Marshmallow made a screeching sound, and I looked back at him. He'd frozen right under the bridle.

"Are you all right?" I asked.

His whiskers quivered. "It's the same smell from Professor Villanueva's house. A whiff of horse."

The professor had talked about being an animal lover. I turned to Barbra. "Weird. My cat acted this way at Professor Villanueva's house. Do you know if the professor had any contact with horses?"

"He almost seemed uncomfortable at the mention of horses," Barbra said. "Nervously fiddled with his locket when I offered to have everyone meet at my place for our group's initial business meeting. Told them I had plenty of land, including acreage for stables. But, instead, we went with Lloyd's suggestion."

"Lloyd? What's he got to do with anything?"

She finished with the paper clips and laid the metal chain across her desk. "Why, he's the one who suggested meeting up at that run-down park. Guess his buddy has connections there."

Lloyd again. And that same suspicious park.

twenty-seven

N THE MORNING, I still felt like I'd received a breakthrough during my chat with Barbra. I sat up in my bed, stretched, and reflected over the information I'd uncovered. All the signs seemed to be pointing at Lloyd.

Barbra had told me he had connections to the park, and I'd bet money that it was the same downtrodden space where Davis had been found. The man, after all, had even issued a letter to Davis, threatening him to leave Pixie's property "on pain of death." How much clearer could it get than that?

Plus, he'd been the one to "hide" the painting of Buttercup. When he realized it'd been painted by Astral, maybe he figured Barbra would be too deep in mourning to notice it missing. Stolen from right under her nose. And what about the Marilyn Monroe headscarf? Even with my constant urging, he hadn't wanted to report the theft to the Avalon police. Perhaps because he'd been guilty. Maybe this property manager had his hands all over not only the houses but the contents inside them as well.

I tucked my cozy comforter around me and thought some more. How exactly were Lloyd and Davis connected? Maybe Lloyd had wanted Davis to leave the rental house, so he could swipe the Marilyn Monroe headscarf and the framed photo off the bedroom wall. Had Davis found out somehow? Then Lloyd would have needed to get rid of the guy before Davis snitched to the police. It sounded like some sort of mobster movie, but the pieces fit.

Marshmallow crept through my open door and broke my reverie by his continuous meowing. I bet he wanted some breakfast. However, I thought food for him and me ought to wait a little longer. I had something else to feast on, after all: victory.

I grabbed my cell phone from the nightstand and punched in the detective's digits.

Without an ounce of enthusiasm, he said, "Miss Lee, to what do I owe this call?"

"Listen to what I found out recently. That shady property manager is at the core of everything." I proceeded to regale the detective with my theory about stolen items and Lloyd getting caught in the act by Davis, which had led to premeditated murder.

"I don't think so," Detective Brown said, his voice gruff. "Remember, there's that letter written by Pixie threatening Davis."

I blinked in quick succession and said, "I thought Lloyd contacted you and clarified. He left a message on your voice mail."

Sensing my rising tension, Marshmallow lay down on my lap. I stroked his back.

"I never got any message," Detective Brown said.

How could that be? I'd heard Lloyd laying it out to the detective with my own ears. Or maybe I'd been duped somehow. I thought back to that day. Lloyd had definitely spoken into the phone, and I remembered his confession. I recalled presenting him with Detective Brown's business card, and I'd seen him dialing for sure. *But I hadn't followed along and seen which exact number buttons he'd been pressing.* "Lloyd is devious," I said.

"Maybe he's no angel," Detective Brown said, "but there's a flaw to your argument. Why would the property manager need to wait for a tenant to leave to steal? He could've waltzed in any time to take the items. And even if he was a thief, that doesn't mean he would kill someone."

"Isn't greed a big factor in murder?" I asked.

"Lloyd Webster isn't our man for the murder," the detective said. "He's got an alibi for that night."

"What would that be?"

"A well-regarded Avalon resident, owner of The Job Joint, verified his whereabouts," he said.

I gripped the phone tighter. "You mean Lloyd's own brother? He's hardly unbiased."

"There's at least an alibi, which is better than the case for Miss St. James. Your friend has no one to vouch for her, unless you count her shih tzu."

Marshmallow must have been eavesdropping because he said, "I can't believe I'm saying this, but please don't discount a dog's word."

"Her signature on the incriminating letter was a cut-and-paste trick," I said, "so no motive there. And I bet you still can't come up with the murder weapon." I almost snickered, remembering how he'd once swiped a porcelain mug from my apartment, insisting that it was a means to murder.

"I've looked into things, and Mr. Webster doesn't have access to the weapon in question," the detective said. All of a sudden, I heard an uproar of meowing from his end of the line. I pulled the phone away from my ear.

At the same time, Marshmallow leaned in.

I could overhear Detective Brown trying to shush Nimbus.

Marshmallow purred at the phone.

Then everything quieted down.

I placed the phone back against my ear. "Everything okay over there?"

"I don't know why Nimbus started acting up right then. It's not like her."

"Cats," I said, "you can never predict what they'll do."

"Well, if that's all you called me for," Detective Brown said, "you've wasted your time."

"I don't know about that," I said as I eyed Marshmallow preening on my lap.

"Please stop investigating on your own, Miss Lee. Let me handle it," the detective said and then hung up.

I turned to Marshmallow, who still seemed to be congratulating himself. The hissing and purring between Marshmallow and Nimbus must have meant something important. "What'd you find out?" I asked.

"My protégé has been listening in on our bumbling detective's conversations with his colleagues. She said the weapon in question is . . . a Taser."

"Wow. Great work." I scratched Marshmallow on the head as a reward. "Now we've narrowed down the means."

He purred. "What would you do without me?"

"I really don't know." I yawned and checked the time. "Enough complimenting, though. We've got a shop to open up."

After our lengthy conversation with the detective, we rushed through breakfast and hurried over to Hollywoof. I'd barely unlocked the door and Marshmallow hadn't even settled into his usual sunny spot when Nicola arrived for cashier duty. A few minutes later, a customer sprinted inside with her cocker spaniel.

The usual fluffy dog appeared freshly shorn, and the woman paused before me, her hands weaving around in an animated fashion. "I saw your tagline and had to come in," she said.

Where we treat your pets like stars did have a nice ring to it. "How can I help you?" I said. "It seems like your dog's already been to a groomer."

"That's the problem." She wrung her hands. "I need your professional opinion because I think they might have made a mistake while shaving him."

"I know it's neither here nor there," I said, "but you really don't have to shave off his coat."

She glanced out the window at the bright sun. "Well, it's summertime, and I thought it might help with the heat."

"It's your choice, of course, but once shaved, the coat will never quite return to its usual condition."

"I don't mind that." Her voice took on a keening quality. "But he's got these red spots on him."

"Let me see." I knelt down and examined the dog's body. "Oh, it looks like the poor guy has razor burn."

"Huh? I made sure the guy used clippers. It's not like an actual razor."

"It's a common issue," I said, holding out my hand to the dog and letting him lick it. "Sometimes the tool can get overheated. That's why it's important to let the clippers cool down every so often while working."

"Is it too late to do anything about it?" The woman looked like she was about to yank her hair out.

"Ma'am," I said, "why don't you have a seat? I think I might have something in the back room that could help."

I nodded at Nicola, who took my cue and led the woman to our cream benches.

As I walked away, I also heard her say, "I'll put on a fun movie to watch while you wait. How about *Benji*?"

In the grooming area, I rummaged through my supplies and found a sample size bottle of pure aloe vera gel. I returned with the clear green ointment and offered it to the woman. "This might reduce his irritation. You could also try vitamin E oil."

The woman gushed her thanks. "I'll make sure to come here next time for grooming and tell all my friends about your store, too." The woman darted to the register and grabbed a handful of business cards. Then she toted her dog away.

Nicola nodded at the door the woman and dog had just exited. "Is razor burn very painful?"

"The pup might lick and scratch at the area, but he'll survive," I said.

Once those words left my mouth, I had to sit down on the nearby bench as I made a mental connection to the murder case and Davis Argo. He'd also had burn marks on his body, according to the photos that Nimbus had seen. Burns that had lasted all the way up to the time the police discovered him. I shuddered. How bad must he have been shocked by a Taser, the now-known murder weapon, to have sustained those injuries?

"Are you all right, Mimi?" Nicola stepped toward me, but I put my hand up.

"I'm fine," I said. "Just thinking through stuff."

How could the detective have thought Pixie had done such a cold-hearted thing? And why would he think she even had a weapon like that at her disposal?

I'd better update my friend on her suspect status with the cops. I texted Pixie to come in as soon as she could to "talk about the investigation." She said she'd wrap up some business things and then pop over.

It took Pixie an hour before she could slip in through the door. By that time, I'd already had a chance to cellophane wrap a dozen dog biscuits with a big bow for her.

"Thanks for driving all this way." I extended the bag of treats to her. "Here's a little something for Gelato."

"You're so sweet." She took hold of the gift.

After I plopped myself down on the bench, Pixie followed suit and sat next to me with the wrapped treats balanced on her lap.

I glanced at Nicola. "Could we have some privacy for about fifteen minutes?"

"Sure." Nicola meandered away, taking a glossy magazine with her to peruse.

Once she was out of earshot, I started in. "First," I said, "I should probably tell you about your property manager. He forged your signature on that letter the cops are saying is evidence against you."

Pixie wrinkled her brow. "But how?"

I fidgeted with my hands. "He copied your signature by using the machine in his office. He basically admitted as much to me."

A glint appeared in Pixie's eye. "The nerve of that man. The only time Lloyd's had access to my signature was the contract I'd written up for him to serve as property manager. Why did I ever agree to let him do it in the first place?"

I patted my friend's hand. "Because you're a generous woman, and you take chances on people. I know my shop wouldn't be around if you hadn't invested in it."

"Yes, but this was a great investment. Hollywoof is wonderful." She looked me in the eye. "And you're an amazing friend, trying to help clear my name."

I shifted my position. "Unfortunately, you're still in the hot seat with the police. I tried to tell them to chase after Lloyd as a suspect instead, but Detective Brown won't bite. He says the man has an alibi."

Pixie fiddled with the bow on the treats. "I see, and all I have is my precious shih tzu to back up my innocence."

I tapped my bottom lip with my finger. "There's still a way to beat back his suspicion. The crime was done with a Taser, so if you don't have one in your—"

She raised her eyebrows. "But I do, Mimi."

I stammered. "What?"

"Not exactly a police-issued Taser," she said, "but a stun gun nevertheless."

"Oh." This put a wrench in my defense of her.

She crinkled the cellophane wrapping. "I'm a single female, and it makes me more secure to carry it at night or in unsafe places."

My mind flashed to a certain green space. "Like at that park where you and the other Catalina Chalet owners met up?"

She flushed pink. "I don't think we should judge by outward appearances."

"Barbra told me that you guys went there based on Lloyd's recommendation," I said.

Her eyes widened. "I'd forgotten about that, even though the profile pic should have reminded me."

"What profile pic?"

"For the guy who handles the park reservations. The photo he tied to his phone number." Pixie tapped at her cell and flashed the contact up at me. I squinted at the pic, which had three people framed in the profile image.

It was probably a recent photo, too, because I recognized a current-day Lloyd wearing his favorite seersucker suit. He stood on the left side.

Pixie pointed to the man in the middle, a head above the other two, who had freckles and a goofy grin. "This is the parks guy."

And the other man on the right? I felt a chill creep up my spine. He had crazy wavy hair and didn't appear to be smiling. A ruffian look, Barbra had said when she'd described those exact features. The third man had to be Davis.

CHAPTER
⩵ *twenty-eight* ⩵

AFTER PIXIE LEFT Hollywoof, my mind ran around in circles. What did it mean that the three men had known one another? And what about Pixie's stun gun? I wondered if Detective Brown had already squirreled out that damning detail.

My pacing irritated Nicola so much that when lunch closure came, she practically sprinted for the door. Even Marshmallow snapped at me. "Your soldier marching is disturbing my beauty sleep," he said.

I'd just started eating the bologna sandwich I'd slapped together for lunch when I received a call from my sister. She offered me a much welcome distraction to cool off both my mental churning and my physical body by asking me to meet up for a frozen treat. It was a hot summer day (well, above eighty degrees), which kind of felt like an oven compared to the typical temperate weather in Los Angeles.

I finished the sandwich in minutes and left Marshmallow to happily nap away while I drove to the dessert place. It was located in Chinatown in a strip mall decorated with intricate pagoda-style roofing. The eatery, Let It Snow, was flanked by a dim sum restaurant and a boutique clothing store.

My sister was waiting just inside the door in the air-conditioned interior. "Mimi," she said, pulling me into a hug.

I returned her embrace. "Thanks for the invite, sis. I needed a break."

"No prob," she said, looking away from me.

I checked out the extensive menu on the wall and asked, "What are you thinking about getting?" The photos of the various snow bowls (kind of like shaved ice but a lot fluffier) made me salivate.

She shrugged. "I'm going to share with you. The serving sizes are massive here."

It was my first visit to this particular shop, so I took my time selecting the snow flavor and the accompanying toppings. I finally went with the classic condensed milk drizzled over the snow, along with medicinal-tasting dark grass jelly tempered with fresh mango chunks and sweet potato balls.

Alice selected a table for two near the entryway to sit at while we waited for the order to arrive. She tapped the toe of her shoe against the floor.

"Why are you so twitchy?" I asked.

She stopped moving her foot. "No reason. I think I'm just worrying about what other disastrous date Ma will set up for me."

"I take it she hasn't let up yet?" I pulled out napkins from the nearby dispenser and piled them before us. Eating snow meant potential melting ice messes.

"Ma *is* taking a short pause to regroup after the fail with the Malaysian forum." Alice shook her head. "By the way, she left the group." I felt a jolt of pleasure on hearing Ma standing up on our behalf and leaving that toxic online environment.

Alice picked up a napkin and started wadding it up into a ball.

I removed it from her fidgeting hands. "Why are you wound so tight? You're on break. It's not like you're teaching summer school."

"It's a good thing I'm not. Donna said her kids are horrendous. She's been confiscating items left and right: water pistols, Swiss Army Knives, and more." She pointed at the wadded-up ball. "Even a DIY slingshot."

The snow bowl arrived at our table, looking like the size of a small grapefruit.

"Dig in," I said, but Alice proceeded to place her plastic spoon on a napkin.

"Nah, I'll wait. I'm still digesting lunch." She patted her stomach.

Her eyes drifted to the door, and I saw Ma walk in.

She came over to us and then zeroed in on my sister. "Time to shop lah. New outfit will add oil to your social life."

Huh. I guess Ma's idea of a matchmaking break was to doll up Alice and ensure her success with potential new partners.

"I gotta go now," Alice said to me. "Ma and I will be shopping at the boutique next door."

I gazed at the mound of snow before me. "Er, how will I finish this all by myself?"

My sister winked at me. "I'm sure things will work out."

No sooner had they left than another familiar figure walked in. His dark brown eyes sought mine, and he slid into the seat opposite from me.

"Josh," I said. "What are you—of course, it was a setup all along."

"I had to get your sister involved." He slid a palm down his face. "You weren't answering my calls. Or the door."

Up close, I noticed that he had subtle bags under his eyes. I made sure to place the second spoon out of his reach and scooped up some of the delicious snow for myself.

Josh leaned in toward me. "I'm really sorry about Gertrude showing up at the complex like that. She was really overstepping the line as a paralegal."

"Para-lethal," I muttered, in between spoonfuls.

His brown eyes sparkled at me. "Is that your personal nickname for her? Are you jealous?"

"Maybe a little," I admitted. "Wouldn't you be in my position? Texting your work all night long. Cutting short our vacation."

He held his hands up. "I admit I goofed up on our Catalina trip."

I dug deeper into the snow, excavating the sucker out of it. "I don't get it. Did you just fall asleep on the couch the whole night? Or had you wanted to stay away from me and just sleep there?"

He ran a hand through his hair. "Sorry for conking out like that. I really didn't mean to. Guess I was just exhausted. Gertrude really did miss the filing deadline, so I collapsed on the couch after putting out that work fire."

Gertrude. I was glad he didn't use the more intimate Trudie nickname.

I chewed on a sweet potato ball, processing everything he'd divulged. "I get it," I said.

Josh used his hand to flop his bangs to the other side. "Thanks for understanding, Mimi."

"Sounds like we're on the same page." I now knew I needed to apologize for my own recent behavior. "I'm sorry for freezing you out, Josh, and not taking your calls."

"And I'm sorry for avoiding the topic during Catalina and afterward," he said.

"You're forgiven," I said, finally relinquishing the second spoon to him. He took a tiny scoop and smiled.

"I've missed you, Mimi." He half stood to lean over me.

I closed my eyes, expecting a kiss even sweeter than the dessert I'd been eating when his cell rang with a sharp trill.

Opening my eyes, I glared at his phone. "Who could have such horrible timing? Is it Gertrude?"

Josh silenced the ringing but let me peek at the screen.

"Murph?" I said. "Isn't that the last name of your boss? Maybe you should pick up."

"No." Josh rolled his eyes. "I mean, the partner's name *is* Murphy, but this is his son. We call him by his last name but shorten it to Murph, so as not to be super confusing within the firm."

"The guy doesn't like his first name?"

Josh chuckled. "I don't think anyone would."

"Now you've got to tell me what it is." I scooped up a spoonful of snow. "Or you'll get some ice down your collar."

He waved his hands in surrender. "No need. The guy's first name is Dumbdore. They messed up on the birth certificate. His parents had wanted to name him after Albus from the Harry Potter series, but left out a couple letters in their exhaustion."

I laughed. "Wow. What does a Dumbdore even look like?"

Josh ate another scoop of snow. "Oh, you've seen him before."

I gave him a blank stare.

"He's kinda tall." Josh indicated the height with his hands.

"Not a superb hint."

He sighed. "You know, Mr. Bras before Bruhs."

"No way," I said, but then I remembered how the law partner at the chocolate cake table had told him to mingle and called him "son." At the time, I thought he was using a term of endearment, but now I knew better. Come to think of it, I had seen "Murphy" listed as a last name before. Under the "Associates" section in Josh's spiral-bound law firm directory.

An idea surfaced in my head. "Hey," I said to Josh, "Can I swing by your apartment after work, around eight tonight?"

"Sure." He beamed at me. "Looking forward to it."

We finished the snow together, and every last bite of it tasted delicious.

• • •

When I returned to Hollywoof, I caught Nicola watching something on her phone instead of flipping through her usual glossy magazine. Even Marshmallow perched on the counter near the cash register to follow along on the screen.

"What's so interesting?" I asked as I put my purse away.

"It's that YouTube channel Henry and Shirl mentioned, *One Man's Junk*." She angled the phone, so I could see the show.

I spotted an older man with expressive eyebrows who had a distinguished Sean Connery look about him. Maybe Henry and Shirl felt a bit of camaraderie with the aging gentleman. "Is that the host?"

"Yeah," Nicola said. "It's no *Antiques Roadshow*, but he still makes sure people get some money out of their goods."

I followed along as one woman waited breathlessly for an evaluation of her crockery.

"Two hundred dollars for the matching set," the host warbled.

The woman screamed and ran around in circles.

Marshmallow flicked his tail up. "She was about to give her dishes away for free in a yard sale before she heard about the show."

The credits started rolling while a catchy jingle played: *One man's junk is another's treasure. Getting you money for stuff is my pleasure.*

Marshmallow bobbed his head along to the beat.

I watched as a familiar name popped up on the screen and then scrolled away. "Can you rewind it?" I said to Nicola.

She did.

"Stop right there."

The cameraman for the show. It was none other than Davis D. Argo.

Interesting. Davis had worked for someone who knew all about pricing items, and I bet the host of *One Man's Junk* also had buyer contacts to boot. Since Davis and Lloyd were buddies, I bet they'd formed some sort of partnership together. Lloyd could scout out the possessions in his rental homes and give Davis easy access to them. Hadn't Davis's own boss called him "flaky" on the job—maybe Davis had wanted easier money than manning a camera and turned to looting to pay his bills?

I'd have to revise my prior theory about Davis getting killed by Lloyd for attempting to stop a robbery. Instead, maybe they'd had an intense clash over that pricey piece of fabric, the Marilyn Monroe headscarf.

I spent the rest of the workday mulling over this idea, examining it from various angles. In between trying to see if there were any holes in my new theory, I did a few sets of pedicures (well, *paw*-dicures).

After work ended and we'd returned to the apartment, I relayed my ideas to Marshmallow, who grunted at them. He didn't seem to agree or disagree with my theory. But then again, maybe he was just hungry.

I made sure to feed him well and microwaved a plate of leftover Chinese takeout for myself. My quick meal of orange chicken and sautéed string beans reminded me that I had a date that evening.

"Be good," I said to Marshmallow as I grabbed my keys and ran out the door.

I was half an hour late to visit Josh, but he gave me some slack. "Traffic plus dinner, right?" he said.

"Yeah, pretty much."

"What do you want to do tonight?" he asked.

"Maybe find something on Netflix?"

"Sounds perfect." He grinned at me, and I was happy to see his dimple flashing.

"I need to take care of something first, though," I said. "Can you go get your company directory?"

He gave me a confused look but proceeded to retrieve it.

After I flipped through the spiral-bound book and found the page on the associate lawyers, I fumbled in my pockets. Oops. I'd forgotten my cell at home in my rush to come over. "Can I borrow your phone?" I said.

He handed me his iPhone, and I took a shot of the page. "Is Gertrude in here, too?" I asked.

"Yes . . . why? You're not going to do anything rash, right?"

"Of course not," I said. "I remembered our girls' conversation from the mixer and just figured out a way to help her."

"Okay, Mimi. I'm trusting you on this." He showed me where Gertrude was listed.

I logged into my email account to send her a note. The subject line read, "One gal helping out another." I attached the photo as well as a short message: "Hey, did you know that this Murphy on the Associates page is the son of one of the partners?"

I sent the message, hoping the new info would be tasty bait for her man-fishing ways. Hopefully, it'd be enough for her to leave my guy alone.

After signing out of my account, I went back to Josh's photo gallery. He didn't need a shot of a directory he owned taking up space on his phone. I deleted the image. "Do you want me to take out your other old photos while I'm here?"

"Nah, you can just leave them."

I scrolled through all the images. "One day you'll run out of space when you really need it."

"But I bet that's not today."

I paused to admire some previous photos of his Post-its I'd taken on the sly. "See, my idea of there being a digital collection of your sticky notes works great."

"Yeah," he said, "I tried following your lead, but then I got too lazy."

"Really?" A well of happiness bubbled inside me. He'd taken my suggestion to heart, and he didn't see it as nagging. I checked out the images he'd taken. "You weren't twiddling your thumbs that much. This note is marked with a deadline of July first."

"What?" His eyes widened, and he took the phone from me. "Huh, so I really did tell Gertrude the right deadline, to file it by July first. Not July seventh, like she'd insisted."

More trouble for the para-lethal? Bring it on.

"How about that movie?" I was definitely in a mood to enjoy my time with Josh now.

We ended up watching a sappy rom-com on Netflix, and it didn't matter about the muddled storyline or that the actors launched into frequent histrionics. It felt right to lean my head against his shoulder while watching and to have his clean pine scent wash over me.

Josh placed a soft kiss on my lips when the film ended. "Thank goodness we've forgiven each other. And can you tell Alice thank you for arranging the convenient meet-up at that dessert place?"

"I will." I thought back on Alice's behavior and wondered why my little sister's nervousness hadn't clued me in on her ploy in the first place. After all, I'd seen her wadding up the paper napkin while babbling on about her fellow teacher confiscating water pistols and slingshots in summer school.

I left Josh's apartment, turning over a thought in my head. Might misbehaving student behavior apply at the college level? Could Professor Villanueva also have confiscated some unsavory weapons from his students, including something along the lines of a stun gun? I intended to find out.

CHAPTER
twenty-nine

STROLLING THROUGH THE UCLA campus in the early morning hours, I yawned. Beside me, though, all the students seemed to be striding purposefully to various buildings. The smell of percolating coffee floated in the air, and I noticed everyone passing by held a foam cup or a travel mug in their hands. The nearby coffeehouse on campus must have been raking in the dough.

I walked by the Murphy Sculpture Garden. While the posed figures seemed artistic enough, I didn't quite understand the one that looked like metal Tetris blocks stacked on top of one another. Shaking my head, I focused my attention on the building I was looking for: the Luskin School of Public Affairs. It was a modern-looking building, a bold rectangular design with square columns and plenty of glass to let the sunshine in.

Bursting through the clear doors, I searched for the Department of Public Policy. Nobody bothered me as I hunted down Professor Villanueva's office. Everyone probably thought I was just a student who attended the school.

The door to Professor Villanueva's office was open, and I peeked in to see him seated behind a hefty desk, hunched in a black leather chair and peering at some papers on the polished wooden surface. An intimidating bookshelf with heavy tomes on the top half and closed cabinet doors on the bottom made for a fine backdrop, indicating refined intellectual interest perfect for a professor.

I took tiny steps into the office. "Knock, knock."

His head jolted up. "Mimi? What a surprise to see you here. Is there an alumni event happening today?" He turned his head to peer at an affixed bulletin board on the wall. I saw it advertising different upcoming student events, along with a document highlighting the tough zero-tolerance policy on campus.

I slipped into the bright turquoise chair opposite him. Unfortunately, it wasn't as nice as his black leather one, but at least it had padding. "Oh no, I'm here to pick your brain, Professor."

"Really, now?" He folded his hands on top of his papers.

"Yes. I've been making some headway with the stolen objects. In fact"—I gave him a broad smile—"Barbra's gotten her painting back."

"Oh, well, that's wonderful," he said, and I didn't bother to correct his likely assumption that I'd played a key role in returning the valued pet portrait to her.

"I'd love to work on retrieving your jewelry. Could you remind me what kind of item you're missing again?" I asked.

His chair creaked as he shifted away from me.

I glanced around his desk, looking for framed photos as corroborating evidence. Nothing. "Could it have been a locket?" I remembered Barbra talking about it, but he'd never worn one since we'd met.

His eyes darted left and right. "Locket? Why would you say that?"

"Barbra told me about it." He'd also touched his neck during some insistent questioning from me during my interview at his home.

"Yes . . ." He hung his head. "It *was* that locket that went missing."

"Can you tell me some more? Describe the necklace and what's inside. You can rest assured that everything you say to me will be kept in the strictest confidence."

He darted me a skeptical look.

"Okay, how about this?" I said. "Let's make a trade. You tell me about the locket in return for a small favor from me."

"What kind of favor would that be?"

"I have teacher friends, Professor." I pointed to the zero-tolerance poster tacked onto his bulletin board. "The no-weapons rule applies to everyone on campus, including faculty."

His eyes shifted to the closed cabinet behind him. Gotcha, I thought. Professor Villanueva would make a horrible poker player.

"I'm guessing you've kept some of your students' loot," I said.

"How will I know you won't report me?"

"Give me one of the items you've confiscated, and I'll keep quiet."

He drummed his fingers on his desk, considering. "Guess that's not a bad deal. I accept. But first, we need to make sure nobody is listening."

"Of course." I sprang over to the hallway, peeked out to see no one around, and shut the door for good measure.

Once I'd settled back into the padded chair, he started talking. "I'll tell you a secret. The locket has . . . hair in it."

I goggled at him. He'd asked for us to speak in secrecy about something as mundane as a strand of hair? "From a past love?"

"No, it's not human hair. It's from *Traveler.*"

I blinked at him. "Am I supposed to know that reference?"

JENNIFER J. CHOW ·

He sighed. "The horse."

"Sorry, still nothing."

"I thought you were full of UCLA pride. Traveler is USC's mascot and the magnificent white horse that they use for their games. Their school's warrior rides around the stadium on it."

I hadn't attended many rival games, but I dropped my jaw in astonishment. He'd somehow snipped off a strand of hair from our rival college's horse. "Wow. How did you manage that?"

"Wouldn't you like to know." He beamed with pride. "It was the prank of the year. No, the decade. Maybe the greatest trick of all time."

No wonder Marshmallow had detected an equine odor around the man and inside his house. "So why'd you take the necklace off?" I asked the professor.

He tapped the stack of papers on his desk. "I'm up for Distinguished Professor standing. If word got out that I'd been involved, let alone coordinated, such a prank, others in the department would call my unblemished record into question."

"Is that why you hid it on Catalina Island?"

"The farther away from me, the better." He pointed at the poster on the bulletin board. "That zero-tolerance policy isn't just for the kids. Pranks are no longer considered the rite of passage they used to be by the current administration. More of a crime, really."

"Times have changed," I said, "but I do still hope you get the promotion."

"Thank you, Mimi."

I rubbed my chin with my thumb and forefinger. "Can you give me more details about the locket? So I'll know what it looks like if I ever spot it."

"Sure." His eyes got a misty look in them. "It's heart-shaped and golden, with the initial 'T' on it in cursive."

"Easy enough to remember," I said. "Thanks, Professor."

"And now to seal your secrecy . . ." He wheeled his chair away from the desk and swung open the cabinet doors at the bottom of his impressive bookcase. "Have a look in there, and take whatever you'd like."

I scanned the inventory inside. Mostly stacks of vaping devices and cigarette packs. A few pocket knives, a can of pepper spray, and even some nunchucks. I peered into the back recesses. "You don't happen to have a stun gun, right?"

"No, nothing like that. Why?"

I borrowed Pixie's line of reasoning. "For self-defense. You know, being a young woman and all."

"You sure you don't want anything in there?" His hand gestured wildly. "Do we still have a deal on your silence?"

"Of course. I can sign some sort of nondisclosure agreement if you want, but"—here I placed a hand over my heart—"I'll offer you one better: a true Bruin's promise."

He stared at me for a moment and then nodded, seeming content with my vow.

All through the drive back to my apartment to pick up Marshmallow and traveling to Hollywoof, I mulled over Professor Villanueva as a potential suspect. He didn't have the (smoking) stun gun in his cabinet of wonders, which didn't rule him out, but it did decrease his chances. He'd be less likely to have a murder weapon somewhere that could be tied to him, say on his body or at his house. The confiscated student effects would have been a great place to hide a crucial piece of evidence and camouflage it. And I'd popped in for an unplanned visit, which meant he wouldn't have had time to squirrel it away.

At Hollywoof, I ushered Marshmallow into the store but realized that with my early start we were still ahead of schedule to open up. After the requisite flipping of the sign to read "OPEN" and the dusting down of the cash register, I still had time to do odds and ends. I proceeded to sweep the floor, swishing the broom along the golden stars with canine names on my Bark of Fame walkway. I'd just managed to put away the broom when my cell phone rang.

"Josh?" I said, picking up.

"Are you busy?"

I glanced at my still-locked store. "No. What's going on?"

"So, I had a meeting with the partners earlier this morning and told them I no longer wanted Gertrude as my paralegal."

I cheered internally.

After a loud exhale, Josh continued, "Of course, they wanted to know why, so I told them she'd messed up the filing date, not me."

I sat down behind the cash register. "Did they believe you?"

"They ended up calling Gertrude into the office as well," he said. "And she must have known something was up because she had a defense at the ready. She showed them the Post-it I'd given her, but with my July first date altered to read July seventh."

I clenched my free hand into a fist. "I hope you got out your phone and proved her wrong."

"Yeah, I did," Josh said. "It's a good thing I never delete any photos."

I felt the side of my mouth quirk upward. Point for Josh. I'd need to remember to needle him less about preserving phone storage space. "Anyway, go on with your story."

"The partners said they'd discuss it among themselves and told both of us to get back to work."

I clutched the phone closer to my head. Marshmallow, curious, jumped up onto the counter and crept toward me to eavesdrop.

"In the end," Josh said, "they believed my word over hers."

"Did they fire her?" I looked around my store for something to celebrate with. No champagne to pop, and the only food reward I saw were my homemade doggie biscuits.

"Actually, she wasn't let go," Josh said. "Murph swooped in and requested that she be reassigned to him."

Marshmallow hissed, and I let out a muffled boo. Gertrude must have read my email and had stuck her claws into Mr. Bras before Bruhs. And nepotism had beat justice.

"Whatever," I mumbled. "One problem down for me, one to go."

"Still trying to clear Pixie's name?" Josh guessed.

"Yes, the investigation's ongoing according to Detective Brown." I gave Josh a quick summary, stressing the new higher stakes, since Pixie had in her possession a suspected murder weapon. "I wish the death had never happened. If only his sister had reported him missing earlier, then the police would have tracked Davis down faster and he might still be alive today."

"I don't understand," Josh said. "Didn't his sister call Pixie pretty early on to ask after Davis?"

"Yes." I played with the jar of dog biscuits. "But she didn't report him missing until after the required forty-eight hours."

"What required forty-eight hours?"

"Isn't there a mandatory wait period before requesting the police to act?"

"No," he said. "That's only what you see on TV. People can report somebody as missing as soon as they want to."

"Oh."

From his end, I heard a deep voice call out, "Akana." A second later, Josh said, "Mimi, sorry, I've gotta go."

We hung up, and I put my phone away with glacial slowness while pondering. Why hadn't Dorris reported her brother as missing earlier? Had she been misinformed, swayed by TV shows on the proper protocol to follow when somebody disappeared from your life? Or had she done it on purpose?

CHAPTER
thirty

WHEN SATURDAY ROLLED around, I knew I needed to figure out what Dorris's motivation had been to report her missing brother only after forty-eight hours had passed. I called into What's In Store and was told she'd just left the premises and had headed home.

Okay, it was off to her apartment complex then since I couldn't reach her through her nonexistent cell phone. The bright side? I knew Marshmallow was welcome there, so I took him along again.

After I got to her apartment and knocked, Dorris opened her door with a startled expression on her face. "Mimi. You weren't whom I was expecting."

"Sorry I didn't call before dropping in. I just wanted to do a quick run-through of the timeline regarding your brother to help me get a better grip on the case—if that's okay?"

Her thin body seemed to waver.

"Maybe we should sit down to chat."

"Oh, right." She motioned us inside, and we took over the frumpy couch from before. Dorris and I sank into the cushions while Marshmallow perched on a couch arm. "Do you have any more insight into Davis's death?" Dorris asked.

I folded my hands on my lap and clasped them tight. "I'm working on things. I've done a number of interviews so far."

Her head tilted my way in interest.

"But first, I need to understand something on your end. You waited forty-eight hours to call the police to report that Davis was missing . . ."

"Uh-huh." She shivered. "I told the cops as soon as the forty-eight-hour mark passed, but I couldn't wait around even that long without doing something to find Davis. That's why I phoned Pixie."

"But she didn't even recognize his name."

"Yeah. I told her I was looking for Davis D. Argo." She played with a strand of her straw-like hair.

"He applied to rent her home under the name of Dwayne A.," I said.

She stopped messing with her hair. "Yes. Davis Dwayne Argo. Sometimes he went by his middle name, especially with his friends."

"Speaking of his buddies . . . that park he was found at. Did you know that one of his friends worked there?"

She turned her gaze to the ceiling. "I think you must mean Chris."

First time I'd heard his name. I should double-check on the new guy as a potential suspect. "Do you think Davis and Chris might have had a falling out?"

"No way. They've known each other since preschool, and Chris idolized my brother." She reached for Marshmallow and placed him on her lap. With a trembling hand, she patted his head. "What did you uncover from Catalina, Mimi?"

"I do have some new intel," I said. "It seems like the murder weapon involved was a Taser or some kind of stun gun."

A flicker of surprise crossed her face. "Isn't that something only the police carry?"

"No. People can and do purchase stun guns for their own protection." Much to Pixie's plight.

Marshmallow purred and reached a paw out toward Dorris's neck. "What are you doing?" I asked him.

He continued, aiming for the necklace she was wearing. I could spy a delicate gold chain but the actual pendant had disappeared underneath her multicolored tank top.

"I think he likes your necklace," I said.

She fished the pendant out. "It's pretty, right?"

Then she took the necklace off and dangled it before Marshmallow. Something registered in my brain. "Can I see what's inside the locket? Do you mind?" Professor Villanueva had described his locket as having Traveler the horse's hair stuck inside it.

Before she had a chance to answer, I clicked it. The locket swung open to reveal . . . a grainy picture of Davis and Dorris.

She closed the locket and wore the necklace once more, tucking the pendant underneath her tank top. "I place this next to my heart because it reminds me of my brother."

"That's very sweet," I said.

Her eyes had started misting up when her phone rang. She cleared her throat before picking up the call. "No, the intercom's busted. Can you wait a few minutes before entering? I have a guest over right now, but she's just about to leave."

That sounded like my cue to depart. I took Marshmallow off her lap and said goodbye.

I walked out of her building with my cat following behind me and almost passed by the figure at the entrance. Then I stopped short and did a double take. The man holding a cellophane-wrapped tray of brownies in his hand was none other than Lloyd Webster.

I gaped at him. "What are you doing here?"

"Visiting Dorris." He showed off the brownies. "To send her my condolences. I don't get to come into L.A. much, but I finally got some time off to drop by."

I narrowed my eyes at him. "How come you didn't tell me before that you knew Davis? That you two were buddies." At our first meeting, Lloyd had stumbled over Dwayne's name and almost revealed the man's true first name, Davis.

The tray wobbled in his hand. "That wouldn't have sounded so great, me needing to drum up business by asking friends to rent the properties I'm in charge of."

It seemed like a flimsy excuse, but I let it go. I had never asked him directly about the last renter at Pixie's home. And, besides, I had another way to turn the corkscrews a little more.

My voice dripped with honey. "Well, I'm glad I ran into you because I talked to the police. Seems like the call you made confessing about the fake letter was never received."

He gulped. "But you heard me—"

"Cut the crap, Lloyd." I crossed my arms over my chest. "I spoke with Detective Brown. He never got the voice mail."

"Ick." Marshmallow moved away from us. "Lloyd stinks of rising fear."

I pressed my advantage. "Did you even send Davis that letter? Or was it some kind of cover-up to pin it on Pixie and absolve you of murdering your friend?"

He almost dropped the tray but managed to catch it. The brownies had all crowded to one side, but he didn't seem to notice. "I didn't kill Davis. Why would you think I'd do something like that?"

"Look," I said, unfolding my arms, "I know all about your lucrative partnership with Davis. Come on, every time he stayed in one of your managed properties on Catalina, something got stolen."

Lloyd gave a forced laugh. "What a ludicrous idea."

"Really?" I arched an eyebrow at him. "Barbra tells you where her horse painting is hidden, and you offer to keep it out of sight. Then it gets stolen. That pet portrait went up on Amazing Online Bargain recently, and I bet I can link the defunct seller account to you."

Lloyd glanced at the entryway into the building, looking like he wanted nothing more than to flee from my questioning. He continued to stay silent with a frown pasted on his face.

Sounded like Lloyd needed more persuasion to open up, involving a little white lie from me. "While Detective Brown hasn't made this connection quite yet—after all, nobody formally reported any thefts—I can connect all the dots for him. I bet that headscarf was worth a pretty penny, enough to kill for."

"You're barking up the wrong tree," Lloyd said. "I've got an alibi for that night."

I harrumphed. "Your brother. *Family* vouching for you. Kinda flimsy, don't you think?"

He gritted his teeth. "Look, I didn't do it, okay? The one thing I'm guilty of is that letter, which I already apologized for. And I only did it to scare him away from stea—"

Lloyd turned red, knowing he'd admitted too much.

"Were you about to say 'steal'?" I asked, glee evident in my tone.

"Sounds like a murder motive to me, and I've got a direct line to the detective."

"Wait, don't," he said. "I told Davis not to take that dratted scarf and the photo, but he said he had a foolproof plan. Really, I was trying to be a good friend and steer him off the wrong path."

I tapped my toe. "Maybe you can enlighten me. How exactly did Davis get the headscarf out of a locked cabinet without your help?"

Lloyd grimaced. "Pretty sure he made a copy from mine. Said he'd lost the house key. All of the master keys were together on a ring, and I gave him the whole set."

I reflected on this new thread of information. Davis could have been acting solo by taking the headscarf and the Marilyn Monroe print, but I still thought he and Lloyd had a kind of buddy system. Plus, something else bugged me. "What I don't get is why Davis would want to overstay his rental time instead of getting a move on and leaving with the stolen goods."

Lloyd scratched the top of his head. "Beats me."

I drummed my fingers against my thigh. This line of questioning was getting me nowhere.

Lloyd must have seen my frustration. "If you're trying to find Davis's killer," he said, "you need to follow the real trail, and for sure it doesn't lead to me. Find the headscarf, find the murderer."

I admitted that Lloyd had a point—*if* he wasn't the one who'd ended up with the Marilyn Monroe scarf.

Maybe he saw the lingering suspicion in my expression because he shook the tray of brownies, redistributing the treats, and said, "I've gotta go inside. Dorris will be waiting for me, and I told her I'd help sort through stuff, maybe go through Davis's bobblehead collection. It'll probably take the rest of the weekend to organize things."

I let him go but wrapped my fingers around my phone. Should I call

Detective Brown? Lloyd had just admitted to knowing about the rob-bery. Too bad I hadn't recorded him saying it.

Would the detective believe me—or even listen to my thoughts? He'd told me to stay out of *his* investigation more than once. I relaxed my grip on the phone. I needed hard evidence to convince the detective to hear me out. Also, I wanted a better sense of the whole picture. I still had so many questions floating around.

Turning to Marshmallow, I asked, "What do you think about all this?"

My cat fluffed out his fur. "Lloyd is playing the best-friend card. His forged letter could be read one of two ways: Either he was trying to kick Davis out before he did some damage—or it served to cover Lloyd's you-know-what."

I looked into Marshmallow's intelligent blue eyes. "How so?"

"Because if it came out that the headscarf was stolen, the letter would definitely call into question Davis's rep. It'd mark him as a troublemaker, and if he ratted on Lloyd, everything coming out of his mouth would be that much less believable."

I clicked my tongue as I thought. "Lloyd is definitely a slimy guy, but would he kill his friend?" What would be the benefit to Davis of his buddy dying? Particularly if they'd had a partnership with all the robberies.

Also, there was something about what Lloyd had mentioned that tickled my brain . . . Davis had "a foolproof plan." Which involved stay-ing a little longer on the island. What could it have been? Maybe it would take a quick day trip to nose out the answers.

CHAPTER
thirty-one

AFTER MY FERRY ride to the island, I really felt like a gumshoe, taking a cropped blurry profile pic of Davis Argo on my phone and walking around Catalina. However, I had a hunch on why he'd wanted to lurk around Avalon longer. How might an expensive missing item not be considered gone? If a substitute for it was found.

To that end, I planned to track down all the clothing goods stores in the area and talk to the staff there. First, I'd offer the picture of Davis to see if they even recognized him entering the store around the end of June. If they felt like it was a maybe, then I'd continue probing. If not, I'd walk away.

I didn't find any dirt at the first two stores I tried. The third one I visited was called Catalina Clothiers. Despite its upscale name, all I saw when I entered the brightly lit interior were rows of T-shirts and a wall rack of hoodies. A table positioned between those clothing items sat laden with baseball caps. At the front register, I noticed a spinning rack of vibrantly colored magnets.

Approaching the woman at the counter, I asked her if she'd seen Davis before and showed her the photo.

"Why?" she asked, her hazel eyes brightening with curiosity. "Are you a PI?"

The excuse I'd given to the other two stores was that my friend had wandered off on the island, and I was searching for him in order to make it to our glass-bottom boat tour on time. But I could tell this woman with her dangling skeleton earrings wanted a juicier backstory. I glanced around the empty store, lowered my voice, and said, "I'm helping the police department with a crucial investigation."

Her hazel eyes assessed me. "You don't look like a cop, even one fresh out of the academy."

"I'm asking around informally, on behalf of my uncle. I can give you his name if you'd like." I'd provide her with Detective Brown's information if I needed to make things seem authentic.

"Nah. Even if you're feeding me a whopper, this is the most excitement I've ever had at this store. And I work here a lot."

She'd be a good person to ask then.

I put my phone on the counter, and the woman peered at the small photo. After a few moments, she said, "Maybe. It's hard to say from this fuzzy shot."

"The man's name is Davis. Sometimes he goes by his middle name, Dwayne."

She shook her head, making the skeleton earrings dance. "Sorry, no dice. But most customers don't ever give me their name. Do you know what he was browsing for?"

I hazarded a guess. "I think a headscarf."

The woman snapped her fingers. "Oh yeah, I do remember him. It was such a weird request. First, I thought he said 'scarf.' Of course, we don't stock winter gear during the warm months."

I pressed the conversation forward. "So, he described it as a head-scarf?"

"Yeah, he even showed me this black-and-white photo of one. I remember laughing at him and telling him we definitely don't sell that kind of fashion anymore."

"And the photo was of . . ."

"Marilyn Monroe in her younger years. Tongue-in-cheek, I even told him to check out the museum on the island. They'd probably have something like that in a display case. Then the guy just fled, without even a thank-you to me. Very strange behavior."

I took my phone back. "You've been extremely helpful."

"I hope you find the guy real soon," she said.

I gave her a noncommittal dip of my head. No need to get into the specifics about his death.

My intuition had been correct. Davis had been running around town trying to see if he could swap in an item from a nearby store to stand in for the headscarf. Maybe he would've made it look vintage it if he could. Make it a little more yellowed or something to keep the facade up.

Speaking of facades, I figured I could also peek into The Job Joint while I was in the area for my day trip. I knew I wouldn't run into Lloyd there because he'd already committed to helping Dorris sort through Davis's belongings all weekend long. Besides, I really wanted to question Lloyd's brother in depth.

I walked over to the job placement center. It looked the same as before, with its tidy rows of desks. Lloyd's brother was busy helping a prospective employee at one of the identical stations, so I waited until he finished before I waltzed over and dropped into the seat opposite him.

He peered at me through his horn-rimmed glasses. "Have we met? You look so familiar."

"I came the other week with my boyfriend. We were looking for your brother, Lloyd, and his business, Catalina Chalets."

He sat back in his swivel chair, and it shifted with his weight. "Sorry, Lloyd's gone for the weekend."

"Not a problem." I flashed him a smile, ready to go into my spiel. "I'm actually here to ask about your brother's credentials."

He tugged at his ear.

I propped my phone's screen in front of his face, so he could see the document Pixie had forwarded to me. "Look familiar?"

"Yeah. That's my brother's résumé."

"Everything about him looks excellent on paper." I scooted closer to him and lowered my voice. "But ever since my friend hired Lloyd as a manager, she's had nothing but trouble on her property. Something was stolen from the house, and now she's even implicated in a murder case."

Lloyd's brother pushed one hand into his dark hair. When he took it away, a swath of inky black hair remained upright, creating a comical effect. "That's got nothing to do with my brother."

I placed my phone back in my purse. "The man killed was someone Lloyd had rented to."

Lloyd's brother shrugged. "A stranger. So what?"

"Davis D. Argo and Lloyd were friends. Lloyd told me so himself."

He picked up a ballpoint pen and started chewing on its cap.

"I even have a photo of them together as proof of their friendship." The uncropped version of the blurry profile pic.

He sighed. "Yeah, they knew each other. But that doesn't mean Lloyd was involved in Davis's murder."

I noticed that he'd omitted commenting about the possible thefts.

Great re-framing, if he knew about the partnership between Lloyd and Davis. No wonder he crafted such polished résumés. "I talked to the detective on the case. Didn't he swing by here to chat with you?" And you'd given Lloyd an alibi, I thought.

He started tapping the ballpoint pen on the desk, fast and hard, like a drumstick. "My brother was on the island when the death happened. We were watching a game together."

"I believe you," I said, my voice silky. Now I needed to switch gears, so he could pour all of that pent-up nervous energy into another angle of conversation. "But tell me more about Davis."

He let go of the pen, and it clattered on the desk. "Davis was a bad influence, a terrible friend back when they were in high school. He only dragged Lloyd down, and I was glad when he left for Los Angeles."

"Did he go away for college?"

"Hardly. He barely made it through high school, and I bet my brother helped him out on some of his school assignments." He pointed at the nearby laptop. "Davis was one of those people who actually used 'password' for his password and one-two-three-four for his PIN."

My disbelief must have shown on my face because he continued, "Seriously. Anyway, I did him a favor by crafting a résumé for him. He landed that job in Los Angeles because of me."

I stroked his ego by ooh-ing. "How'd you do that? Embellish it so he could find work over there?"

"Easy peasy because of my expertise. I drew up a functional résumé for him."

I furrowed my brow.

"You know, the kind that lists skills and abilities, instead of the standard chronological one. It helps those who have gaps in their employment or inadequate work history, as in Davis's case."

"Well, it sounds like you did a bang-up job on it."

He leaned back in his chair, arms crossed, expression smug. "I sure did. He got that cameraman gig, and I kept him on the mainland, away from my brother."

Indeed. Davis had snagged a nice job at *One Man's Junk*. Had filming those episodes inspired him to reconnect with his old high school buddy to *snag* things to sell? And I bet the host of the show had just the right connections to help Davis get a hefty sum for all those stolen goods.

CHAPTER

thirty-two

I T TOOK A simple call to my friend Lauren Dalton, the wife of a famous Hollywood producer, to track down the host of *One Man's Junk*. Through her husband's contacts, Lauren was able to set up an appointment shortly.

We met up at the YouTube Space in Playa Vista, also known as the Silicon Beach of the area, with its growing number of tech companies overtaking the region. From the exterior, the modern building didn't really seem like a renovated hangar. It had a sleek look with glass panels and bright white letters spelling out the name of the building.

I walked inside, and the space opened up. The high ceiling made me feel even smaller than my usual petite self. I noticed the host of *One Man's Junk* sprawled across a black leather futon. I marched over to him and said, "Hi, I'm Mimi Lee."

The host straightened up in a languid jellyfish-like motion. "Salinger, but you can call me Sal." He pushed aside one of the bright red cushions on the futon and patted the seat next to him.

I made sure to slide to the side farthest away from him, closer to the foosball table several feet away.

"Thanks for taking the time to chat with me, Salinger," I said.

He had a prominent widow's peak of black hair that looked almost villainous in its sharpness against his forehead. It didn't help that he offered me a wolf-like grin in welcome. "It's my utmost pleasure. Now, I hear that you know Dalton—does he want to make a documentary about me?"

"Not exactly, but I do have a few questions for you."

His dark eyes swept up and down my frame. "Ah, I see. You must be a journalist. First, let me tell you about the atmospheric number of subscribers on my channel—"

"While your numbers must be quite high, I'm actually trying to dig into the truth about something." A pretend interview would be a great angle to get specific answers out of him. I whipped out my phone to record the conversation and lend authenticity to my reporter status. "I wanted to ask about your cameraman, Davis Argo."

"What about him?" Salinger frowned. "The man was always flaky with his work. I swear I threatened to fire him a dozen times. Actually, he left me in the lurch recently, and I had to find another person to take over his duties."

"Did you know that Davis was recently found dead?" I asked.

"Yes, the police came by to talk to me." Salinger leaned in toward me, his green eyes seeming to almost spark. "Have you uncovered what happened?" He'd moved so close to me that I could also see the brown flecks in his irises.

I grabbed the cushion from behind me and shifted even farther back on the futon. For good measure, I placed the red pillow between us as a barrier. "The police are still investigating the case, but I have a theory. I've uncovered that Davis had some sticky fingers. Did he ever show you any items and ask you to assess their value?"

Salinger squinted his eyes, as though trying to remember. "Maybe once or twice. When you're an expert like me, people always come to ask favors of you."

I pushed my phone forward to better record him. "Did you connect Davis to any potential buyers?"

Salinger flared his nostrils. "I'm a television personality, not a match-maker."

I couldn't tell if he was being honest or merely redirecting my probing.

He continued, "Is my good name getting dragged in the mud because of a lousy cameraman?"

I waited a beat, wondering if he'd reveal more as his anger heated up.

His face started turning red. "I've done nothing wrong here. If any buyers are connected to me, it'd only be from some offhand comment I made to Davis."

"Would you care to elaborate on whom you might have mentioned?"

Salinger swished his long pale fingers in the air. "It would've been from so long ago that I couldn't even begin to remember."

"I see. Anything else you'd like to add?"

He pointed his finger at me. "If my rep is sullied in any way because of this article, you can bet I'll be lawyering up."

"Don't worry," I said, pulling the phone away from him. "This article might not even get printed."

I thanked him for his time and shuffled out the door.

Salinger had seemed defensive during the interview, but I *had* ques-
tioned his reputation, which might have made him less than forth-
coming. He'd responded by covering his bases, and it sounded like he
wasn't in the direct loop from stolen goods to payment. Otherwise, I'd
think the police would've discovered the link already, despite my doubts
about Detective Brown's competence at times.

I drove back home and had just walked through the front door of
my apartment when a notification rang out on my phone. It was the
Google alert I'd set up for the missing headscarf.

A silky piece of fabric had shown up in the classifieds section of a
neighborhood networking site. I wondered if it was the same one Pixie
had acquired for her collection. The description of the headscarf mentioned it as having been worn by Marilyn Monroe while her husband
had been stationed at Catalina Island. What were the chances that it'd
be a different item than the one I was searching for?

I sent the link to Pixie, who verified that it was the same headscarf
that had been stolen from her rental home. If I could hatch a plan to
suss out the online seller, then that person might be the missing link to
the stuff taken by Davis Argo. If I followed the trail of access, I might be
able to uncover the killer.

* * *

I arranged to meet with the seller in the parking lot of a Trader Joe's that
very evening. Despite the darkening sky, something about the bright
red lettering of the store's sign put me at ease. That, and the glimpses of
colorful Hawaiian shirts on the crew members inside the store. I figured nothing bad could happen to me here. Or if something did, at least
I'd have eyewitnesses.

I parked my little Prius in the southeast corner of the lot, far enough away from the hurrying grocery store goers to not bother them, and with enough extra spaces for the unknown contact to park in. The local community site where the classified ad had been placed didn't require verification of their members, so all I knew about the seller was their online ID: SwellSeller.

Sitting in my Prius, I waited for the person to show up. We'd agreed to meet at half past seven. Ten minutes later, and I started drumming my fingers against the gear shift. My little car felt stuffier the longer I waited, so I rolled down the windows. Five minutes after that, I propped the door open. I wasn't sure if it was the tight space of my car getting to me or my anxiety heating up my body.

I noticed an increase in traffic in the parking lot. Perhaps I shouldn't have set up a time so near to the store's closing. It seemed like last-minute shoppers kept rolling in to get their supplies and stock up their fridges. Either that, or people had waited until nighttime to beat the earlier heat and venture out. One older lady even honked at me to close my door, so she could park next to me.

Could that be SwellSeller? My contact had mentioned they'd be driving a black sedan. I patted my hair and pretended to tie an invisible scarf around it as a kind of signal to the lady.

She reared her head back as if I'd given her a rude gesture.

"Sorry," I mouthed as she shook her fist at me.

Spots were filling up fast, and I needed to make sure there would even be a place left for the seller to park. I walked around to the passenger's side of my car and stood on the asphalt to keep someone from parking in that space. Just in case the contact knew me (say, if it was Lloyd), I'd gone for an incognito look for the meet-up. I'd pulled my hair up into a high ponytail, donned oversized celebrity dark glasses to cover my face, and wore loose baggy clothing.

Finally, a dark sedan did arrive with a roar of an engine, its high beams blaring. The sharp blast of light assaulted my face, searing my eyes. My heart thumped like a jackrabbit in my chest.

As they sped closer, an alarming thought occurred to me. Why were they driving so fast unless they wanted to run me over? I jumped out of the way, hurtling to the front of the car to hide.

Bright spots danced before my eyes while I tried to calm my frantic heart. Then I peeked around the frame of my car. The driver had sped away, their tires screeching. They'd moved so fast I couldn't even make out the make and model of the vehicle, much less anything about the person behind the wheel.

It took several minutes of deep breathing to center myself. What had spooked them? I wondered if they had somehow recognized me through my disguise.

CHAPTER
thirty-three

ALTHOUGH UNLIKELY, I still checked in the morning to see if I'd received any further messages from the seller. Nope, and, of course, they hadn't bothered to reschedule the meeting.

On the plus side, I noticed the headscarf listing was still up. If they'd been worried by my presence last night, at least they hadn't been terrified enough to take down the item.

Good. I knew the online community site wouldn't give me any info about the seller due to their privacy policy, but I figured I could find a back door to unearth their identity.

Detective Brown didn't have any lost love for me, but I knew he could pull some strings. That morning, I waltzed into the police station with an air of righteousness.

I found the detective at his usual scarred desk. It seemed like he'd wanted to multitask but was failing miserably. With a document gripped in one hand and strawberry jam–slathered toast in the other, he kept fumbling both things.

"Hi, Detective Brown," I said. "I'm here to report a crime."

He made sure to put down the paper and the toast before focusing on me. "Have you stumbled onto another dead body, Miss Lee? They seem to turn up everywhere you go."

"Haha. No, I'm here to discuss a theft."

He picked up his toast and took a big bite. With his mouth full, he said, "Not my department."

"But it has to do with the murder of Davis Argo," I said, enunciating my words for effect.

His eyes widened.

"I found Pixie's headscarf—the one that was stolen from her rental home—being sold online," I said. "All I need is for you to work your police magic to trace the seller."

He finished chewing and swallowed. "What exactly are you thinking I would do for you?"

"Track the IP address of the person listing the headscarf for sale."

He held three jam-stained fingers up. "First off, do you even know if it's the same headscarf? Second, I don't feel like using police resources on a wild-goose chase. And third, this 'theft' happened on Catalina, so it's not my jurisdiction even if I went along with your unfounded theory that stolen goods equals murder down the road."

I heard a purring from underneath his desk.

"I've missed you," I said, scooping Nimbus up and sitting with her on the guest chair before the detective.

"Yes, why don't you have a seat and waste some more of my time," the detective said. "Not like I don't have enough to do with all the paperwork and documentation I'm behind on."

"Fine. If you don't want to help me track down this likely killer, why don't you tell me which other suspects are on your list besides my dear friend?"

"You know I can't do that, Miss Lee."

"What can you tell me then?" I threw my hands up in the air, startling Nimbus. Her paws waved in the air, and I bent over to examine them. "Why are they red . . . and sticky?"

Detective Brown pulled his toast toward him, and I could see where some gray fur decorated his plate.

"I can clean her paws up for you while we discuss the case." Rummaging through my purse, I found a pack of cat wipes. On-the-go cleaning at its best.

He gave me a terse thanks.

"Can you at least talk to me about what you found at the park?" I remembered its dismal state, but even when I'd visited, there had been two moms strolling by. "Weren't there eyewitnesses around since it's such an open space?"

"Not relevant," he said and started in on his toast again.

I pulled out a cat wipe. "How can it be irrelevant? The park was the scene of the crime."

"No, it wasn't," he muttered.

"I'm sorry?" I paused, holding the wipe aloft. Like a silent game of chicken, I stared into his light blue eyes and waited him out.

"Fine," he finally said. "This won't help you much, but the victim was *moved* to the park. The original crime scene was elsewhere."

"Wait, what?"

"Based on the victim's lividity, the body was moved."

I furrowed my brows at him. "What's 'lividity'?"

"The way the blood pools in the body after—"

I let out a choking noise and focused on wiping the jam off Nimbus's paws. They were a startling red that made me feel even more nauseated. The faster I cleaned them, the better.

"Hey, you asked," Detective Brown said, leaning back in his chair and clasping his hands behind his head.

I hoped he ended up with sticky jam in his hair.

Once I'd cleaned off the kitty, I stood up and handed Nimbus back. I tossed the used wipe in a nearby trash can.

I stumbled out the door, still feeling a bit queasy from all that talk about blood and death. Although I couldn't think about it right away, I knew I'd have to eventually mull over what the detective had told me.

• • •

I filled Marshmallow in about the details of my police station visit as I opened up Hollywoof. After I finished tidying and had flipped the sign to "OPEN," I stood before him and asked, "Do you have any idea why the body would have been moved?"

He blinked at me, slow lazy blinks with his ocean-colored eyes. "No. We need more leads. Are you sure you can't trace that IP address?"

"I don't think so. I'm not a computer whiz, and Detective Brown wouldn't budge."

"Maybe there's some sort of hint you can find with the item for sale. Let me see the ad."

I took out my phone and scrolled to the site. As I was flashing the image to Marshmallow, Nicola sauntered in.

She clambered over to us. "What do you have there? Juicy celebrity gossip?"

"Nope, sorry. Just a picture of a headscarf."

She peeked at the image and then looked between Marshmallow and me. "Is it a fashion accessory for Marshmallow? It's cute."

He bristled. "Do I look like a cat who would need accessories? I'm perfect as is."

Nicola went on to read the description, muttering every word beneath her breath. She then got a dreamy look in her eyes and seemed to change topics. "You know I thought I saw MJ in line the other day at Starbucks."

"Who?"

She gave a wide smile. "Michael Jordan, of course. MJ. He was about two cars behind me in the drive-thru line."

I shook my head, half in awe of her one-track mind, always on the hunt to find famous people. "How did you get from a headscarf to a celebrity sighting?"

"From the initials in the scarf description."

"What initials?" I said.

She pointed at the phone with her shiny manicured finger. "Right there."

I noticed that the item line description had three initials: NJD.

Where had I seen those three letters joined together before? They looked so familiar . . .

Before I could recollect, my phone pinged with a text. I saw a message from my sister saying, Finished my latest K-drama binge. You free to do lunch today?

I texted back. For real? Or another setup?

She gave me a laughing face emoji. A true sisters' date. Pinky promise.

Okay then, I wrote back. XOXO.

CHAPTER

thirty-four

O F COURSE MY sister and I met up at a Korean tofu stew place. How fitting to celebrate her binge watching achievement.

The restaurant looked pretty empty when I entered. Guess bubbling, spicy soup wasn't a major hit during the sweltering summer days. Inside, I didn't find Alice at first glance. I spotted three tables occupied with people, and two of them were taken by couples.

The third table had a girl in a puffy white dress with a giant red bow across her chest. As though she felt my gaze on her, the girl looked up from her menu. My eyes widened—it was Alice.

I walked over to her, barely suppressing my giggle. "What. Are. You. Wearing."

"The outfit Ma got for me." Alice scooted her chair back, stood up, and twirled.

She wore a strange dress with a nautical collar and a giant mushroom skirt on the bottom. Alice looked like a cartoon come to life. "Are you, like, a walking anime character?" I said.

"Basically." She sat back down.

"Why did you agree to let Ma buy you that thing?" Although maybe horrendous clothes versus terrible dates was a pretty good trade-off. "And why are you *wearing* it?"

"She did that sneaky Chinese paying-the-bill technique," Alice said.

I took a seat myself. "The one where she pretends to use the restroom but goes to the cashier instead?"

"Kind of. Except the small shop didn't have a restroom, so she just grabbed something off a hanger, pushed me into a dressing room, and then did the deed."

"You could've returned it."

"It was a mom-and-pop type of store. No refunds, no exchanges."

I chortled. "On second thought, I can see you wearing it to school . . . for show-and-tell day."

"Yeah, maybe my kindergarteners would love this getup. It's a knock-off Sailor Moon outfit."

"A what?"

"Sailor Moon is a manga character. Even had an old TV series before. Except actually, the tag on this outfit reads, 'S-a-y-l-or' Moon."

The name did ring a bell. "Don't you need pigtails to complete the effect?" I said.

"No more questions, please. And stop gawking at me like I'm an alien." She slid a menu my way. "Feast your eyes on this instead."

I glanced at the items displayed but knew I'd get my usual: seafood *soondubu jjigae*. "Why are you wearing this beautiful ensemble on a lowly lunch date with me?"

She sighed. "I ran out of time to change. Ma dropped by the apartment right before lunch and insisted I try it on again to see if it needed any tailoring."

"Well, I think it fits perfectly." I gave her a huge grin with two big thumbs-up.

My sister's voice dripped with honey. "If you're so excited about this dress, Mimi, you can have it. We're about the same size."

"No thanks. I'm sticking to my head-turning tees and jeans combo." To cut off any further discussion of clothes swapping, I raised my hand and waved it to catch the attention of the waitress.

After she came over and took our orders, I turned back to Alice. "Actually, you could pull off the anime look. Maybe make your eyes look cartoon-like with some specially applied makeup."

She grabbed a pair of disposable chopsticks from the holder on the side and threw them at me.

"Hey," I said, managing to catch them in the air by a stroke of luck. "I'm just kidding."

"This is for sure going into my Halloween costume bin." She split apart her own pair of disposable chopsticks with a decisive snap.

"Aw. Why wait three months until October to snag your dream guy?" I said.

She didn't have a chance to throw more chopsticks at me since the server arrived with complimentary iced tea and our food order: bowls of purple rice, *banchan* appetizers, and the piping hot soups. I asked for a raw egg to add to my tofu stew, and then cracked it open and dropped it into my soup.

While the egg was cooking, I grabbed a few kimchi cucumber slices and chewed on them.

"Keep eating," Alice said, "so you don't say anything else stupid."

"You know I love you."

She snorted. "Why can't I have your life? Everything going so perfectly..."

I swallowed a cucumber piece whole and coughed. Grabbing my nearby glass of iced barley tea, I took a big gulp.

"What? Didn't you and Josh make up yet?" She gave an exaggerated pat of her own shoulder. "I mean, I set everything into perfect motion with my snow eatery date."

"Things are better with Josh and me, I think." He told me he'd ditched the conniving para-lethal after all. "But I'm involved in another murder case."

"What? Again? Tell me everything," she said.

"It's Pixie." I gave my sister a brief summary of the rental home situation, the dead tenant, and how the guy had been found in a park, disheveled and almost overlooked.

She gasped. "It's like a real-life drama."

I took a sip of my soup. "Trust me, it's better watching that kind of stuff unfold on the screen."

She used a long metal spoon to swirl around the tofu in her soup. After a few clockwise circles, she said, "Actually, it does smack of K-drama."

I dislodged some clam meat from a shell and ate it. "Want to share more about that series you just finished?"

My sister complied, giving me the ups and downs of the show. We spent our time slurping soup and getting out of the real dramas in our lives during lunch. After we paid the bill and said goodbye in the parking lot, I chuckled at seeing her maneuvering her puffy dress into her compact car.

A sudden realization hit me. I almost hadn't recognized my sister at the restaurant. Was that what had happened with Davis? Had he, in a sense, been costumed as a homeless person? But why?

As my Saylor Moon sis drove off, I also thought about variations on names. That reminded me of the Fantastick Four group and how people tried to skirt the law in their illegal activities, which brought my mind back to the headscarf that was stolen from Pixie's rental home. I couldn't get away from this case no matter what I was doing.

But thinking about the Fantastick Four also inspired me to try a new approach for getting the answers I needed. I'd figured out a loophole on how to get the info on the seller and how to get the headscarf back all in one fell swoop. I just needed to contact my favorite lawyer once I closed up shop and dropped Marshmallow off at home.

• • •

Around dinnertime, I traveled downtown to visit Josh's workplace. The receptionist at his law firm waved me on through. Maybe she finally recognized me, what with my previous visits to Murphy, Sullivan, and Goodwin. That, or because she was busy jabbering away on her headset and working the phone.

I traveled down the rows of desks and found Josh, with his back to me, clacking away on the keyboard. No Gertrude in sight. Good.

After sidling up next to him, I said, "Surprise."

He turned his head, and a smile broke across his face. "Mimi, I'm so glad to see you."

"Sorry I didn't call first."

"No worries." He got up and gave me a warm hug.

I loved that feeling of being embraced by Josh, and the scent of pine rolling off him brought an enticing mix of comfort and excitement.

"Don't mind me. I'll just stand here out of the way." I moved about a foot away from him and let him return to work.

"I'll only be a little bit longer. I'm almost done here, and then we can grab an impromptu dinner."

"Sounds wonderful."

I peeked around the area, checking out the other nearby oak desks. Quite a few people remained, working on papers or making phone calls. I couldn't hear anything coming from the obscured area opposite Josh. Their workspaces were separated by a tall hutch, so at least I didn't have to run into Murph.

Guess I'd spoken too soon, though, because pattering steps soon approached our area. I heard Josh's desk neighbor talking. A high-pitched giggle also accompanied Murph's distinctive reedy voice. The coworker's head popped up above the hutch before settling into his desk.

Their talking must have also disturbed Josh because I noticed he'd put on a pair of earbuds. I wish I kept a set in my purse. Or brought along cotton balls or something, especially when I accidentally eavesdropped on some of Murph's conversation:

"Did I ever tell you what an amazing paralegal you are, Gertie?"

"Oh, Murph." She drew out his name and giggled.

Please, save me now. I glanced at Josh, whose brows were knit in concentration as he speed-typed.

I focused on hearing the tap-tapping of his keyboard and ignored our neighbors' voices. Thank goodness Josh's fast typing skills paid off. In less than five minutes, we were out the door.

"Where do you want to go?" he asked as we stood outside the sandstone office building.

"How about the place where we first ate out together?"

He interpreted my suggestion correctly. "Great idea. I love animal style burgers."

We'd gone to In-N-Out early on in our relationship, and the food still brought good memories with it. Josh and I had ordered the same type of burger back then, with the extra spread and the grilled onions.

He hooked his arm through mine. "It's a date then. Except we can't walk there. The closest location is driving distance away."

"I'm up for a joy ride," I said, giving him a happy wink.

When we got to his Lexus, I slid into the passenger side and luxuriated in the leather seat.

"It's nice to have you sitting here next to me," he said.

As he put the car into gear, I said, "Oh, you might regret those words, mister. I've got you trapped in this car now, and I intend to pick your brain about something."

Since he drove along the streets at the actual legal speed limit, it gave me plenty of time to ask away. "I'm wondering if you could help me out. I found Pixie's stolen headscarf on some online classifieds site. Maybe you could create some legal document, send it to the seller, and get the item back for her."

"What are you suggesting?" he said.

We'd pulled up to a stop light. "A cease and desist letter," I said.

He puffed his cheeks and blew out his breath. "I do write those—for threats on intellectual property. I'm not sure they're really applicable in your case. Couldn't you just flag the administrator of the website?"

I chewed on the side of my cheek. Then we started moving again. "I guess so. They could probably give me the seller's contact info, right?"

"It's worth a shot," Josh said as he pulled into the parking lot of the In-N-Out. "I can't write an official cease and desist letter for you, but I can give you some special legal terms to make things official-sounding. Throw around phrases like 'monetary damages' and 'seeking all appropriate legal remedies' when you contact the administrator."

"Ooh." I fluttered my eyelashes at him. "I like it when you talk *legally* to me."

Josh snorted. "Come on, Miss Flirt. Time for some grub. I think your hunger pangs are getting to you."

I grinned up at him. "Let's go wild. Not only should we get the special burgers, but we should also split a Neapolitan from their secret menu."

A shared strawberry, chocolate, and vanilla milkshake sounded like just the right sweet ending for our dinner date.

CHAPTER
≈ thirty-five ≈

'D SENT AN email to the administrator of the online auction site that evening, but I still hadn't received a response the following morning. I sure hoped my hinting at legal consequences would do the trick. Maybe by my lunch break, the administrator would reply.

At Hollywoof, Marshmallow and I settled into our typical opening routine. Not that he did much. My cat napped while I had the honor of wiping down surfaces, checking to make sure the television worked, and flipping over the sign.

Nicola came barreling through the door, flustered. "I can't find my phone anywhere," she said. "But I swore I took it out the door with me."

"Deep breath," I said. "It's not in your purse?"

She dumped out the contents of her bag onto one of our waiting benches. I noticed packs of bubble gum, wadded tissues (hopefully clean), and a mass of cosmetics. No luck with the phone, though.

"Did you check your pockets?"

She flipped them inside out but found nothing except the lint coating their interiors.

"I know. I'll give you a call." Pulling out my cell, I dialed her number. I let it ring until it went to voice mail.

She wrung her hands. "What am I going to do without my phone?"

Marshmallow opened one eye from his slumbering spot. "See, humans do have leashes," he said. "The digital kind."

Checking the clock on the wall, I said, "We've still got a few minutes. Why don't you retrace your steps along the plaza? I'll keep calling you. Maybe you dropped it on your way to the store."

She stuffed all her belongings back into her purse, and then we walked out of the shop and onto the paved area in front of Hollywoof and the other stores near the beach. I dialed while we searched high and low, near the planted palm trees, by the scattered bike racks, and to the back area where the metered parking spots lay. We went right up to her vehicle, a used mint green VW Beetle.

"It's not here," Nicola said, yanking on her hair, perhaps literally trying to tear the strands out.

I glanced at her car. "Have you tried looking inside there?"

She wrinkled her nose but unlocked and opened the vehicle door.

I called again.

A loud ringing blasted the air.

"Oh." She scrounged around in the vehicle and located her phone from under the passenger side's seat. "Got it."

Nicola deposited the phone in her purse, zipped it up tight, and locked her vehicle. We proceeded back to Hollywoof, where I made an extravagant bow in front of Marshmallow. "Guess who saved the day?" I said.

He kept right on napping.

Nicola patted down her hair, glossed her lips, and seated herself behind the register. Disaster averted, we looked forward to some relaxing time filled with much shampooching.

Hours sped by with suds flying around and the requisite fur shaking from our doggie clientele. At noon, I closed up for lunch and a much-needed break. In the waiting area, I scarfed down my prepackaged salad using the tiny disposable fork.

Putting the plastic bowl with dregs of dressing off to the side, I checked my email again. This time around, a new message popped up—from the administrator of the neighborhood networking site. The owner didn't give me any contact info about the seller due to "confidentiality" issues. However, the account had been suspended, and the administrator promised to conduct an investigation into the entire matter.

I still didn't have a solid link to who had been trying to hawk Pixie's stolen item, but at least Pixie wouldn't lose her valuable headscarf for the time being if the seller couldn't list it.

I tapped my fingers against the pleather bench, considering. Reflecting on the headscarf made me go over all the other items that had gone missing from the Catalina Chalet owners. I used my Notes app on my phone and made an actual checklist to sort through my thoughts:

1. Pixie's headscarf—listed in the neighborhood community's classifieds section
2. Barbra's pet portrait—found on an online auction site
3. Professor Villanueva's locket—still missing
4. Riku's phablet—also unaccounted for

I blinked at the last item on my list. A *phone* plus tablet. If only Riku's model was as easy to locate as Nicola's had been this morning.

Then I could give it a call and just walk around listening for the ringtone.

Of course, who knew where the phone was located right this minute? If only I could find it using some other method. And then it hit me— there was a way. I needed to talk to Riku pronto.

CHAPTER

thirty-six

I ASKED NICOLA IF she could stay overtime after I closed up Holly-woof to watch over Marshmallow. He growled at my suggestion. "I don't need to be kitty-sat."

"Sorry, buddy." I patted him on the head. "I just need to hop by and see Riku, and I'm pretty sure they don't let pets into that fancy tech building."

"I'll be expecting treats, lots of them, when you return."

Taking that as acquiescence, I thanked Nicola and waved goodbye to the two of them.

I drove at a snail's pace through the evening traffic until I found myself again marveling at the mirrored building that housed Riku's company. At the lobby, I needed to sign in to gain access to the fifth floor, and the receptionist also called upstairs to make sure I was a welcome guest. The security guard making the rounds paused nearby and patted his full utility belt while he waited for the verdict.

I must have passed with flying colors because the receptionist led me to the elevator bank, pressed the "hold" button, and scanned her badge for the fifth floor. Then she stepped away. The doors swooshed closed after she exited.

A smooth glide deposited me on the fifth floor. It was hard to miss Riku's office, since it took up a quarter of the entire space. Enclosed in glass on three sides, he was sitting behind multiple monitors at his sprawling workstation. He waved me through his open door.

I spun around the room in awe. "Not quite a window office, but it's really spacious."

He laughed and jerked his thumb at the wall behind him. "Yeah, not bad, but my only scenic view is tacked on this wall."

I took in the blown-up image of Santa Monica, a shot of the crashing waves and the iconic pier with its Ferris wheel, bathed in sunset pinks and oranges. "Sure is postcard pretty."

"It's even better up close. Of course, it costs a lot to live here, and I've certainly had to work hard to afford it." I could almost guarantee that he didn't live in any of the rent-controlled places still operating in the city.

"May I?" I gestured to one of the seats in the office, an uncomfortable-looking utilitarian metal chair.

"Go ahead." Riku, in his typical mock turtleneck ensemble, sat in a black ergonomic swivel chair with padded arm cushions. I could see the power hierarchy displayed through his office furniture.

I slid my hands beneath my bottom to cushion it better and said, "I think I know a way to retrieve your phablet."

He leaned forward. "How?"

"Using a 'find your device' feature." I removed my hands, immediately regretting the decision, and dug into my purse to extract my own phone. I showed him my tracker program.

Holding up his hand, he said, "I know how a locator app works."

Of course he did. Heat rushed into my cheeks. "Anyway, I thought if you had a second phone, and they were linked . . ."

His eyes probed mine. "The new phablet's a prototype."

Did that mean it had been the only model around? I stood up to get out of the uncomfortable chair and moved around the desk to his side. There, I found myself drawn to his extensive work setup.

I peeked over at his monitors. One seemed to display a dizzying amount of code. I rested my eyes on the other, which featured a screensaver of a lovely Santa Monica home. "Yours?" I said, tilting my head toward it.

"Yes." The image was of a picturesque house, complete with a white picket fence, on a tree-lined street. Only the metal sign by the sidewalk with its resident-only permit parking rule ruined the friendly vibe.

A new thought entered my mind. "What about by computer? Can your tech track down a phone that way?"

He pulled his shoulders back and sat up straighter. "No doubt. As long as the phablet is activated."

"Oh." I bit the inside of my cheek. "There's probably no carrier, since it was only a model."

His nostrils flared. "The phone still works, as long as there's Wi-Fi around. That way we can easily test its features."

I shuffled my feet. "So, how did others get ahold of it in the first place? Didn't you lock it up in the rental home?"

Riku shot me a withering look. "Are you putting the blame on my shoulders? I'm the victim here. Anyway, I kept the phablet in the extra drawer of my desk. I didn't realize that vacationers would be snooping around people's private stuff like that."

"Sorry, I didn't mean to accuse you." I sat back down on the metal chair in contrition. "Since you know the phablet can work on Wi-Fi, did you already try tracking it?"

He ran his hand through his hair. "That's the problem. I've tried everything I could think to find it. Nothing works as long as the phablet's turned off, and I'm sure I powered it down when I stored it away."

It would've looked like a dead phone at first glance, but perhaps the thief had tried to use it to check and see if it worked? "Maybe it's on now," I said.

He gave me an icy stare. "Do you really think you know how tech works better than me?"

"You can at least try," I said. "So we can catch everybody who's responsible for the thefts."

He startled, rolling his chair back a few inches. "Mimi, you think there's more than one culprit involved?"

"Yeah. At first, I thought it was just Davis stealing everything—the same renter at all of the Catalina Chalet homes and the missing items at each residence couldn't be a coincidence. Now, though, it looks like he was in cahoots with someone else."

"What makes you think that?"

"The other items the owners have." I ticked them off my fingers. "Pixie's headscarf, Barbra's painting. They've all gone up for sale since after Davis died."

Riku rubbed his chin. "Guess there's no harm in trying to see if the phone's on."

It took only a few minutes of tapping on the keyboard, and Riku's jaw slackened. He turned to me. "I must have checked at least a hundred times, but I can't believe a noob like you managed to get lucky. I've homed in on a location."

My eyes boggled. "Where?"

"Let me write down the address." Peering at the screen, he wrote something down on a slip of paper.

When he handed me the note, the hairs on the back of my neck stood up. That address looked familiar to me—because I'd mapped it out before.

Riku must have seen my tremor. "I'll go with you, Mimi."

I steeled my nerves. "No, I can handle things myself."

He frowned at me. "My stuff is there as well."

"Good point."

I followed Riku outside to the parking lot located at the side of the mirrored building. As a Tesla owner, he had a specially reserved spot for his vehicle. We got in and buckled ourselves, and I couldn't help but admire that his vehicle still retained that new car smell.

We drove to the address in silence and soon arrived at the public storage facility. I didn't blink twice at its familiar name: What's In Store. The place where Dorris Argo worked. Except now the headquarters' lights were off, and it looked closed for the day.

"Shucks," I said, but Riku headed for the gated entryway.

"Unit number twelve," he said. He peered at the keypad before the gate, brows furrowed.

I groaned. "We were so close, but this isn't one of your tech devices, Riku. You won't be able to hack your way in."

We waited a few minutes, hoping for another car to arrive to let us in. Nobody showed up. The sun started setting, making splashes of brilliant color against the sky.

"There's absolutely no one around," I said, jerking my head toward the storage units on the other side of the gate. All seemed quiet in there. No cars or people roamed the place.

Riku drummed his fingers against his steering wheel.

"We can't stay here," I said, noticing something for the first time and pointing it out. "There's a camera recording our every movement. It'd be suspicious if we sat here waiting around."

Riku blanched and reversed the car. "You're right," he said. "Besides, the criminals aren't even here."

Using my phone, I searched for What's In Store's opening hours online. "Seems like there's nothing to be done right now. But the storage facility is open bright and early in the morning."

"We'll have to wait until tomorrow then," Riku said. "Contact me around ten in the morning, and we can make a plan to catch the culprit."

I nodded in fake agreement, but I didn't like working with others and knew I couldn't wait that long before springing into action. Maybe I'd even be ready when the business unlocked their doors at dawn. I'd storm into the place and collect the footage from the camera and get evidence for what really went down the evening of Davis Argo's death.

CHAPTER

thirty-seven

I CALLED WHAT'S IN Store right after dawn. A sleepy male voice answered, and I double-checked to make sure Dorris wasn't working the morning shift. He responded in the negative. Good. It'd probably be better not to run into her as I tried to uncover the video evidence.

Though Marshmallow groused at me for stomping around the apartment so early in the morning, I was glad he was awake. "I need a partner," I said, swooping my cat up and placing him into the car. Perhaps his feline senses could ascertain more than my own. At the very least, he'd provide a furry distraction in case I needed one.

The young man working at the counter at What's In Store seemed of Marshmallow's early morning mindset; he yawned his way through my forged intro as a potential client who was searching for storage space. His rumpled clothes appeared like they'd been slept in, and maybe they had. He seemed fresh out of high school and not invested enough to look very presentable for his summer job.

Marshmallow moved around the front office, staring at all the cardboard options. "Look at this collection," he said, swishing his tail. "Boxes of all shapes and sizes."

I ignored his covetous commentary and focused on my rehearsed speech to get the worker to talk more about the potential video footage. "So"—I leaned on the counter in a confidential manner—"I saw a camera near the gated entryway to the locker units. Do you have a pretty good security system here?"

He scratched behind his ear. "Uh, it's okay."

Not much of a talker, this one. "What kind of cameras do you use?" I could look up the actual models later.

"I'm not really sure," he said.

I blew out a breath. "Well, how many devices do you guys have here?"

He started bouncing on his heels. "Just the one, I think."

I scrunched my brow. "You don't know the number of cameras covering the facility? How long have you been working here?"

"About a month."

At this point, Marshmallow jumped on top of the counter.

The young man reared back at my cat's sudden appearance.

"Oh yeah," I said. "I brought my lucky cat. To suss out the best storage unit."

"That's not all I can figure out." Marshmallow cocked his head at me. "While you've been wasting your breath talking, I scouted out the joint."

Mm-hmm. I wouldn't call checking out the boxes the best investigative snooping.

"Look around you, Mimi," he continued. "Where are the monitors showing live coverage?"

Marshmallow had a point. I searched the walls for monitors and grainy moving pictures. Usually, secured areas would mount the screens up to convey the safety of the place for customers.

Peeking around the counter, I asked the young man, "Hey, where's the running feed for the cameras?"

His voice came out as a whisper. "Fine. I don't get paid enough to lie. The camera, the one mounted on the car gate, is a fake."

Oh. I couldn't hide the disappointment in my voice. "Does that mean you don't actually have surveillance on the lot?"

"Well, we have workers here at the office during open hours watching over everything. And the locked gate, of course. You need a code for the keypad. Plus, customers can place their own special approved locks on each unit for good measure."

I stared out at the storage spaces. I'd need to find other evidence besides the video feed then. "Mind if I take a tour?"

"No problem." He led me outside to the units with their rolling garage-like doors.

I paced back and forth across the lot. "Could you give me a few moments to think?" I said.

"Sure." He slunk back inside the office.

Marshmallow joined my side. "You want me to take a peek at the unit?"

"Space number twelve," I said. "See if you can find an opening."

He padded over there and sniffed around. "Nothing doing. Not even a gap under the door for me to squeeze through."

I hazarded a glance at the main office. The worker seemed to have his head propped on his hand, staring at the phone with half-lidded eyes. I casually strolled over to the unit marked "12" and nudged the door with my foot. Nope, not unlocked by accident.

As I examined the four-digit combination padlock, I wondered if I could smash it without creating a scene. Or maybe I wouldn't have to. I remembered something Lloyd's brother had mentioned about Davis. The guy had used less than stellar security combos like "password" and . . . 1-2-3-4. Could it be that easy?

I scrolled until I had entered the four numbers on the lock, held my breath, and pulled. It tumbled open into my hand. Eureka.

"Quick," I said to Marshmallow. "Let's go inside."

We entered the enclosed space, and I pulled down the door. We were left in sudden darkness. Using my phone, I switched on the flashlight feature. Then I looked around.

The small beam from my phone didn't illuminate very much, so I had to walk slowly around the locker space to determine its contents. I found a mishmash of accumulated belongings, all old and dusty according to my nose. I sneezed every few moments as I riffled through the items.

There really did appear to be piles of junk stored here. I found a set of old, but unchipped, porcelain dishware with swirling designs. Vintage clothes folded up in neat squares took up another box. I even saw a stack of old toys: board games, building sets, and jump ropes.

I did all the hunting because Marshmallow seemed fixated on examining every cardboard box in the area instead of investigating. It was a cat's fantasy playground because the boxes ranged in size. He attempted to squeeze himself into something that looked like a cereal box, and I was shocked he was able to do so.

He wouldn't be much help, distracted as he was. Since I couldn't gather all the items in the storage space and leave with them, I figured I should take pictures of them. The digital photographic evidence would serve to put away the guilty party. I tried snapping some shots, but the dim lighting really wreaked havoc on the photos.

"Stupid phone," I muttered. "Can't take any good pics in the dark." I turned on the flash, but it still didn't cut it.

I needed better lighting. Going over to the door, I bent over to start rolling it up—only to find it had started moving of its own accord. Was there some sort of automatic spring feature?

The door slid up with a loud bang, revealing an angry figure. Dorris stood before me, scowling, her feet planted shoulder distance apart. Guess she did have strength in those thin arms of hers. "Mimi Lee," she said, "what are you doing going through my storage unit?"

I blurted out the first thing that came to mind. "But I thought you weren't working this morning."

She jerked her head toward the front office. "My coworker told me about how you trespassed and broke into my unit."

Whoops. Guess the guy hadn't been lazily looking at the phone earlier.

I took a few steps back into the locker and gestured around. "I know all the stuff in here is stolen."

"Reclaimed," she said with a sniff. I noticed she didn't sneeze. Not even one sniffle. "People forget about their possessions all the time here. I'm just giving them a second life. Nothing wrong with that."

"What do you mean, Dorris?"

"Think of it this way," she said. "I'm truly helping the owner of What's In Store when I clear out items from irresponsible people who forget to keep paying for their units. I remove all the boring paperwork and red tape. Instead of waiting to give those slackers overdue notices or hold public auctions for their discarded items, I tidy up for them. I turn their junk around and change it into another person's treasure."

I snapped my fingers. "*One Man's Junk*, the show your brother worked on. I bet Davis asked the host for a favor to get you the right connections to do your trading."

She smirked at me. "Nothing's wrong about helping people unclutter. Sal's connections helped me find people who snatched up well-worn treasures. You could say I'm aiding people with some Marie Kondo-ing. In their heart of hearts, they must not really want their old belongings."

I blinked at her. Maybe she could justify her deviousness to herself, but her Good Samaritan act wasn't fooling me. I also noticed the heart locket around her neck again. Aiming the flashlight beam at the necklace, I trained it on the pendant hanging outside her shirt. Even with the scratched-up facade, I could still discern the letter "T" engraved on it. "T" for Traveler, the USC horse mascot. "I'm certain that necklace belongs to Professor Villanueva, one of the Catalina Chalet owners."

"Does it?" she said.

"Your brother stole from the homes he rented."

"What's that got to do with me?" she said. "I'm not my brother's keeper."

Oh boy. Did she really want to feed me that old line? I pointed at her jewelry. "Don't play innocent. Even if you kept that one item out of sentimentality's sake and placed a picture of your brother in it or if Davis had really given that necklace to you, I'm aware that you've been trying to sell the other stuff. I know about Barbra's pet portrait, Pixie's headscarf. They all went on sale *after* Davis died, and you're the one with ties to this storage space where he kept his loot."

She crossed her arms over her chest. "I call your bluff," she said.

I arched my eyebrow at her. "I think you're forgetting about the phablet." Once I found that item in her storage unit, she wouldn't be able to explain its presence away.

"The 'phablet'?" she said, her brows furrowing.

"A phone plus tablet. It's how I found your unit in the first place . . ." My voice trailed off as a new thought struck me. I actually hadn't seen the tracking beam on the screen and had only been given the familiar address on a slip of paper. How accurate were those locator apps anyway? Not within several feet, surely.

Suddenly, I noticed someone clad in black move up behind Dorris. A sizzle. And then she crumpled to the ground.

CHAPTER
thirty-eight

CRIED OUT IN alarm. Dorris had been attacked by a stun gun. She'd hit the ground pretty hard when she fell. I retreated from her unmoving body, stepping farther inside the storage unit.

"Should have realized it was you," I said to Riku, a chill creeping up my spine. The man stood there with a wicked grin, a Taser in his hand. "You knew the exact number of the storage unit while we were blocked by the gate last night."

"Yes," he said in a grim voice. "I suppose I told you a little too much."

"That, and"—I waved my hands around the small space—"I never found the phablet in all these piles of junk."

He gave a small head nod. "Once I tracked down Davis and followed his car to this facility, I took the device. It's too valuable to let fall in the wrong hands. The innovative phablet belongs with me."

Something didn't compute. "If you couldn't bear to be without it, why did you go and tuck it away on an island in the first place?"

He shook his head at me, as though disappointed with my ignorant questioning. "Mimi, that was just a spare. Remember, I told you I kept it in my 'extra' drawer on my desk." Guess I'd misheard his phrasing. Riku probably carried around another copy (always within his reach, I bet).

"So if you have an extra, it doesn't really matter that the other one got taken."

He snapped at me. "Of course it does. The design could've gotten copied or leaked before the IPO."

"Did you really have to kill Davis for it?"

He held the Taser with one hand and let the other dangle by his side. I noticed the utility belt wrapped around his waist. The same kind I'd seen on the security guard at his building. No wonder he'd had quick access to the murder weapon. I shuddered.

"It was done in defense against the theft of my property," Riku said.

"I don't think the police are going to see it the same way." I shifted a few inches to the side, attempting to peer around his taller frame to peek at the front office and see if I could signal for help.

"Don't worry, Mimi. No one is going to bother us. I made sure to first stun the worker. Crept up on him while he was shelving something, so he won't be able to ID me. I tied him up, the same as I'll do to Dorris. They won't be able to identify me, not like you."

I swallowed the lump in my throat.

"From experience, this won't take too long." He crept forward, and I retreated more into the interior of the storage space. "At least it didn't with Davis, but then again, he did have a preexisting heart condition."

"You knew about that," I said. "How?"

"Not only did he get greedy and take my phablet, but he even used the built-in health app on it and entered in his information." He snorted, shaking his head.

"So you knew about his weak heart."

Riku steadied the Taser with both of his hands and aimed it at me.

I took a deep breath in to steady myself. Could I maybe run past him with a burst of adrenaline? Some assistance would be nice. I checked on Dorris, who still lay immobile on the ground. She wasn't going to get up anytime soon, so no help from there.

"It's your turn, Mimi," Riku said with a hint of glee in his voice.

I heard an echo of my name from somewhere. "Mimi," my cat repeated. "Go backward for five steps."

I followed Marshmallow's directions. In the meantime, I engaged in conversation with Riku. Best to distract him with questioning, so he would use his Taser later rather than sooner. "Heard that Davis's body got moved. I assumed you took him from here after you retrieved your phablet and planted him farther away," I said. "Why the park, though?"

Marshmallow encouraged me. "You're doing great, Mimi. Now turn left."

I copied his instructions, and as I did so, Riku crept closer to me.

"Davis was riffraff. A greedy robber," Riku said. "I hate jerks like that. Stealing what hardworking people like me have spent their entire lives creating."

Riffraff. An unkempt image came to mind. "Was that why you disguised him as a homeless person, to show what you really thought of him?"

"And so I wouldn't get caught, obviously. I figured he'd get overlooked, that maybe his death would get ruled as accidental. No one cares about the tramps of the world." He cocked his head and reflected. "I heard that back in the good old days, Santa Monica used to have an unofficial relocation program for the unhoused."

I'd listened to the same rumors myself. How Skid Row in downtown Los Angeles had started filling up because other nearby cities would use the area as a dumping spot.

Marshmallow whispered, "Almost there, Mimi. Two more steps backward."

"I'm not sure how you're going to explain my presence here in this place," I said as I backed up, right against the edge of a table.

Riku tilted his gun toward the unmoving Dorris. "The way I see it playing out is that you snooped around too much, kept on playing your little sleuthing game. You decided to confront the thief in her storage space, except she zapped you to death."

"You would pin the blame on Dorris?"

"Two-for-one," he said, "She gets locked up for murder—she's just as bad as her brother—and you'd be gone as an eyewitness."

I gulped and peeked behind me, hoping that Marshmallow had directed me to a nice cache of weapons. All I found on the table was a tower of cardboard boxes. In front of them lay a stack of lacy dishtowels. Really, Marshmallow? I grabbed one anyway.

"Sweet dreams," Riku said as he approached. "Forever."

I saw him tighten his grip on the Taser, and I threw the dishtowel at his head. He easily ducked it and kept on coming, an ugly sneer on his face.

CHAPTER

thirty-nine

THE LASER BEAM from Riku's Taser aimed straight at the middle of my chest. Before he could fire, though, a fierce snarl reverberated in the air. From behind me, Marshmallow launched himself in the air—he must have been hiding in one of those cardboard boxes on the table. His claws sank into Riku's arm. Riku yelled out in pain, and his arm swung down, firing the probes into his own leg by accident.

He fell over, writhing in agony. I made sure to kick the gun out of his reach with my sneaker.

"Quick," Marshmallow said. "Tie him up."

I hurried over to the toy bin and extracted an ancient-looking jump rope with wooden handles. After making sure to truss Riku's arms tight, I placed a call to the police.

Within five minutes, the cops showed up with their lights flashing and their sirens blaring. A familiar figure clad in a gray sport jacket strode up to me. "Miss Lee," Detective Brown said, "what happened?"

"I found the murderer for you . . . again," I said, pointing at Riku. The cops swarmed around him.

"Are you all right?" he asked.

I nodded.

Detective Brown gave me a long, assessing look. Seemingly satisfied, he said, "Okay. Now tell me everything."

I proceeded to explain the entire scenario to the detective, about how Riku found Davis with the stolen phablet and decided to exact revenge since Davis had stolen innovative new tech that could've derailed a lucrative IPO.

Detective Brown scribbled down notes in his pad, his attention riveted to my story.

"Also, there's a Taser in that corner," I said. "Probably the same one used on Davis, and the weapon should have Riku's fingerprints all over it."

"We'll make sure to collect the evidence," he said. "What's all this other stuff?"

"Stolen goods," I said. "I think Davis, Dorris, and Lloyd worked together to take advantage of people. Even the necklace Dorris is wearing doesn't belong to her. But she won't admit to anything quite yet."

From the corner of my eye, I noticed Dorris stirring.

"The Wicked Witch is awake," Marshmallow said, slinking over to her.

Dorris sat up, groggy. She touched the back of her head and winced.

I crept over to her and nodded at Detective Brown and the other cops on the scene. "See, Dorris, I have friends in the police department. And now they've found your secret stash."

She rubbed her skinny arms. Bet she'd get more than a few bruises there from her hard fall. "You still can't prove anything, Mimi. No one's going to claim this old junk."

"Once the rightful owners are contacted, you may be proven wrong about that," I said. "Besides, what about the stuff from the vacation homes?"

"That's all Lloyd and Davis's doing, not mine. They orchestrated stealing from those Catalina Chalets."

I spun in a circle. "Didn't you mention to me earlier that this was *your* storage unit? Don't act like you're innocent. I think you knew about Lloyd and Davis keeping their stolen goods here."

She played with the locket around her neck.

"You must have been handling those new sales, like with the Marilyn Monroe headscarf."

"NJD," she mumbled.

"Exactly. Why choose those specific initials for the classified ad? On Catalina, Lloyd corrected me about Marilyn Monroe's name on the island: Norma Jeane Dougherty. Those same letters were used to describe the headscarf recently. I'm sure you and Lloyd worked together."

She placed a hand against the back of her head. "I must not be thinking clearly after my tumble. It was entirely Lloyd's fault. He orchestrated the selling off of the Catalina items all on his own after my brother died."

"Really?" I rubbed my chin. "Except, as I recall, he'd gone back to Catalina when I was supposed to meet up with the seller in the parking lot of a Trader Joe's."

Her eyes darted left and right.

"That same seller hightailed it when she saw my car." I nodded at Dorris. "The color, model, and license plate of which the security guard at your complex had informed you about when I visited your place."

Her lips tightened. She wasn't going to say anything to incriminate herself.

Okay, time to play hard ball. I raised my voice.

"Detective Brown here can trace the online account to your IP address."

Hearing his name, the detective responded and picked out his words with care. "We do have that capability."

While he wouldn't waste good police sources on my hunches, Dorris didn't have to know that.

She slumped in defeat, while I gave her a winning smile.

Meanwhile, the EMTs had been cleared to enter the scene and check on everyone inside the storage space. They assessed a groaning Riku, a slouched Dorris, and even Marshmallow and me for injuries.

We were okayed to leave after giving the necessary statements. The police recorded everything, and Detective Brown promised to "set things straight" before I left.

"What a morning," I said to Marshmallow as we headed over to my parked car.

"Mimi, I was really worried about you back there." My cat paused before the back door of the Prius and looked at me with wide blue eyes.

"Thank goodness you were there to sneak attack Riku. I mean, I wasn't sure when you first gave me those directions and all I saw were dish towels . . ."

He huffed. "You should know by now, Mimi. It always pays to listen to your cat."

"I agree. Thank you so much for saving me." I patted his head. "And you didn't help only me in the end, but all those owners with stuff locked away in her storage unit. Do you realize what you accomplished back there?"

"What?" He preened himself.

"You put a stop to all that purr-loining."

He groaned but let me pet him some more.

CHAPTER

≒ forty ≒

TWO DAYS AFTER the takedown of Riku, I sat in Pixie's home at her breakfast bar. She'd already placed bowls of purified volcanic water out for our furry pals. Marshmallow had been clearly getting all kinds of doting. I'd stocked up the pantry with special cat treats and had given him quite a few in reward for his heroics. And right now, he was lounging across the massage mat, purring in harmony with the vibrations.

Pixie pulled out a pitcher from her refrigerator and came over with two clear glasses. We both got the fresh peach and kiwi iced tea she'd made, complete with chunks of real fruit.

"This drink is in honor of you, Mimi." She raised her beverage up.

I did the same, and we clinked our glasses together.

"Cheers to the both of us," Pixie said. "You cracked the case, and I got my name cleared."

I sipped the refreshing homemade drink and smiled at her. "Did Detective Brown give you the official scoop on what happened with everyone involved?"

"Yes." She placed her drink down and concentrated on filling me in on every detail. "Mimi, due to your excellent work in cornering Riku—"

Marshmallow gave a loud meow in protest.

"My cat was instrumental on the scene, too," I said.

Pixie peeked over at the massage mat. "Right. Because of Marshmallow's and your help, they arrested Riku. The guy's fingerprints were all over that Taser."

I swirled the contents of my glass, watching the fruit pieces chase one another. "What about the thieves?"

"Lloyd and Dorris wanted to save their own skins naturally, so they couldn't wait to rat each other out."

Marshmallow purred even louder from his spa spot of pampering. "Apt analogy," he said.

"Serves them right," I said, taking a gulp with satisfaction.

"Looks like they'll be charged with grand theft. The belongings discovered in the storage unit will all be returned to their rightful owners."

I chewed on a kiwi chunk in thought. "Might take a while with all the stuff that's there."

"Yes. Plus, the detective seemed focused on restoring the missing items to the Catalina Chalet owners first. Excuse me for a moment." Pixie disappeared into another room.

When she returned, she placed a large padded envelope before me. She opened it and slid out the contents with care. I saw a beautiful silky fabric headscarf along with a framed print of Marilyn Monroe a.k.a. Norma Jeane Dougherty.

"He found your stuff," I said.

She beamed at me. "Not only that, but he hand-delivered these two items. Along with a heartfelt apology."

"About time," I said, shaking my head.

"Mimi"—Pixie took my hand in hers—"you're a wonderful friend. I don't know what would have happened to me if you hadn't been there to clear my name."

I blushed at her earnest compliment.

She let go of my hand and placed the picture and headscarf back into the envelope. "There must be some way I can pay you back."

I waved her offer away. "Come on. Your continued friendship is its own reward."

But she snapped her fingers and said, "I know just the thing."

• • •

On Saturday morning, I made sure to inform Marshmallow about my busy schedule. "I'll be gone until late tonight."

He groused for a bit. "Why would ever you want to ditch *moi*?"

"Maybe I'm tired of waiting on you hand and foot, an upsetting trend over these last few days," I joked.

Marshmallow hissed. "Please. Take it as Human Training 101 . . . so you don't forget the hierarchy of the animal world. Lions are the natural kings."

I scoffed. "Domestic cats really aren't in the same category."

He turned his back on me.

"Don't worry," I said. "I do know someone who will pamper Your Majesty. Let me just make sure she's free."

Then I called up Alice to see if she could drop by and check on Marshmallow at least part of the day.

"Not a problem," my sister said. "Maybe it'll help get Ma off my case at the same time. I could tell a little white lie—hint that I have a date with a decent male for once."

"Yeah," I added, continuing with the joking. "Feel free to dress up and wear your Sailor Moon outfit while cleaning out his kitty litter, too."

"OMG. Wouldn't that be unfortunate. Oops, I ruined the dress you bought me, Ma, while taking care of the cat. Can't possibly wear it anymore."

I hung up, leaving my sister to hatch devious ways on how to get rid of her unwanted dating outfit. (Though I knew that would only put a pause and not really stop Ma's wedding planning in the long run.)

When I told Marshmallow my sister would be coming by, he came to my side and licked my hand. "Smooth move," he said.

Then I pulled out the big guns, finding the fish-shaped massager Pixie had gifted me from Catalina, and dropping it at his feet. "I'm sure Alice won't mind acting as your masseuse, either."

Marshmallow pounced on the toy and looked at me. "Okay, you win, Mimi."

I jingled my keys at him when I left the apartment to go and catch a plane. The private jet provided by Pixie for my day trip with Josh to Catalina Island.

During the quick flight, Josh and I updated each other on our lives. We filled in the details about office hijinks (him) and solved murder cases (me).

Once we reached the island and saw it laid out before us, we quieted down. It was as though we'd entered a sacred space. My mind blocked out the stress of my usual life as we hovered above the glittering turquoise water. I promised to carve out time for reconnecting with Josh.

On this beautiful summer day, we stood in the quaint downtown area and admired the bevy of fun candy-colored shops. I'd left my schedule wide open. The only thing definitely off the list was revisiting The Job Joint or that breakfast diner where I'd gotten intel on the Fantastick Four. I didn't want to be reminded of the case whatsoever. No distractions this time around, I promised myself. The quick Catalina jaunt would be a do-over trip focused on solely Josh and me.

As we ambled along the cobblestone streets, Josh took my hand. "Anything in particular you want to do?" he asked.

"I don't know. Snorkeling maybe." I wouldn't mind seeing him in swim trunks. "Or just tasting some fresh seafood. Maybe spotting a bison or two. But really, nothing's set in stone."

He squeezed my hand. "I don't have any plans at all, Mimi, except to spend all day with you."

I kept my tone light. "No work-cation this time?"

He shook his head, flopping his bangs from one side to the other. "No way. I didn't even bring my phone with me."

I gave a mock gasp. "That may be the sweetest thing I've ever heard."

"Yeah, call me Mr. Romance." He paused to offer me a lopsided grin.

I chuckled, feeling carefree by the warm sunshine and the calming crystalline waters only several feet away. "We can do whatever we want then. This island's our oyster."

"A mixed metaphor," he said, "but I'll take it."

"Excellent," I said, squeezing his hand back in solidarity.

We continued along the picturesque street. As Josh and I strolled, we swung our arms in the air for fun, our hands clasped together in perfect unity.

ACKNOWLEDGMENTS

This book would not exist without the amazing gals from the Chicks on the Case blog: Becky Clark, Cynthia Kuhn, Ellen Byron, Kathleen Valenti, Leslie Karst, Lisa Q. Mathews, Vickie Fee, Kellye Garrett, and Marla Cooper. Thank you for making me do writing sprints and finish my word count goals. Confetti and sprinkles to Becky, Ellen, and Leslie for being insightful beta readers.

Book bloggers who I'm thankful for are Lori Caswell from Escape with Dollycas and the kindhearted Dru Ann Love of Dru's Book Musings. Amazing podcasters I've talked to include Eric Beetner of Writer Types, Charlie Jensen of The Write Process, and Diana Giovinazzo and Michele Leivas of Wine, Women and Words.

Thank you to all you superstar readers who have emailed me or tagged me on social media. Always feel free to connect with me through my newsletter (sign up on my website, jenniferjchow.com) or @jenjchow on Facebook, Twitter, and Instagram.

Speaking of Instagram, I want to acknowledge fab bookstagrammers who've gone the extra mile to not only review my books but create lovely backdrops for them. These people include @catsandpages, @jenvido, @mybooksandplants, @litchick4ever, @katherineholom, @thephdivabooks, @abigailba_, @momming_and_reading, @bookslibrariesalsocats, and @suspensethrill. Sorry if I forgot anyone!

Thank you also to bookstores like @bnmishawaka, @bntorrance, @changinghands, @belcantobook, and @bookcarnival for carrying my books.

I've felt very supported by fellow authors and am grateful for First Chapter Fun and The Back Room. Special thanks go to Robert Lee Brewer, who has been supportive ever since we first met at a *Writer's Digest* conference. Gabriel Valjan is the best booster of everyone's books—thank you.

Never-ending gratitude to the hardworking folks at Berkley. Along with my copy editor and proofreader, Angela Kim is a fantastic editor and saves me from myself. Thank you for killing my darlings, making me sound youthful, and improving the romantic threads in my stories. Applause and cheers to my marketing and publicity team, who work wonders: Stephanie Felty and Natalie Sellars.

My writing career is in the trustworthy hands of my agent, Jessica Faust, and her canine literary assistant, Olive. Thank you also to James McGowan and the entire BookEnds team.

I'm happy to be a part of many stellar writing groups. These include my local critique partners (hurrah for Lisbeth, Robin, Sherry, and Tracey). Online author friends include those from the 2020 Debuts, particularly Nicole Mabry, who created a great IG still shot; Julie C. Dalton, who sewed sassy cat–themed masks; and A. H. Kim, who keeps our 2020 Debuts of Color group organized. Thank you to Crime Writers of Color, including the Mystery Maven, Naomi Hirahara, Sarah M. Chen, Marla Bradeen, and Tori Eldridge, for all the support.

If you made it through this long list and didn't see your name specifically mentioned, know that I'm also grateful for you.

Of course, I can't forget about my immediate family! They (graciously) lived with a grumpy writer unused to sharing her writing space during lockdown. All my love to Steve and my kids, the treasures of my heart.

JENNIFER J. CHOW is the Lefty Award–nominated author of the Sassy Cat Mysteries. The first in the series, *Mimi Lee Gets a Clue*, was selected as an OverDrive Recommended Read, a PopSugar Best Summer Beach Read, and one of BuzzFeed's top five books by AAPI authors. She's active in Mystery Writers of America, Sisters in Crime, and Crime Writers of Color. Connect with her online and sign up for her newsletter on her website.

CONNECT ONLINE

JenniferJChow.com

🐦 📘 📷 JenJChow